RAVAGE MC #2

SEDUCE
me

RYAN MICHELE

Fifth Edition Published December 2022
Fourth Edition Published: October 13, 2019
ISBN-13: 978-1-951708-01-6
ISBN-10: 1-951708-01-6
ASIN: B00KVI3TKG

Previous Edition Information:
First Edition Published: May 11, 2014
Second Edition Published: June 8, 2014
Third Edition Published: November 17, 2017
ISBN-10: 1499529090
ISBN-13: 978-1499529098
ASIN: B00KVI3TKG

CONTENTS

RAVAAGE MC FAMILY TREE

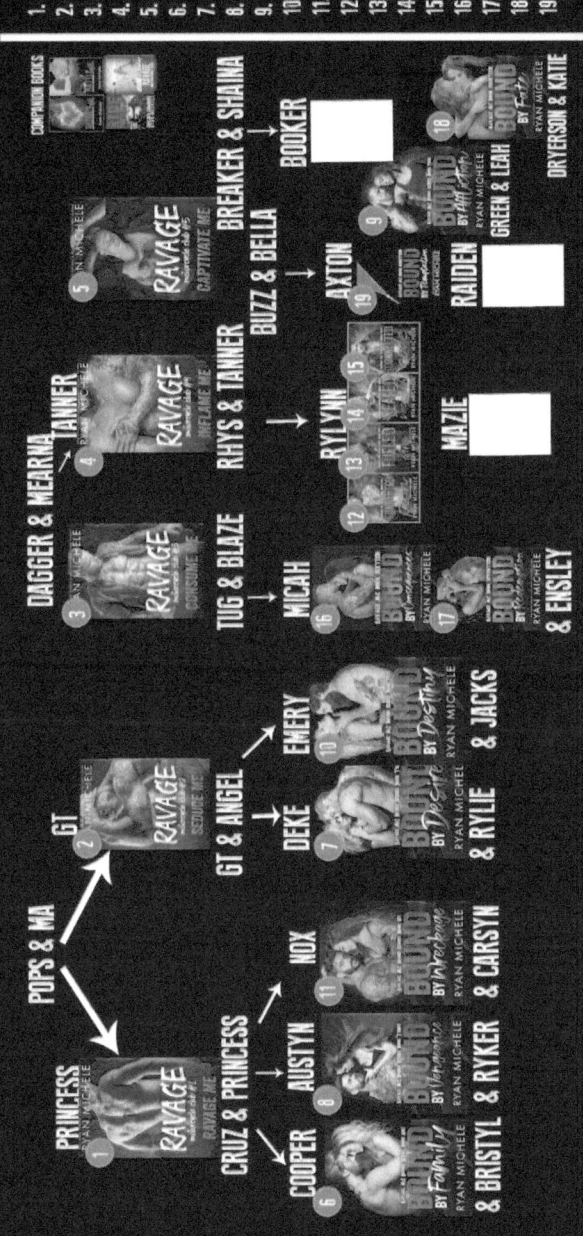

1. Ravage Me
2. Seduce Me
3. Consume Me
4. Inflame Me
5. Captivate Me
6. Bound by Family
7. Bound by Desire
8. Bound by Vengeance
9. Bound by Affliction
10. Bound by Destiny
11. Bound by Wreckage
12. Connected in Pain
13. Fueled in Fire
14. Sealed in Strength
15. Connected in Code
16. Bound by Consequences
17. Bound by Redemption
18. Bound by Fate
19. Bound by Temptation

POPS & MA

PRINCESS — RAVAGE ME
CRUZ & PRINCESS

GT — RAVAGE: SEDUCE ME
GT & ANGEL

COOPER
& BRISTYL

AUSTYN
& RYKER & CARSYN

NOX
BOUND BY FAMILY — RYAN MICHELE
BOUND BY INNOCENCE — RYAN MICHELE
BOUND BY WRECKAGE — RYAN MICHELE

DEKE
& RYLIE

EMERY
& JACKS
BOUND BY DESIRE — RYAN MICHELE
BOUND BY DESTINY — RYAN MICHELE

DAGGER & MEARNA

TANNER — RAVAGE: INFLAME ME
RHYS & TANNER

RAVAGE: CONSUME ME

TUG & BLAZE

MICAH
BOUND BY CONSEQUENCES — RYAN MICHELE
BOUND BY REDEMPTION — RYAN MICHELE
& ENSLEY

RYLYNN
12 13 14 15

MAZIE

CAPTIVATE ME — RAVAGE
BREAKER & SHAINA

BUZZ & BELLA

BOOKER

AXTON
BOUND BY TEMPTATION — RYAN MICHELE

RAIDEN

GREEN & LEAH
BOUND BY AFFLICTION — RYAN MICHELE

BOUND BY FATE — RYAN MICHELE
DRYERSON & KATIE

BLURB

Secrets can destroy...

Tragedy strikes the **Ravage MC** and **Casey** must **return home** to a family she's never really felt she fit into.

The **secret** she carries deep inside her **is sure to destroy** what's left of the relationship with the **one man she's loved** since she was a child.

GT rides hard and plays harder. The club is **his blood-- his legacy.** He **breathes** for it. He'll **die**for it.

Causing Casey to **leave him** was the **hardest** thing he's ever had to do, but it was for the **best.**

Except when she returns and **life goes to hell**, she's the one person he wants to turn to, but he doesn't know...

Sometimes the **pain** is too much to **overcome.**

Sometimes it **consumes** a person until there is **nothing left.**

Sometimes **forgiveness** isn't an **option.**

Some secrets you **never come back from.**

Come and join the ride with the Ravage MC!

To all of you who want to be Ravaged and Seduced.

CHAPTER ONE
Casey

THE MORNING AIR STRIKES ACROSS MY SKIN AS I STEP OUT of the clubhouse slowly walking to my car. I've had to say good-bye to Harlow twice now, but this one is by far the hardest. The weight on my shoulders is bogging me so far down; my legs find each step difficult. I do not want to leave. This is my home, the only life I've ever known.

And my only connection to my father Bam, but it's what must be done.

I place my hand on my stomach closing my eyes and breathing in deep, the air rushing through my lungs. It's funny how life repeats itself. I think that it's Dr. Phil that says 'past behavior predicts future behavior' and to hell if that isn't the truth.

Walking up to my white and red Chevy, I slide in slowly turning the key in the ignition, the car roaring to life. My eyes focus on the garage and my heart sinks as I slouch in my seat, the weight becoming too much. Hours I've spent inside that building learning, but the best were the ones I spent with my Dad, side by side under the hood of this car. He spent so much time teaching me everything he could, always patient and answering the thousands of questions I had repeatedly. It was the best time of my life.

Growing up in the club had its difficulties, but with each challenge that has been thrown in my face, I came out a stronger woman because of it.

I never knew my egg donor of a mother, who happened to be a club momma. As soon as I popped out of her stomach, she handed me over to Bam and never looked back. I don't even know her name and at this point in my life, I have no intention of ever finding out.

I rub my stomach and disappointment scatters through my body. How could someone just dump their child and never contact them again? Never want to watch them grow up? The thought is just inconceivable to me.

Even though it doesn't make sense, it's what mine did. Bam never had a choice on whether to raise me or not, but I never once felt like a burden on him. True, my life growing up was very different from the life of my other schoolmates, but I loved it and wouldn't change a thing.

For me, being strapped to a Harley before I could walk and attending parties where guys smoked cigarettes, drank booze and kissed barely clothed women was the norm. Watching fights break out over stupid shit almost every single day is the way of the club. Don't get me wrong, I was always cared for, mostly by Bam, but he was busy a lot. When he was, a throng of club mommas entered in and out of my life to temporarily care for me, none ever staying long enough to form any kind of connection to.

Bam was there as much as he could be. He'd have tea parties with me and play this wrestling tickle game that always sent me into fits of laughter. I loved him... I still love him. His life lessons were the best education a little girl could have. I never had to ask him, it was like he knew what I needed when I needed it.

When the time came for boys, he always told me that *no man is good enough for my baby*. At the time, I rolled my eyes, but now I crave to hear those words come back out of his mouth.

I hang my head down to my chest willing the tears to stay at bay. *I will not cry. I'm stronger than that.*

Bam was able to do it, raise me that is. Even with the struggles, he did it. I can too, but in order to, I need to get away from here and find out who I am. I need to do better for myself and for my baby, my family. I want a life here, but, unfortunately, that is not possible right now. It's not my choice, but that of my baby's father.

Even though he doesn't know about this precious gift I have growing inside of me, he's made it perfectly clear that he doesn't want a life with me anywhere in it. It seems he's too interested in chasing pussy to ever settle for just one. It guts me and shreds my heart that I'm not good enough. But I'm learning to accept it, even if it kills me. He left little room not to.

But I need to get myself together and stop with the ever impending pity party of poor me. I am not a poor me kind of woman. Thanks to Bam, I'm a grab life by the balls, deal with the consequences and make myself a future kind of a woman. That is what I am doing by leaving. I have every intention of coming back, every intention of introducing my child to his father and every intention of making my relationship with Harlow work. As soon as I have my head on straight.

Lifting my shoulders, I put the car into drive and set off for the new life that I have planned for my baby and me.

CHERRY VALE IS ONLY an hour's drive away from Sumner, but it feels like thousands and thousands of miles away, a whole new world. With each landmark that I pass, floods of memories seep through my body, tearing me away layer by layer. The pizzeria where Bam used to take me on special occasions flies by the window warming my heart and slamming me with sadness at the same time. The water tower where Harlow and I used to hang out to get away from everything and escape is seen high up in the sky. The old mill is still untouched after years of nothingness. I keep telling myself that there is a reason for my madness and it's for my baby that I am moving away.

Pulling up to the apartment I rented, I park the car on the side of the street by the front door and stare at the four story brick building. Windows line the front with the sun shining so brightly on them they have a glare. The white shutters around the building give it a homey feel along with the flowers planted around the base of the building.

My apartment is located near campus giving a short walking distance to class, but yet not on campus. When I did my search for living arrangements, I didn't want to live in a place where only students were, instead wanting one that had some families in it also.

I don't know the first thing about kids, but I didn't want to deal with frat boys and sorority sisters after drunken nights when I have a crying baby.

Before I met Harlow at the shop earlier tonight, my car was already loaded with my life and ready to go, everything else left with the truck yesterday. I didn't want to go back to the apartment I've lived in for so long, afraid that I wouldn't leave. It was my every intention to help Harlow with Rocky and get the hell out before anything else happened. I needed to make sure that was exactly what happened.

Sighing, I reach for the door handle and push open the door. The morning is still crisp, but nothing like an hour ago, the heat and humidity have begun to set in. Popping open the trunk, I reach in and grab a box. I made sure to pack all the really heavy stuff for the movers to bring, not wanting to lift too much.

Walking into the building and punching the elevator button to up, I stand and wait, my thoughts drifting to Bam. When I was younger, he always said he wanted me to go to school and get my degree. He told me that I was a smart girl; with a good head on my shoulders and I want to prove him right.

I hope that he wouldn't be disappointed in me. After all, I went and got knocked up just like my club momma of a mother. Like mother like daughter, except one big difference, I will not give up on my baby. Everything that I'm doing now is for him or her.

The elevator dings. Balancing the box, I step in carefully. Reaching over to punch in the number three and the doors begin to close.

"Wait!" A deep voice from the other side rumbles. The voice is commanding yet soft. I try to find the open button on the panel while juggling the box, but have no luck. A large hand jams between the doors making them jump back with a clang, effectively opening them.

The man's smell fills the elevator. It's a mix of sweat, testosterone and something minty. His red running shorts, tennis shoes and a white tank show off an impressive set of muscles throughout his body. His blonde hair is dripping wet with sweat and his breathing heavy. When his brown eyes land on mine, a small smile quirks the side of his mouth. My body is on instant alert and I put up my defensive walls inside.

"You need help with that?" His voice reverberates off the small enclosed area.

"No, thank you," I say straightening my shoulders. One thing you learn being around a bunch of badass bikers is presence. The more confidence you have, the less likely you are to be messed with and with not knowing the guy, I will not give an inch.

"Here." The box in my arms disappears and instantly my arms feel the relief. "I can just help ya to your apartment. I won't even go in." His full out smile is waiting for me and it's so infectious I find myself doing the same.

"Thank you." I look away to watch the numbers move from one to two.

"I'm Jace." I feel his eyes staring at me burning a hole right through me, but I will not give this man an inch. No one is getting an in... again.

"Casey." I continue to watch as the numbers move from two to three willing them to move faster.

"You need help with your other boxes?"

"I'll get them, but thank you." The elevator dings on three and it just occurred to me that Jace didn't push a number. Exiting the elevator, I look for 303 finding it on the right hand side of the hallway. "I'm right here, you can set it down. Thank you."

He makes no attempt to set the box down, but stands next to the door, his shoulder pressed up against the wall. Out of my peripheral vision, his muscular arms flex as he holds the box as if it weighs nothing at all. I swallow and quickly reach in my pocket for my keys trying not to fumble them.

Opening the door wide, I take in the room. Boxes line the room and walls, my furniture is piled in heaps, but the good part is I don't see the bed so hopefully it's been moved to the bedroom. I let out a deep sigh and walk into the apartment relishing in the mess that will take me days to organize.

I turn to the door. Jace is still standing with his shoulder propped against the door attempting to hold it up, but I don't think it needs any help and nonchalance is not his strong suit. I walk quickly to him and hold out my hands for the box. He hands it to me hesitantly.

"Thank you." I say pulling away from him and setting the box on top of the massive pile everywhere.

"Anytime. I'd really like to help you with the others that you have. My mom always taught me to help a lady. She'd smack my head if she found out I didn't help you." He smirks but covers it up with his hand.

"I only have two and a suitcase. I can handle it, but

thank you." I say ignoring the mom comment. I turn back around my eyes lock with his deep chocolate brown ones and instantly look to the floor, my confidence wanes a bit. His interest in me is clearly written on his face, but it will not happen and I do not want to give him any indication that it will.

"If you need anything, you let me know. I'm down in 306 across the hall." He moves away from the door frame but does not step into my space. He's kept his word about not coming into my apartment and I do appreciate his respect.

"Thanks, but I'll be just fine. Going to unpack." I grasp the door getting ready to shut it.

"Got it. It was nice to meet you Casey." His lips form into a heartbreaking smile, one that would curl most women's toes. If I were any other woman, in any other situation, I'd probably be putty in his hands. But I'm not.

"Same here." I clutch the door a bit harder, Jace turns and walks down the hallway only a few steps to his door. Without looking, I quickly shut the door, lock it, and turn, allowing my back to sag on the door in relief. I made it. I got here. I can do this.

I HATE UNPACKING. I've only had to do it twice, once when I moved in with Harlow and now this. It's taken me most of the day, but I think I finally have everything where it needs to be, at least furniture and clothes-wise. The rest will wait for another day.

Plopping down on the couch, I lean my head back to

rest it. My entire body aches from the top of my head down to the tips of my toes. My stomach growls reminding me I haven't eaten. Since I haven't gotten to the grocery store yet that means no food here either. I sigh to myself. I'll need to remedy food before bed.

Both my hands instantly reach my stomach. I'm nowhere near showing yet, but I know the life inside me is growing. I did not plan on getting pregnant. When the doctor says that birth control is only 99% effective, believe him. I'm graced with the lucky one percent, but I can't say that I'm disappointed. This pregnancy may not be what I have envisioned for myself, but I would not change it for the world.

G.T. and I didn't use condoms. It was a huge fuckup on my part as I should have insisted we did. I knew him, I knew he'd never commit to one person, but did it anyway like some stupid love struck teenager, hoping I'd be the one he'd change for. Stupid. He did get tested for me though and got the all clear, but even that should not have had me tempting fate.

My relationship with G.T. has never been what one would call stable or healthy. As kids, he's the little brother Harlow and I loved terrorizing and manipulating whenever we got a chance. We had him do some pretty disgusting stuff, like drink stale beer with cigarette butts and someone's loogies in it. With only a couple year age difference, we spent a lot of time together, but mostly it was the eww-he's-gross kinda time.

Part of me fell in love with Gage Thomas Gavelson when I was seven years old though, he threw mud in my face because I wouldn't jump in it with him. That sealed the deal for me.

Shortly after he started hanging around the club, I noticed a cute little brother starting to turn into a man and I went from a sickening case of puppy love to a full-blown crush. But around thirteen, Pops, G.T.'s dad, started bringing him around the club more and more. I would see him from across the parking lot occasionally while Bam and I were working on cars, but it wasn't the same. I missed him. Then, the women started coming around. Much older women. At first, I thought maybe they were just helping him with homework or working for Pops. How wrong I was. I quickly learned they were helping him, but definitely not with homework.

The intensity of my feelings for G.T. continued to grow, never lessening. If anything the longing became intensified to a degree it ached to even see him at all. He continually held a special place in my heart; one I kept locked up tight inside trying desperately to keep contained. But every smirk he'd give me or every bump on the shoulder would crack that container a bit more.

One fateful day, he actually saw me. Really saw me. The emotion in his eyes when they locked on mine lit my body on fire. That day was fast, fierce and beautiful. That day also started our short love affair.

I should have known better. All common sense left me when it came to that man. I saw the women in and out of his room at the club throughout the years, but stupid me, I thought I was different. I thought I meant something to him. But I didn't. I was just one of many. There is no changing a man like G.T. As much as I want to be the special one he sees, I'm not and I have to live with it.

Our time together was a whirlwind and went by so

quickly, but with such deep rooted feelings for G.T. I was sucked into everything that is him. But after only three weeks together he broke it off leaving me with a parting gift. As sick as it sounds, I'm happy to always have a part of him with me. And the even sicker part is I am my mother. I'm the club momma that got knocked up by a brother. I'll be the one that everyone looks down on as the whore. But the major difference with me is I will not give up my baby or abandon it.

The day will come here in the next few months when I will need to tell G.T. I'm not a heartless bitch that would try and keep his child from him. No matter how much he hurt me, I'd never do that to him. It may kill me to have my son or daughter around the throng of club mommas G.T. has in and out of his bed, but I'll deal, just like I deal with everything else. And I'll let him or her chose whether they want the same life, as their father. I will never make that decision for them.

But the whole point of me coming up here is to get myself together. I have no doubt G.T. will provide financially for his child, but I want to be able to do it on my own as well. This baby is mine and I want to give G.T. the option, unlike my father ever had. Part of me desperately wants him to step up and be the father I know he can be, but I will not force him like Bam was. I will get my degree and I will provide for my child. I will not rely on anyone, ever.

Not only that, I need to come to terms with Bam's death. Thinking about it sends chills down my body and my hands shake. Even after four years, his death still haunts me. I close my eyes, tears well up inside of them. I try keeping the tears at bay but am finding it hard to do.

Bam is the only family I have, was the only family I had. Even though I grew up around the club, I never felt part of it. Instead, I always felt like an outsider looking in. The brother's kid, therefore, everyone put up with me.

Harlow is truly the sister I always wanted, not by blood but by bond. Even though I do consider her my family, she now has her own to deal with. Not only that, she has the club. Now that she's an ol' lady, she's in a whole different bracket than me. Where once we were similar in status, to a degree, now she's on a whole other field and I respect her place there.

Even growing up, I always felt the difference with her. Harlow is the *Princess* and I always felt like the court. The brothers always fawned over her, and were nice to me, but never to the extent of Princess. Looking back now, it sounds damn petty and jealous, but to a thirteen year old girl who's trying to come into her own, it was everything. I don't even know if the brothers realized they were doing it or if they cared. But *I* cared.

When Bam died, all the brothers stepped up to take care of me, but again I felt like a spectator just watching from the sidelines. There, but not feeling part of it. And part of it could have been the grief I was in, considering I didn't come out of my room for a couple of weeks. But the club was Bam's family, not mine, even though I wanted it to be. I have always been an obligation to the brothers. I don't need anyone's pity, ever again. But I'll always have Harlow to some degree, maybe not like before, but I do know if I called her right now she would come. Granted we have some things to work out, but I know we will.

I can't tell her about the baby though, not yet. I almost did last night lying in bed with her after the intensity of what we found out about Rocky being an undercover cop. I want someone to talk to about the pregnancy, but I could not add more shit to her already huge pile she's dealing with, even though I craved to lean on her. I ache for her to wrap her arms around me and take away all the hurt and confusion. But on the flip side, I know she will be pissed that I left and would drag me back and force me to tell G.T., but he's not ready to know yet. More importantly, I'm not ready to tell him yet.

A loud bang on the front door causes me to jump and clutch my chest, my heart pounds. Damn. I walk hesitantly to the door and look in the peephole where Jace is standing with a plastic bag in one hand and a pizza box in the other. My stomach growls, but chastise it to shut up.

I open the door slowly and give a small smile. "Hi."

"Hey Casey. I just figured you were busy unpacking and thought I'd bring ya something to eat."

"Thanks. But I'm just heading out to find a grocery store." My chest tightens. I don't want to be a bitch, but from the gleam in his eye he is seriously interested in me and I can't have that. There is too much in my life that needs to be sorted out before any of that will happen and leading him anywhere is a mistake. Especially when he finds out I'm going to have a kid, insta-dad doesn't work with a lot of men. But it is a nice gesture to bring a new neighbor food.

"I've already got food. You've gotta be tired from unpacking all day. Look. It's just a friend thing. I can see the wheels in your head turning. I've gotta eat. You gotta eat. Let's just eat and when we're done, I'll leave." Jace changed into a pair of cargo khaki shorts and a blue polo shirt that is tight around his biceps. His hair looks like his fingers have been through it a thousand times, but still put together. His eyes gleam as they stare into mine.

"Just friends." I emphasize for him, not myself.

"Got it." I sweep my arm in front of me ushering him into my apartment my heart continuing to beat rapidly.

"Ignore the boxes. Crap. I don't know if I have plates or anything." I step into the kitchen that sparkles with white cabinets, a slightly lighter blue-grey color on the walls and large island that has two bar stools. I reach for the chrome knob on the cupboard door to get plates and Jace's touch on my hand shocks me and I instantly retract it.

"Sorry. I have paper plates and pop. No worries." I instantly feel like shit for my reaction. I sigh and reach for the countertop to steady myself. *Pull your shit together.*

"Great, thank you." I give him a small smile. "Please have a seat." I turn and point to the stool at the island.

He sets all of the things on top reaching into a plastic bag pulling out two plates, napkins and two pops. A grumble from my stomach declaring its hunger sends Jace into a fit of laughter.

"See, I knew you'd be hungry." He opens the box pulling out pieces of oozing cheesy pizza and setting one on each of our plates. The smell of garlic and pizza sauce instantly hits my nose and my mouth waters. The realization of just how hungry I am hits me hard.

"It's been a rough day." I smile reaching for the pizza and taking a large bite. A slight moan escapes my lips as the sauce hits my tongue, so good. He smiles and begins to eat.

"I remember when I moved in last year, I was dead on my feet." He starts obviously not liking the silence.

"Thank you for bringing me food." I wipe my mouth and quickly dive back into the pizza devouring it, also if my mouth is full, I can't talk much.

"You are very welcome. What are neighbors for?" He smiles and pizza sauce drips on his lip.

"You've got some." I point to my lip, his tongue darts out catching the sauce. It's definitely appealing, but I enforce the wall I have separating friendship from attraction.

"Thanks. Are you in school?" I nod. "What are you studying?" He asks.

Part of me didn't want to answer him, didn't want to give him any information about myself. But I didn't want to be a rude bitch either. "Business, but I'm just starting so I have to get through all my gen eds first."

"I'm business too. This is my second year, I'm mostly gen eds too. Hoping next semester, I'll get some guts."

I laugh at his description. "How are classes?" I grab another piece of pizza out of the box and immediately start eating.

"Alright. Nothing too exciting." He shrugs before taking a large bite out of the slice in his hand.

"I'm looking forward to it." I grab the pop taking a deep swallow, surprised that talking to him comes so natural as my body begins to relax a bit.

"So, Casey tell me about yourself." I still, the relaxation I felt moments ago drifts out of my body and I stare at him. He notices my hesitance, "Just getting to know each other. Nothing more."

It would be nice to know someone here and he does

seem like a pretty decent guy. Hell, he brought me pizza. I can tell him, just not much.

"I'm from Sumner. I love working on cars and that's about it." I dig back into my pizza.

He grins. "I'm sure there's more to it than that, but I'll go with it." He pauses. "I'm from here actually. Started school last year at the insistence of my father, I worked for him as a paper pusher so he thinks he can boss me around. Well, I guess he can." He chuckles. "I run quite often, love to watch football and am an all-around *great* guy."

Now it's my turn to laugh. "You sure think highly of yourself there."

He chews the pizza and swallows. "Nah. Nothing like that. Just thought I'd get to hear you laugh, and I'm glad I did."

I turn away quickly at his flirtation, filling my mouth with more pizza.

He holds his hands up in surrender. "Sorry. I'll stop. I'm making you uncomfortable and it's the last thing I want."

I wipe my face and slowly stand. "I really appreciate you bringing dinner, but I'm really tired."

"And there's my cue to get-the-hell-out," he grumbles as he slides off the stool. I can't deny his words. "Thanks for letting me eat with you. I'm sure we'll see each other around."

"Thank you again for helping with the box and bringing dinner. It was very nice of you."

"What every guy wants to hear. It was nice." He laughs. "It's really no problem. If you need anything, I'm in 306. Come by anytime."

I nod as I move quickly towards the door and open it. "Thank you. See ya Casey." He smiles his eyes squinting in mischief. It's best for him to go. He needs to go.

"Bye." I shut the door and lock the deadbolt, clean up the remnants of dinner and head to bed. I wasn't joking, I'm beat. I need sleep, now and it consumes me as soon as my head hits the pillow.

CHAPTER TWO
Casey

THE FIRST WEEK OF SCHOOL FLASHES BEFORE MY EYES AND the second is almost over. I really like my classes and my professors seem alright. My job, on the other hand, not so much. Work is rough. Finding my place in a male dominated industry is a challenge and Foster's Garage is no different and it's what I expected. Back in Sumner, I paid enough dues and demonstrated my abilities daily to all the guys, and for that I am respected. Here... not so much.

The guys make their dumb ass comments about my ass, but I let it roll off my back. If I let that shit get to me then I'm in the wrong business. What gets me is the condescending tone some of them have when I talk engines. In reality, I can walk circles around them when it comes to an engine and more than likely take apart and rebuild one faster than they ever thought possible. Again, it's all about paying my dues and I accept that, I just don't have to like it.

Luckily, I only work two days a week for a couple of hours. I really don't need to work at all. Bam left me enough money to survive on for quite some time and I've skimped and saved over the years. Bam taught me well when it came to money. Never live above your means and if you want something you work for it. That is exactly what I'm doing now. Plus it doesn't hurt I love being under an engine and am not quite ready to give it up yet.

One of the best things that happened is meeting Bella. She's really the only friend I've made here at school. We met in the two classes we share. She sat next to me one day and I couldn't keep my damn eyes off of her. Her hair was so unique, dark black, but its silkiness is caught my attention; I wanted to touch it to see if it was real. And that was the first thing I asked her. She laughed replying yes. After talking more, we found out we have a ton in common and have been friends since. We began hitting up the coffee shop down the road to chat after class.

Bella lost her dad about a year ago, in talking about our experiences our bond formed instantly. We also have the same major which made us a match made in heaven. She actually lives in the next building over from me, which was a happy surprise.

When I walk into the coffee shop, Bella is instantly noticeable. Her long jet black hair flows uncontrollably down her back. Her eyes are blue, but they have a purple tint to them making them utterly unique. To say she looks exotic is an understatement. Add in a rocking body, smarts and kick ass personality, the guys at the club would eat her alive.

"Hey! So how's it been going?" Bella asks as I slide into the table next to her.

Wrapping my hands around the mug of coffee she so generously had waiting for me, I smile. "Great. You?"

"Alright. Absolutely nothing exciting going on what so ever." She grunts staring at her mug.

"You still seeing that guy..." My voice trails off as I wave my hand not remembering his name.

"His name was Ethan and no. He's gone. I don't have anyone at the moment." Her evil smirk graces her pouty lips.

"You're kidding me." I egg her on smiling. In the short time that I've known her, I've learned quickly that Bella always has someone she's with and someone waiting in the wings to take their spot. So far, she's been through two.

Her laugh breaks out of her lips. "Nah. Need a break. This last one was too much of a pussy. I need a man... A real one." The wiggle of her eyes up and down instigated my full out laugh.

"You sure you could handle that?" I say between breaths of fitting giggles thinking of all the brothers in the club.

"I'm tougher than you think. Why don't you hook me up with one of your biker men?" Her tongue darts out running across her top lip. Telling Bella about my home life went so much smoother than I imagined. I am always apprehensive of telling people how I grew up especially with how others reacted in grade and high school.

I've been called everything from a biker brat to a biker slut and everything in between. Most of my classmates' parents told them to stay clear of Harlow and myself; we were bad news, bad eggs, and bad seeds. Now that I look back on that, everything turned out for the best. Harlow and I didn't have to deal with the superficial friendships that seem to be part of the high school experience for most people. But that didn't mean our time was easy.

Even now as an adult, I still get weary, but Bella's only reaction was the utter desire to come to the club and meet the guys. But there is no way I'm letting her turn into a club momma. Not going to happen.

"Girl, they'd eat you alive."

"Maybe that's what I need. To be eaten... hard." The mug that almost made it to my mouth slams down the table as a roar of laughter bellows out of me uncontrollably. This is why I love hanging out with Bella, her mouth.

"Well, that's sure a beautiful laugh." My eyes gaze into the chocolate brown ones that were in my apartment. I have seen him a few times, but never enough to talk to him since our pizza night. He's either coming in or going out of his apartment. I smile slightly, but never engage in conversation and to my surprise he just smiles back and goes on his way.

"Hey Jace. How are ya?" I ask turning to look at Bella whose eyes are bugging out of her head. Jace is a very attractive man from his toned muscular arms and legs to his sharp nose and cheekbones. I smile knowingly.

"I'm good. How's school going for ya?"

"Good. This is my friend Bella. She lives in the apartment building next to ours." He smiles politely to Bella.

"Hi there." To my utter shock, his eyes jet right back to mine, not giving Bella his attention. My first thought is what the hell is wrong with him and the second is damn. I look over at Bella, who shrugs her shoulders, but no words escape her lips.

"You wanna hang out Saturday night? My friends and I are going to this bar, Dixie's and I'd love for you to come with us. Bella's welcome to come too."

Before the words can leave my mouth, Bella answers for me. "We'd love to. What time do you want us to meet you?"

My mouth drops to the floor and I stare into her beautiful blue eyes wanting to strangle her. Her knowing smile only infuriates me more; she knew I'd say no. Damn her.

Instead of having it out with her, I look up into Jace's triumphant face. "I can pick you up instead."

"No." I shake my head. "I'll drive."

"Alright, alright. Eight. Meet us at eight."

"We'll be there." Bella adds. Jace smiles over at Bella, but not in an I-want-to-sleep-with-you-way, but a thank-you.

"I've gotta run. I'll see you two Saturday." He smiles. "Oh wait. Here's my number. Give me a call or text." He hands me a paper with numbers scrolled on it and leaves the coffee shop.

I glower at Bella. "What the hell was that?"

"Oh, stop it. He obviously has the hots for you and you were going to say no. You need to get out and meet people. Hell, I need to get out and meet people. This is perfect." She smiles and I want to slap it off of her.

I haven't told her that I'm pregnant. Hell, I haven't told

a soul that I am, and going out drinking is not my idea of fun.

"I'm not interested in him Bella. I'm taking a break from guys at least for a while." A long while once they find out that I'm about to be a mom.

"You got one at home?" Bella questions and my eyes widen. We've talked a little about the club and my life there, but never has she asked me if there was a man in my life and I'm not sure I want to answer her.

A baby in the distance begins crying and my eyes dart to the sound. A young mother a little older than myself pulls a small infant from a car seat. The baby's covered in pink from head to toe and screaming like a banshee. I watch in awe as the mom stands with the baby and lays a blanket out on the table. She begins doing this weird magic thing where she wraps the baby up binding its hands and legs together. When she picks her up, she looks like a little burrito all nice, snug and tight. What-ever mom magic she just did, instantly has the baby calm, not even a whimper.

The mom bounces softly as she looks down at her baby, love just pouring out of her eyes. My heart constricts at the sight. I catch my hand quickly not wanting to touch my stomach in public, but everything inside of me is yearning to feel the baby inside of me.

I will do anything and everything for it.

"Hello!" Bella's voice snaps, pulling me back to her. "Where did you go?"

It takes me a couple of beats before I register her words. "I'm here. Sorry."

"So you obviously have a man at home." She muses.

"I had one, but it didn't work out." That's putting it mildly.

"Do tell."

"Really it's not something I talk about." I look down at my mug willing Bella to drop it, but knowing she won't.

"Tell me." The tone is stern and absolute.

I sigh. "His name is G.T. I've been in love with him since we were kids, but it didn't work out. Now I'm here and he's there. It's what's best for everyone."

"Why is that?"

My head begins to ache and I rub my eyes, letting out a deep breath. "G.T. has made it perfectly clear that he wants nothing to do with me." Or anything I'm associated with. "I refuse to beg him to love me. I refuse to grovel at his feet. I'm not that woman. It's his choice and since that's what he chose, we both have to live with those consequences."

"What are you hiding?" My eyes dart to hers, my shoulders tighten and my heart may just beat out of my chest. I'm at a loss for words. My mouth opens, but nothing comes out. There is no way that she can know.

"Never mind." She dismisses. "Look whoever this G.T. guy is... Is a fool. I'm not saying you have to date Jace. Let's just go out and have fun."

I breathe in a sigh of relief closing my eyes for a moment to open them to Bella's intense stare. I feel like she's looking through me, looking through the bullshit. But I'm not ready for her to know.

"I'll go." My voice comes out shakier than I anticipate, clearing my throat I repeat myself quickly.

"WOULD you hurry your ass up already?" I yell to Bella. She is in the bathroom where she's been 'fixing her face' for the past twenty minutes. I spent all week dreading this night out, and it seemed time went by faster than normal. But it's here and there is no way Bella is letting me out of it.

We are due to meet Jace and his friends in twenty minutes, but will definitely be late if she doesn't move her ass.

"I'm coming." She snips walking down the hallway. As she came into sight, her long black hair cascades down her back and shoulders while her eyes are dark and unbelievably tempting. Her very tight jeans with tears in the knees and a wraparound purple top bring out the color of her eyes even more. I need to take lessons from her quick, the girl has style.

"Damn girl. You look hot!" Bella smirks and shrugs her shoulders as if it's nothing.

"As do you babe." I'd gone for a less straight-laced approach choosing my jeans that hugged every curve of my hips, ass and legs perfectly. My navy blue top is cut low giving the girls a beautiful show as it hugs my waist. A couple of days ago, I went and got the underside of my hair colored a rich black with my blonde still flowing on the top. I think it looks hot. I curled the ends and it flowed down my back hitting my ass. I have also taken meticulous time on my makeup and I don't even know why. I slip on my boots, the ones with the heels and zip them up tight.

"Thanks. We gotta get going." I say pulling out my cherry lip gloss and smearing it on my lips. I've been using the stuff for years and don't leave home without it.

The ride there, Bella had me laughing so hard I thought I'd pee myself on several occasions. Anything from some of her past sexual encounters to penis sizes of her men. Damn that girl. My good mood courses through me for a change.

Entering the bar, the music is pumping and the dance floor is hopping. The crowd is just starting to come alive as we walk inside. I'm not stupid. I can feel the eyes on us everywhere as we walk through the bar. Searching through the bar, my eyes lock on chocolate brown ones and instantly take in the others at the table as we approach.

Two men and two women's eyes dart to us as Jace gets up smiling at us. "You came." His infectious smile spreads across his face.

"Told you I would."

"Hey Jace." Bella says standing next to me her arm brushing mine.

"Hey. Let me introduce you guys." He turns to the table. "This here is Alex." Alex's dark hair is styled and gelled to perfection. Part of me wants to put my fingers through it just to mess it up. I smirk at the thought. His brown eyes spark with excitement and even though he is attractive, he's way too clean shaven and gives off an uppity vibe, unlike Jace. I smile and give a slight wave.

"This is Jared." Jared, on the other hand, has a definite

rough edge to him. His long brown hair seems a bit out of place when looking at Jace and Alex, but to each their own. He's wearing a long sleeved black shirt and jeans, his body lean and muscular. But it's when his eyes lock with mine that I hold in my gasp. The intensity there is a bit more than expected, but I school my features and smile.

Jace brushes my arm and I lose eye contact with Jared. "And these are their girls. Joey is Jared's and Ella is Alex's." The irritation on the women's faces does not go unnoticed, but as soon as Jace looks at them, they school their features and put on a one hundred percent faking-it smile. All my flags wave like crazy. I will definitely be keeping an eye on these two.

Ella is pretty in the girl-next-door-never-get-a-tattoo-to-mar-her-body sort of way. Her flawless skin and light brown hair are styled to perfection. Joey, on the other hand, is layered in fake, fake nails, fake boobs, and fake eyelashes. Her eyes are gleaming with hate and disdain, why, I can't puzzle together quite yet. Their eyes dart up and down on both Bella and myself.

I inadvertently straighten my shoulders. This woman definitely has an issue and I'll be damned if she even thinks of starting shit with me. I'm not just protecting myself, but my baby as well.

"Please sit. What can I get you to drink?" Jace asks pulling the chairs away from the table.

"Sprite for me," I say looking at Bella, who eyes me, but doesn't confront. I've been reading all of these baby magazines online and learned that I'm not supposed to have caffeine, which blows. But I will do anything for my peanut.

"Beer. Draft, please." Jace nods heading off to the bar to get the drinks, quickly returning.

"So, Casey what's your story?" Joey asks snidely. I ignore it and it baffles me that no one at the table catches it besides Bella.

"Not much to tell." I tell them where I'm from and my major. We even discuss how Jace and I met, very idle chit chat. I continue to sip on my Sprite as Bella does a quick recap of her life.

"So what about your family, Casey?" Ella asks, her question seems genuine. I don't feel the snideness I did from Joey. I flex my fingers and move my knuckles back and forth. Bella handled my family life just fine, but I'm not sure about telling all of them about it all.

"I don't have any. My dad died a few years ago and now it's just me." And my baby.

Jace turns to me shocked. "You have no one else?"

"Don't let her fool ya. She has a whole club that looks after her." I turn to Bella my mouth gaping. What the hell?

Jace's head snaps to mine, his eyebrow raised. "What club?"

I breathe out a deep. "My dad, Bam, was part of Ravage Motorcycle Club. My best friend Harlow is an ol' lady in the club, but I'm not part of it."

"What in the hell is an ol' lady and why the hell would someone want to be called that?" Joey clips and Ella nods her head, both Alex and Jared sit quietly and listen. I really did not want to have this discussion. It seems that anytime I explain it, people get this notion that it's a horrible thing, that being someone's property is against all moral code in the world. But for me, I would have given anything to be G.T.'s. I sigh shaking my thoughts.

"An ol' lady is a sign of respect. It's the highest form for a woman in the club. It is not a derogatory name nor is there any negativity associated with it. It is an honor to be an ol' lady. It has the same weight and commitment as being a man's wife."

"Have you ever been an ol' lady?" Ella asks.

"No. Never. If I were an ol' lady, my man would be right by my side and every single person in this club would know exactly who I belong to." The thought makes my stomach clench. If only.

"You probably just go around fucking all the guys and be their bitch." Joey laughs, but to my amazement the entire table turns to her and glares.

"What the hell is wrong with you Joey?" Jace chastises.

What the table does not realize is this is exactly the shit I've had to deal with my whole life. It is one of the reasons I never wanted to become a club momma. "She's just not educated in the club life. It's alright." I wave my hand and look directly at Joey.

"I did not go around fucking all the guys in the club. Number one, I'm a club member's daughter and was raised in the life. I have seen and know better than to ever do that shit. Two, what you're referring to is a club momma. Those are the women who come in and hop in different guys' beds each and every night. They enjoy it."

"Who in the hell would want to do that?" I think back to G.T. The only reason I was ever in his bed was because I loved him. Nothing more.

"They all have their reasons. I wouldn't know them

what each is, but it can range from just wanting to have a good time to craving to be an ol' lady and thinking this is the way to get there."

"So is this like a motorcycle gang?" I roll my eyes.

"Not a gang. It's a club." Over the years, the term gang has been thrown around relentlessly. The brothers always get pissed at the word because first and foremost Ravage is a club of bikers who love to ride.

"So…"

Jace cut off Joey's words. "Enough about the club. She's squirming in her seat. She doesn't want to talk about it."

The realization hit that I am, in fact, moving my hips and I immediately stop.

"I think you need a break. Wanna dance?" Jace asks. Suddenly cold shivers flow through my body and I'm in desperate need of a drink. I grip the straw between my lips and begin to suck, the liquid coating my throat. "It's just a dance. No big deal."

Bella nudges my arm and I want to elbow her, but refrain. I slide slowly out of the seat. "Sure."

Jace grabs my hand pulling me to the dance floor. A very slow beat engulfs the room. Jace wraps his arms around my waist linking his fingertips behind my back. Not wanting to pull him too close, I rest my hands on his shoulders.

Why do I get the sudden feeling that we are in high school at a damn dance? Not that I ever went to one.

"Sorry about all that." I look at Jace's face. His forehead is wrinkled and his eyebrows press together.

"It's okay." My voice is soft compared to the blaring music.

"I am glad that I got to know a little about ya." He smiles.

My eyes dart away searching for what I have no clue, but my eyes keep jumping from person to person in the room.

"Hey." He says tilting my chin. I meet his gaze. "I want to get to know you. I like you Casey. There is something about you."

I remove my head from his grasp. "I can only be friends with you."

"I can still get to know you." He chuckles and all I want to do is leave, get away from this man. For some reason, he's making my insides tangle up and I'm not ready for this. I'm not ready to take a step with someone, anyone right now and leading him to believe I do is plain out shitty of me. On top of that, if he knew about the baby, he'd be high tailing it as far as he could away from me.

I pull away from him. "I really think that Bella and I should get going. Thanks a lot for inviting us out."

Jace reaches up and grips my arm, not hard, but firm. "Please don't go."

"It's for the best." I turn away from him and spot Bella at the bar. I quickly walk up to her.

"I need to leave now. If you don't want to come, you'll need to find a ride."

"What's wrong?" She says her eyes widening in panic.

"Nothing's wrong. I just need to get out of here."

"It wouldn't have anything to do with the man coming up behind us would it?" Shit.

"I just need to go. Are you coming or not?"

"Let's go."

I turn just as Jace approaches. "Thank you so much for everything. We're going to head out."

"Casey. I'm sorry. You don't need to leave."

"Yes. I do. Thank you."

I grab Bella's arm pulling her out of the club and to the car. She doesn't say a word until the door's closed.

"What the hell was that?" She turns in the seat facing me.

"Bella, I get he likes me. I do. But I don't feel the same way and it will be totally shitty of me to let him think otherwise."

"I get it. I do. You like him, but there is something else going on here. What is it?" She eyes me and I want to spill it. I want to tell her everything, just so I have someone to talk to besides the doctor I saw just once. But I don't.

"Nothing. Just tired." It's not a full lie because I am; I'm just not admitting anything, not yet.

ONE WEEK FIVE DAYS LATER

Taking the drive down to Sumner, a sense of calm comes over me. And I know it's for one reason and one reason only. Pulling up to the large field lined with stones from one end to the other, I park my car in the vacant spot under the big oak tree.

Walking through the maze, my eyes peer down at the one I'm searching for. *Bam Alexander—Father and Brother.* I sit on the grass facing the tombstone of my father and reach out placing my hand on the cool stone. Closing my eyes, I let go.

"Hi Daddy. You're gonna be a grandpa." I smile. "I know. You're not too happy about it, but Daddy, I am. I love this little peanut inside of me. Every day I wonder what he or she will look like and what type of personality it will have. I read to the baby every night Daddy, just like you tried to do every night for me. I actually just started it this past week, but I'm trying." I let out a deep breath. "I don't want you to be disappointed in me. I'm scared that you are. I didn't have any intention of getting knocked up, and I should have known better. I haven't told G.T. yet Dad." I don't stop the tears from falling down my face, there is really no point.

"I want to wait to find out if it's a boy or a girl before I tell him." I pause. "Well, that's not entirely true. I do want to do that, but I also want to know I can do this on my own. Because that is what it is Dad. I will be a single mom, just like you were a single dad. Funny how things go around in life."

I pull up blades of grass from the ground and begin shredding them slowly feeling their smoothness between my fingers. "I'm going to school Daddy, just like you wanted. I haven't figured out how I'm going to be able to go to class and take care of the baby, but I've been thinking about it. I have a good friend Bella, you'd really like her Dad, and I was thinking of asking her to help out. I'm still working out the whole job thing, but I have some time." I feel a bit scatterbrained with all my rambling, but I need to tell him. I need to tell someone.

"I'm about eleven weeks now and the last time I went to the doctor she said everything looked really good. I'm due to go back in a couple of weeks." I breathe in the warm Georgia air, the humidity clinging to my skin. "I wish you were here to give me advice on how to tell G.T. I know he's going to be pissed at me. One for getting pregnant, even though he had as much to do with it as I did, and two for not telling him right away." I sigh. "Daddy. I've been working really hard since I left here to get my head screwed on straight. And I think I'm almost there. But when it comes to him, I'm still that same love struck kid and I hate it Dad. Hate it."

"I haven't told anyone about the baby but you. Not even Harlow. I want to so bad Dad. But she has a new life right now that she's dealing with and I don't want to add to it. I need her so desperately. Even when we talk on the phone, it's mostly her talking and me listening. I'm sure she doesn't intend for it, but it's there. And I'm okay with it."

"I will do you proud Daddy. I will be the best possible mom I can be. I will tell him or her all about you. I know I can do this because you did. I love you Daddy."

I sit for a long while just enjoying the silence.

I did not tell Harlow I was coming into town, because if I did she would have for sure insisted I came to see her and I can't. I can't look her in the eye and not tell her about the baby. Each time I talk to her, it gets harder and harder to keep my mouth shut.

During the ride back to Cherry Vale, I gather myself back together. I always love talking to my Dad as it gives me relief, but pulling myself together is always the hardest part.

Winding up to my apartment, Jace is standing by the front door. I swear part of me wonders if he has me pegged or something. He always seems to know where I will be. Since seeing him at the bar, he has said hi to me dozens of times and made the idlest of chit chats. He even brought me dinner a couple of times.

Damn if the man wasn't growing on me.

Climbing out of the car, I head to the door. "Hey. How's it going?"

"Good. Just got back from a run. Where you been off to?"

The innocent question doesn't take me aback as it would have a few weeks ago. "I went to talk to my Dad. Now I have to go study. Fun times." I smirk.

"You need some help?"

"Nah. But thanks."

ONE WEEK LATER

I HAVE A HUGE TEST TOMORROW. Huge and in the one subject that I do not freaking get, stupid Western Civ. What is the point of this class? I know some people prob-ably love it, but it is not my thing. After three hours of looking over notes and reading this book, I'm ready to throw the damn thing. Only bits and pieces are sinking in and I need a break.

Opening the fridge, I kick myself for not getting to the grocery store. With school and work, I haven't had much time and looking in the fridge moldy cheese isn't going to cut it. Bella and I have been doing mad dash runs to eat together, which has been really our only time together. We both need to keep our grades up and have been focusing on that solely.

My stomach aches and cramps. I curse myself. I should know better than to not eat especially with the baby growing inside. I take my vitamins religiously, but when I'm studying, all thoughts of eating fly out the window.

Grabbing my cash and keys, I head to the corner deli grabbing a turkey sandwich on wheat and eat it on the way back to my apartment. The day is beautiful and sunny, the warmth caressing me like a second skin.

Images of me walking with my little one flash through my head and excitement and happiness fill me. "Hey, what's got you smiling?" Jace's voice comes from the side of me making me jump a bit. He is in his running gear and slicked in sweat. His breathing is coming out in small pants as he pulls his head phones out of his ears.

"Just a beautiful day." I reply taking another bite and swallowing.

"Yes it is. I needed to get out and run. Can't let a beautiful day like this go to waste. You mind if I walk with ya back?" He asks panting.

"Not at all."

As we walk, I continue eating, trying to ease the ache

in my stomach. Jace talks about his classes and asks with interest about mine. Our conversation is casual and easy flowing. One thing that I've really grown to like about Jace is how easy it is to talk with him.

I yawn, "I'm really tired all of the sudden. I think it's all the studying." I smile softly.

"No problem. I gotta get in the shower and clean up." He smirks walking off to his place.

Entering my apartment a huge wave of exhaustion overtakes me. I crawl into my bed feeling the cool sheets hug my body and fall fast asleep.

HURT. Pain. Hurt. My body tosses and turns on its own accord not being able to get comfortable. My bed feels like a layer of rocks instead of its normal softness. I try to wake up from this horrible dream, from this horrible pain. But can't.

I move from side to side trying to get comfortable, but it's impossible. My eyes shoot open quickly and I immediately know the pain is not a dream. It is full out cramping in my stomach, my hands moving to clutch it. I quickly move the covers, but see nothing amiss. My gut is telling me something is wrong, very wrong.

I slowly get up each movement adding to the already agonizing pain inside. Add to that the frantic fear and I'm lucky I can even move to the bathroom. Pulling down my pants, my underwear is covered in blood. "What the hell!" I scream and panic overtakes me. *My baby.*

As quick as I can, I throw the pants and underwear off

of me and search for my phone. I need to find Bella. She can help me. I dial her number and it instantly goes into voice mail. A cramp hits so powerfully, I drop the phone and hear it clatter to the ground. I double over for a few minutes grabbing on to the counter top so I don't fall until the pain slightly subsides.

I slowly put on new underwear and pants, trying to figure out how to get to the hospital. Jace. Reaching down for my phone, I scream as the pain slices again through me, the pain bringing me to my knees on the floor as the crash to the tile. I reach for my phone and dial Jace's number. He answers on the first ring. *Thank you.*

"This is a nice surprise. See aren't you glad I gave you my number?" I do not have time for his smooth talking and cut him off abruptly.

"I need you to get over here now and get me to the hospital. I'm pregnant, about 12-13 weeks. I'm bleeding and in a lot of pain. Please hurry." I beg him, tears begin rolling down my face at the realization of what may be happening right now. Before I even get the last words out, loud banging echoes through the apartment.

"I'm coming. It's taking me a bit to get to the door." I say grabbing every bit of strength to get up off the floor. I grip my stomach and trying to walk as fast as I can, yet not nearly fast enough each step sending shooting pains through my body.

"Take your time and breathe. I'll get you to the hospital." His voice is calm and sure as he speaks to me through the door. I feel anything but.

I twist the locks on the door and open it wide. "Shit." He mutters, his eyes grow wide with panic as they trail up and down my body. "Come here." He picks me up in his arms, holds me close to his body on the elevator ride down and places me into his car. "Breathe. I'll get you there."

I bite my lip trying not to scream, but the pain is so intense, like nothing I've ever felt before, take cramping times a thousand. I close my eyes and rest my head on the seat biting back as much of the pain as I can. Jace doesn't say a word, he just drives... Fast, but everything is a blur to me.

Entering the ER, I tell the doctors and nurses in a rush as much as I can and they begin checking me from head to toe. They place me on a bed with wheels and move me here and there all the while my hands gripping my stomach tightly. The room they put me in is white and cold and IV's are placed in my arms and big machines that make lots of noises are brought in. They make Jace wait outside the room and I am utterly alone.

Tears stream uncontrollably down my face. I know my baby is gone. Deep down, I can feel the loss already.

After what feels like hours, the doctor pulls his chair up to the side of my bed and sits next to my head. "Ms. Alexander. I'm very sorry, but the baby didn't make it. At this time, we don't know why or if there is a reason you miscarried." Sobs escape my throat; my chest tightens to the point where I cannot breathe. I feel like I'm suffocating... dying. "I need to go in and do a D&C. That's where I go in and clean up your uterus."

"No!" I scream loud. "You are not taking my baby out of me!" I pull away from him and try to get up from the table, but the wires and tubes coming out of my body slow me down. I begin pulling them off of my body in a panic, the plastic foreign to my touch.

The doctor stands over me grabbing my arms. "Ms. Alexander. You must calm down. We must do the procedure, there is no choice." His voice is trying to soothe me, but nothing will at this point.

I stare at him fear ripping through me, my arms wrapping around my stomach. I never even told the father the baby existed and now it's gone. Gone, just like my Dad.

"I'm going to have the nurse give you something to settle you." I continue to stare at the man, my mind coming up a big blank canvas, void and nothingness. I don't have the will to stop him or argue with him anymore. I just don't care. If my baby's gone, I have nothing.

"I'M SO SORRY CASEY." Jace's voice whispers in my ear. I feel his hand rubbing the top of mine and I slowly open my eyes, the realization of what just happened hits me like a Mac truck.

I yank my hand from his placing both of them over my face and sob, uncontrollably. I pour every bit of sadness, frustration and longing into the tears that go on forever. I just can't stop.

I feel Jace by me, but I do not acknowledge him. I don't want him anywhere near me right now. I don't want anyone. I don't need anyone.

The door bursts open, but I don't bother looking, instead I try my best to curl up in a ball, tucking my feet to my chest. The pain is there, but this time I welcome it. At least I can feel something.

"Oh my God!" Bella's voice comes closer and she slides up to me, my eyes only seeing a blur of her from the water encasing them. "I'm so sorry babe. I wish you would have told me."

I continue to sob my words coming out choked. "It doesn't matter. It's gone. Everything is gone."

Bella lays her body next to mine and hugs me while I continue to sob.

CHAPTER THREE
GT

RIDING. IT'S THE ONLY TIME MY MIND IS FREE FROM ALL THE bullshit that clouds my life. Weaving in and out of the winding roads, feeling the breeze slamming my face washes away all the grisly, if only for a moment.

Riding lets me be free.

Some compare riding to sex, for me its better. Don't get me wrong, I'm all in for a good fuck, but even in the throes of lust, my mind doesn't shut the fuck up. Sex subdues it, but it's always there, mocking me, throwing all the shit I've done since I was thirteen in my face. The death and destruction are always there on the forefront mocking me.

There has only been one time in my life that sex was amazing. Where the act of sex actually shut off all the thoughts and let me live in a specific moment. But she is too good for an asshole like me. She deserves all the roses and sunshine bullshit that I can never give her. She's different from my sister, Princess. Even though she grew up in the club, she's not hardened by it. She's tough, don't get me wrong, but she is soft where Princess is rough. I didn't want to break it off with her and when I did it wasn't right, but I fully believe I did it to protect her in the long run. From me. Now, she hates me with every fiber in her being and it's best to keep it that way.

Ravage MC is my life. It is what I've been born and bred to do, to uphold and to protect. Outsiders say that I'm a poor boy whose dad thrust him into a life giving him no choice. Bullshit. There is always a choice. So what? I learned more at thirteen about the real world than most of those fucks know now. I know more about running businesses, making money and protecting what's mine than any of them and how to be successful at it. I may never have a college degree, but I make damn good money.

My brothers have my back at every turn and I can always count on them. How many people can say their family would do that for them? Not many.

This life is what I wanted. Everyone else can just go fuck themselves if they have a problem with it because it's their problem, not mine.

Pops did lay down ground rules for me though before I could become a brother of Ravage. One, I had to have my high school diploma in my hand. Two, I had to be legal.

In actuality, I have been prospecting since thirteen; I just didn't realize it at the time. Each menial task; such as cleaning up from parties or the shit on the bathroom floor were tests from the brothers. Whenever Pops told me to do something, I did it, no complaints. When I turned eighteen, I finally got my official Prospect rag. The party that night kicked fucking ass. I'd never been so happy and knee deep in pussy in my entire life.

After receiving my diploma, my graduation party turned into a full out club meeting with my official rag being placed on my back. Best fucking day ever.

Turning around the last bend with Dagger and Rhys by my side, the warehouse comes into view. Dewey is a supplier that we moved shit for throughout southern Georgia. I was going to come alone considering our long relationship with him, but after the ambush when we met Ransom and his crew, Diamond didn't want any of us going alone.

Scoping out the area, only three bikes sit in front of the old dilapidated warehouse, one I recognize immediately as Dewey's. Parking and keeping an eye on everything around us, Dagger and Rhys move right by my side.

"You ready for this shit?" Dagger asks looking at the door, his piece clutched in his hand.

"Yeah." I grunt, clutching mine as well. One can never be too careful these days. Turning the handle, the doors creak announcing our arrival. Guns up, three men instantly grab their pieces aiming them at our heads. Dewey smiles and begins to lower his. Searching the building, no other people are present except for some poor motherfucker strapped with chains on his wrists and hanging from a makeshift beam on the ceiling. Interesting.

Holding my hands up, I place my gun back in my rag motioning for the brothers to do the same. Dewey's crew follows. "What's going on?" I clip at the man walking towards me with his arm extended to shake my hand.

Extending my hand to his grasp, he said, "G.T. nice to see you. Sorry about our company up there. The boys were just having some fun with their toy before we cut him loose."

Releasing him, I cross my arms over my chest and widen my stance as I tower over him. "What do you need to see us about that couldn't be discussed over the phone?" Dewey's straggly blonde hair comes down to his chin, tats lining his wrists and shoulders. He is not imposing, but that's a hard task for anyone to be for me. Over the years, my resolve has hardened to any of that bullshit.

"New shipment. Guy I know wants two more runs a month." I stare at him, waiting, and my mind instantly running our monthly drop schedule. "It'll be a lot. You'd need your whole crew, but it'll only be a day ride. Best part, 300k in your pocket each run."

"What exactly will we be running?" Dewey snaps his finger as one of the goons who are playing with his hanging meal comes up carrying a duffle bag. Dewey bends down opening the bag. Fuck. Looking at Dagger and Rhys, their eyes dance saying the same thing.

"I'll run it by Diamond and get back to ya. Anything else?" I ask needing to get the hell out of there, just looking at what is in the duffle, will get us all thrown in prison for a long time and I'm not ready to put my ass on the line for this shit yet.

"I need to know by next month. If you don't want it, I gotta find other ways." Find other ways my ass. We are his only way and he damn well knows that shit. I fucking hate games, but that's how the world works. Everyone tries to one up ya, but Ravage does not get one-upped. Dewey may need a reminder of that.

Smirking to my brothers, I nod my chin dismissing the meeting.

These runs for Dewey are huge. All of us will be set for a long time with this amount of cash, but the risk is huge. Not only will every member of Ravage be on the transport, if caught, it will wipe us out, hard. I'm all about the cash, but my gut is screaming that something is wrong, and my gut has never let me down yet.

I'll put it out there at church and figure it out from there, but we will need lots of intel before we attempt this one.

The ride back is smooth, but my mind continuously drifts back to the one woman that plagues me. I should be happy she left to start her own life. Happy that she is going to school to better herself. Happy that she is finding a life that makes her happy. But deep down, I'm not. I'm a fucking selfish prick and even though I pushed her away, I want her home. I can't keep my fucking eyes on her up there and even if I have no damn right, I don't want to care.

Casey has turned me inside out since we were kids. Growing up alongside each other had its ups and downs. Ups when she actually paid me a lick of attention instead of seeing me as her best friend's kid brother, what a fucking pussy. And downs when she avoided me like the plague. I still remember her walking in on me fucking one of the club mommas, fuck if I even knew her name or wanted to. The light in Casey's eyes shattered right before me and I didn't do a fucking thing to fix it. I never thought she actually wanted me until that moment, but I was a fucking moron to never act on it.

Watching her walk around the club in those short ass shorts and hearing hear laugh was the most beautiful torture I could have. I could have fucked her at any time, just for the fun of it, but Casey has never been that type of girl. I never wanted her to be that type of girl and I damn well would have beaten the living shit out of anyone who treated her that way.

One day when I was younger, Bam caught me one day watching Casey. I didn't realize I was doing that shit, but I couldn't stop myself. He sat next to me and his words have stuck in my head since he said them. *'Son, until you're ready to be the man that she needs you to, stay away from her. She is not a piece of ass to anyone. She's too smart for that, I made sure of it. Once you know that you are man enough for my girl, then you will deserve her.'*

Being man enough isn't the problem, it's being able to give her the life that she deserves. I never asked her if she wanted this life, my life.

Even if it killed my heart to do it. Every woman I've been with was just a warm body. What Casey doesn't know and I sure as shit would never tell her... Is her face is the only one I saw. How fucked up is that? I couldn't tell you their names or what they looked like... nothing. Nothing at all. All I see is Casey's beautiful green eyes sparkling at me. Sick. Fucking sick. One of the reasons she's better off without me.

When Bam died, I was the one who told her. Princess was a fucking wreck and couldn't keep her shit together long enough to get it out. When Casey melted in my fucking arms, she stayed there for a week. I busted my fucking ass to make sure she was okay. I even fucking cooked for her ass. At times, it was like taking care of a child, but I fucking loved every minute of it, even if I never told her.

It was during that week that I knew I had to keep Casey at a distance or shit would get bad. A man can only hold back for so long and I kept telling myself it was for her own good, but damn it was hard.

A year and a half after Bam died Princess went to prison for blackmail, which we knew she didn't do, Casey was a fucking mess again, but this time, I stayed away. I knew one look in those green eyes would have me wanting to protect her ass all over again. And I didn't think this time I'd be able to hold back. I caught her crying outside the shop several times, but stayed away.

When I saw Tug comforting her, it fucking killed me because it should have been me. I couldn't watch it. I jumped on my bike and rode trying to get my head on straight. Problem was it wasn't. Nothing is straight where Casey is concerned. While I should have been fucking ecstatic to have cash in my pocket, power and pussy everywhere, I'm fucking miserable and I need to accept that.

I continually did my fucking job with the brothers and did it well. Pops and Diamond have set me up several times over the years in situations to see how I'd react and what I'd do. They didn't think I fucking knew... But I did. I may not have gone to college, but that doesn't mean I'm fucking stupid, especially when it comes to this life. Every test they have put me through is all leading up to the day when I'm at Pops side. Sitting at the side of the table with Pops at the head, when the time came. It is our legacy.

When my Pa, Striker died, Diamond took over. He was Striker's Vice President and that's how it worked. Diamond was voted in and that was that. I've never asked how Pops felt about that, but I knew there were no hard feelings between the two men, just by watching them over the years. But I knew that one day, he'd like to be sitting in that head spot, just like his father. So everything since I was thirteen years old has been preparing me for that day. And I'm more than ready for it when the time comes. I'm in no hurry. I have plenty of time.

One night when I got back from one of Diamond and Pops' tests, I was a fucking mess. I never let it show to the brothers, holding it tight never showing weakness. But that shit wears on a man sometimes. Taking another's life was never easy, even if they fucking deserved it. I remember the night when I got my first taste of my Angel.

Parking my bike, I see Casey still busy at work on one of the engines in the shop. With it being so late, it actually surprises me she is still around and I really don't want to see her. Every time I did, it's just a reminder of what I can't have.

After parking and taking off my lid, I glance over to Casey. Her knee is hoisted on top of the car body while her other foot rests flat on the ground. Her body slowly turned to me as if she could tell I was looking at her. Meeting her eyes, I feel paralyzed. Fuck. Casey smiles that megawatt smile of hers and nods her head up in the air to me.

Nodding back, I know I should walk away. I know I should go find a momma and just get lost in her for a little while. But ... Casey is a magnet that I can't stay away from. She calls to me... And I can't say no. I don't want to say no.

Walking over to the garage, Casey moves, turning towards me, setting both feet to the ground. "Hey G.T. How's it goin'?" My dick pushes painfully against the zipper of my leathers. She did this every fucking time. There is no way of escaping it.

"Fine. You?" I clip a little harsher than I intended to, the frustration within myself rising.

"Here. Trying to get this car up and going. Still haven't figured out what the hell's wrong with it." She says as she turns her beautiful body to the car, staring at the engine. My eyes follow her long back that is covered with the hideous jumpsuit. I knew what was under it though, I've been watching it for years and I want it so badly.

"I'm sure you'll figure it out." I should turn and walk back to the clubhouse. I should, but don't.

She turns back around she shrugs her shoulders, "I'll get it. You doing okay? You seem off?" Her brows crinkle causing her forehead to wrinkle, concern filling her eyes. Boy did that fuck with my head. Shit.

"Rough night. I've gotta go." I say needing to get the hell out of there. I need to get away from her while every fucking bone and muscle in my body was telling me to stay.

A small hand grabs my arm and stops me dead in my tracks. "You know you can talk to me. I'll listen G.T." Her sweet words flow through me as I turn to look in her glassy green eyes and something inside of me snaps.

As Casey's eyes widened, I knew she felt it, whatever in the hell this was, too. I can't keep doing this. I can't keep her away. I need her, more than she'll ever know. With my arm still firmly in her grasp, I reach around her, pulling the hair tie out of her hair as it falls down her back. I thread my fingers through her beautiful blonde hair and search her eyes, hoping and not hoping she will tell me to stop, and when she doesn't... My lips meet hers in a frenzy, where she gives as good as she gets.

Casey's arms circle around my neck pulling me closer as one of her hands threads through the back of my hair. Her tugs and pulls felt desperate as if she thought I'd move away from her. But I wasn't fucking going anywhere. Not this time.

Releasing her hair, my hands instantly land on her round ass pulling her up high, as her legs had no other option but to wrap around my waist. Walking over slowly, I open my eye to find the red button that would close the garage door. Hitting it, the sound of it shutting did not deter Casey one bit, if anything it fueled her. Her hips move in sync with our kisses.

Her tongue entangles with mine as the taste of mint and cherries invade my lips. Walking to the back of the car, I lay her down breaking away from the kiss, instantly feeling the loss. Her breathing comes out in pants as she reaches up to the zipper on her jumper, slowly pulling it down revealing her tight ass black tank top and jeans. She peels the jumper off ever so slowly as she moves, wiggling her body to get it off. When the jumper reaches her feet, her eyes lock with mine. "Wanna help me here biker boy?" She smirks; the confidence in her words makes me regret all of this lost time I could have had with her.

"Boy my ass." I pull her boots off her body along with the jumper as she lay there fully clothed but completely open to me. This is a fantasy that I slept with nightly and it is lying here ready for the taking. And damn it if I wasn't going to take.

My hands snake up her jean covered legs as her head falls back onto the car window. My hands slowly make their way up to the buckle of her jeans. My fingers make quick work as I pull her jeans away from her body revealing a small triangle of fabric, pretending to be underwear. A low growl escapes my lips, the inferno in my body losing control. "I can smell you Casey. You want this."

"Yes" her whisper breathless.

My hands move up her body slipping underneath her tank feeling the soft skin of her stomach. As my hands raise her shirt, my tongue lands below her belly button, licking the path my hands made. Her sweetness mixed with her sweat from working all day causes my heart to beat so fucking fast it may just blow.

Reaching her tits that bounce up and down along with her heavy breathing, I pull one out of the confines of her matching pink bra. In this position, her nipple stands tall waiting for me, but not for long. My lips latch on sucking hard as she cries out my name; her hands reach my head lacing her fingers through my hair.

Pulling away, her whimper made me smile. "Hands above your head and don't fucking move them." I order her. Casey's beautiful eyes widen, her tongue snakes out to lick her bottom lip. Her arms slowly rise above her head, her eyes never leave mine. Something inside of me always screamed that she would instantly obey my commands. I continue my assault on her tits one at a time feeling her body shudder under my touch. I rip her tank off, throwing it to the floor as Casey instantly returns her hands to the exact spot I told her, making me smile. Damn.

"As much as I'd love to play, I can't right now. I need to be inside you." At my words, her eyes roll in the back of her head. "On me Casey. Your eyes are always on mine." Her eyes open instantly and bore into mine. I pull away shredding every

piece of clothing I have on my body quickly, her eyes never leaving mine.

Gripping my fully erect cock in my hand, I move slowly up and down just taking in the sight before me, etching every curve of her body into my brain. Casey laying out for me like a perfect dessert ready for the taking. Her arms stretch up and her legs open wide. Reaching her pink panties, I tear one side of the fabric and then the other, warranting a gasp from Casey's plump lips as I throw the scrap of fabric on top of my clothes. That I'm keeping.

Climbing up her body, my skin sizzles every place she touches mine. I can't wait a moment longer, my need for her overriding my sanity. I plunge into her wet pussy hard and fast, shaking the car underneath us as she screams loudly. "Fuck baby. You're so damn tight, wet. Fuck." Gripping her hips, I pound into her body, never feeling like I've reached deep enough inside her. Casey's eyes threaten to shut, but instantly pop open.

"G.T.!" She screams over and over watching my face, sweat beginning to trickle off my nose and down her body. I'm not going to last, she's too perfect and I've waited too long for this moment.

"Come on Babe. Come for me. Let me hear you." Grabbing her knees, I pull her body down the car, her pussy now in line with my cock as I stand. Over and over and over I thrust in and out of her. Casey's eyes are magnets to mine and I'm relieved for it. I need to know she's here with me at this moment. She screams my name profusely and falls back in a heap on the car as her orgasm hits losing the eye contact I craved.

"Damn Casey. Damn." My cum shoots out hot, fast and my whole body convulses feeling Casey down to my toes. After

the shocks let up, I collapse down over her body crushing her to the car. Her arms come around my sweaty back; her lips kiss the side of my face.

"Yeah... Damn." She whispers in my ear breathing in and out quickly. We lay there for quite some time, neither one of us willing to make the first move. My cock begins to soften inside of her and I feel my cum begin to trickle down our joined bodies. My body goes stiff as a terrible realization hits me.

"Fuck Casey. I didn't wear a condom. Fuck!" I bark loudly as I slowly pull out of her. I'm always fucking covered, what the fuck is wrong with me.

"Are you clean?" She asks me nervously as I stand there watching my cum seep out of her pussy and drip down the crack of her ass. My dick instantly going hard all over again.

"Yeah. I'm always covered. Always."

"Not always." She sighs. "I have the injection so we're covered on the pregnancy end." Casey began to move off the car as I stand there just staring at her pussy. "You can stop staring now." She smiles, hopping down.

"Babe. Watching my cum fall out of you, is the sexiest fucking thing I've ever seen." I lick my lips contemplating if I should just throw her back up on the trunk of the car and lick her clean.

Shaking her head, she walks past me to the garage bathroom. I snap out of my cum dripping haze and throw my leathers back on not bothering to button them. Fuck, I want her again. I need her again. As she strolls out naked, I take in every inch of her fantastic body. The way her tits stand to attention on their own, the curves of her hips, the way her hair flows freely down her back.

As she approaches me, her smile deepens as if she's reading my mind. "That was a long time coming, biker boy." She stands on her tip toes and kisses the tip of my nose. No way. This is not goodbye. I'm not done. Wrapping my arms around her waist, I crash my lips to hers so hard I taste blood for a moment, but don't fucking care.

FROM THAT MOMENT the next two weeks were the best of my fucking life, Casey stayed in my bed and I fucked her every goddamned way I could come up with. I didn't touch another pussy, didn't even fucking look at one. I had the only fucking one I wanted. When she started talking about school and not wanting to move away from me, I knew I couldn't keep her. She had every intention of giving up school just to stay by me and I couldn't let that happen. She deserved so much fucking better than an asshole like me. But I couldn't give her up. Better yet, I didn't fucking want to give her up.

It crushed me to give Casey the final blow, but knew it had to be done. No matter how much I wanted her, I couldn't have her.

"HEY DEDE. YOU ABOUT DONE?" I ask the woman straightening up the bed in my room. I've had DeDe cleaning my room now for the past few months. She's a club momma and I've gotten my fill from her, but a lot of flirting goes a long way in getting shit done. And I need this pigsty cleaned up and I'm not doing it.

"Hey, almost done." She looks up and smiles at me, batting those long eyelashes, the ones that used to have my dick getting hard instantly, but now, nothing. Not with my Angel

in my bed. It's about damn time, I've waited too fucking long to have her.

But I can't get the words out of my head that I overheard earlier today. The words that have been killing me inside. The words that will make me give up the one thing that I desperately want. What a fucking pussy. But for her I'll do anything.

"You need me to stick around?" She asks seductively walking up to me standing at the door.

"Nah babe. I'm good." I step outside the door allowing her through. She stands up on her tiptoes and presses a kiss on my lips in a simple peck that I don't really reciprocate.

A gasp comes from the end of the hall and Casey's eyes are penetrating me. If they were daggers, I'd be fucking dead in a puddle of my own blood. Her eyes shatter before me, the light drifting to dark and as much as it kills me those fucking words travel back in my head and I seize the moment.

"Sorry babe. I need more than one pussy. Variety always works best for me." I shrug my shoulder as if it's no big deal, but inside I'm crumbling to the ground. She doesn't say a word, just turns and walks away. It takes everything in my power to not run to her and tell her that it was a fucking lie, but I can't because this is the only way.

IT'S BEEN weeks since I had her last and I can't fucking stand to be in another pussy. I've tried, but it doesn't happen. I always end up having the bitch suck me off and it's just for the physical release.

I haven't talked to Princess about this shit. I don't even know what to say. I just stay the fuck away from her. If she tries to talk to me, I brush her off or leave. Even with the big blow out, when we fought in the ring, I didn't talk.

The only reason I even fought her was because she challenged me. I couldn't back down from that shit and I knew she could take it. Each blow I landed didn't make me feel any better at all and the only thing the fight accomplished was getting bloody and bruised. It did help give me some release though, even if I still missed my Angel.

Pulling up to the clubhouse, Buzz is at the main gates to move the steel fence letting us in. We are not on lockdown, but Diamond insists we keep the place pretty secure which means a Prospect at the main gates at all times, determining who can come in and who can fuck off. Personally, I think it's a good move.

I know Dagger and Rhys will want to sit and hash out what just went down before bringing it to the table. After parking and entering the club, we side up around one of the tables, chin lifting everyone we see, but keeping to ourselves for a moment. Breaker brings us three bottles of beer, a bottle of Jim and glasses. He knows us well.

"So, what the fuck?" Dagger starts and I have the same thing on my mind.

"Shit. I don't know. It'd be a shit ton of money, but fuck... That's some serious shit. We'd be fucked if we got caught. There'd be no way to get out of that shit." Rhys voices before downing a shot of Jim. He is totally right. I nod.

"Something doesn't feel right guys. I don't know what it is, but something's off." My gut is screaming at me. I've always trusted it. As good as the money is, it'll be hard to turn down, but money is not everything. Freedom is.

"Agree. We'll take it to the table." Rhys says slamming his hand to the table.

"Agreed. So, boys... I'm thinking I need to get laid." Dagger looks over at the couch where the two club momma's are laying staring at the television in front of them. "My dick's hard thinking about all that money."

"I hear ya," Said Rhys. "I've fucked those two one too many times. We need fresh meat in this fucking place." He growls. I lift my chin in agreement, even if I'm not actually fucking them.

Dagger walks over to the couch holding out both his hands to the girls who take them readily, walking off to the back. Dagger has an ol' lady, Flash, but what happens in the club stays in the club.

"What's goin' on brother?" Rhys asks me taking another shot of Jim. Rhys is not a small talk, conversational type dude so when he asked you answer.

"Shit on my mind. I'll be good." He swirls the drink he just poured eyeing it.

"You've been having a lot of that lately." His tone comes across accusingly.

Anger rose. "What the fuck does that mean?" I glare at him.

His poignant stare keeping my anger pushed deep down if only for a moment. "Look. If you need me, I'm here."

"Thanks man. But I'm good." I put off. I need to talk about it, but fuck where the hell do I fucking start.

"You hung up on Casey?" His words stop me, but I brush them off.

"Nah. She's better where she is."

"Didn't ask you that shit. We all know that women are better off away from us. Wanna tell me the real reason you lied?"

Fuck. How the hell did he fucking know about all that shit and when the hell did we turn into a bunch of fucking pussies talking about this? My nostrils flare and I clench my fists ready to fucking punch my brother, but when he continues, I freeze. "Look, since she left, you've been a miserable fuck. You do your job, party, but it's not you. That shit's gonna get you killed. Your fucking head is not in it."

I can't fucking argue with that. My head is everywhere other than where it should be at the moment. But everything's fucking riding me hard. Rubbing my hands up and down my face, "I'll be good."

I swipe my hand across my face standing up. "I just need some fucking sleep."

CHAPTER FOUR
Casey

NOTHING. I FEEL NOTHING INSIDE LIKE I'M A VOID OF A person, a waste of flesh and bones. My heart has no feeling; its only purpose is to keep me alive for some reason. Lying in this bed, all I do is exist breathing in air and taking it away from someone else on the planet. I haven't been to class at all this week and more than likely, won't go next week either. What the hell's the point? My baby is dead. Gone. And what's worse, there isn't even a body to bury. Nothing, like I never had a life in my body, never carried it for weeks, never grew attached. Nothing. I can't go visit my baby like I do Dad. The baby just vanished like she was nothing in this world.

"Casey. You have to get out of bed." Bella comes by four or five times a day trying to get me to leave this bed. I'm now sorry I gave her a damn key to the place because all I want is to be left alone. "You have to eat. Come on." I groan. I hate eating. I hate breathing for that matter. I thought the death of Dad was hard; this is a whole different kind of pain. One that has so many 'what if...' questions that it shreds my heart with each passing minute. I don't even know why I exist anymore. At least with my baby, I had a purpose and a cause. Now, I have nothing.

"Jace is coming over to help me give you a shower. It's either we give it to you or you take it yourself, but girl you are getting washed. You stink. And you are eating. I can see your damn bones Casey."

I tune her out, close my eyes and will myself to sleep.

THREE DAYS LATER

I'M COMING to the realization fast that this pain in my chest will never go away. It's so deeply embedded that nothing will help it or me. But I am trying to move. At least around the apartment. After Bella and Jace had given me their wonderful pep talks, I came to the conclusion that they weren't going to leave me the hell alone and short of shooting them both, I needed to at least appear to want to get myself together.

But I refuse to go to classes. I told them I had a medical emergency and left it at that. My professors gave my assignments to Bella, but they sit on my desk untouched.

I'm never alone though. Either Bella or Jace is here at all times. I should be grateful to have them, but I'd really like it if they left me alone. They walk around on eggshells around me. Always giving each other looks and having some silent conversation between themselves. It feels like they want me to blow, but I have no desire to. There is no reason.

"What do ya want to do today?" Jace asks from the couch where he's lounged with his feet up clicking through the channels on the TV. If I were in my right mind, I would tell him to get out and stop acting like this is his place. But I can't and won't.

"Nothing." It's my answer to his question every time he asks.

"Let's watch a movie, you pick." He pushes.

"No." I walk around to the fridge, opening the door and closing it just as quickly. Nothing sounds good and my stomach roils just thinking about food. Crackers... Maybe crackers.

"What's that noise?" Jace moves towards me trying to figure out where it's coming from. And I listen hearing a slight sound and instantly know.

Shit. "That's my phone. I need to find it." I slowly look for the pre-paid phone that if I don't answer will set off a shit storm back at the club that I am in no way shape or form able to handle at the moment.

Digging through the pile of papers, I find it inside my brown bag. I quickly swipe the screen and put on my happiest voice I can come up with. *Faker.*

"Hey." I answer quickly moving away from Jace.

"Hey Hoochie! When you coming to see me?" The happiness in Harlow's voice radiates through the phone only making me feel lower.

"I can't come right now. Classes and work." Lying to her sucks. I always hate it and rarely do it, but this time it is a necessary evil. The clearing of a throat makes my eyes lift to Jace's who shakes his head. I glare at him not needing his shit right now. Why won't he just go away?

I turn my back hoping to snub him. "How's life up in Cherry Vale?

Horrible. "Great. Everything's going good."

"You're lying to me." My breath catches and I sit there for a beat. "You're never this happy or perky, even when you're in a good mood. Care to tell me what the hell is going on?"

The hand holding my phone begins to shake and my happy resolve is beginning to fade. I think quick, "School's just tough, but I'm getting it. Everything is fine." I try to say reassuringly.

"Yeah. Right. I don't believe you, something is up. And I will find out what it is." My heart stops. "I'll drop it for now, but I won't forget. Cruz and Cooper send their love. Cooper is just a great little boy Casey. He's growing up so fast. I wish you were here to see it." Tears well up in my eyes for the baby that I will never see grow, never see take her first steps or her first bite of real food, never get to hold. I move the phone away from my face and blow out a deep breath, bringing it back to my mouth, trying to calm myself.

"Tell them I miss them too. Low, I have a huge test coming up. I've really got to go." Or else I am totally going to lose my shit.

"Alright. I know something's not right. You'd better be okay. If you don't tell me by the next time I call, I'm coming up there." Shit. Harlow never gives up.

"Yep. Just busy. I'll call you back soon. Okay?"

"Alright. Love you."

"Love you too." I click the phone off quickly; my legs give out, my ass hits the floor with a thud, my body follows behind it. Jace immediately wraps his arms around me, picking me up, cradling me to his chest like an infant. Tears fall rapidly down my face and Jace clutches me tight to his chest.

CHAPTER FIVE
GT

EIGHT DAYS LATER

PULLING UP TO A WIDE OPEN SPACE, RABBIT'S CREW IS waiting for us. These past few months with Rabbit have been rocky as shit. From shootouts, beat downs, destruction of property and Babs, Rabbit's ol' lady, setting Princess up and kidnapping Cooper her son, it's been a giant cluster fuck. We handled it but not exactly how we wanted to. Supposedly, Diamond says it's all fine and wonderful. Sure. Rabbit hasn't gotten what he deserves yet.

Rabbit stands next to his bike with several of his guys lining the way, each having guns in their hands, which is typical. If they didn't, I'd think something is up.

Diamond, Pops, Dagger, Rhys, Cruz, Zed, Becs and myself all climb off our bikes putting our lids on the bars, while Tug, Breaker and Buzz slowly park the large cage that housed everything we would need, just in case. Diamond steps forward, but before a word escapes his mouth, shots are fired loudly all around us. Every brother scrambles to get behind our bikes as shields. It's the best we've got at the moment.

Looking around quickly, each man has their guns drawn firing rapidly. Looking across the lot, Rabbit's crew has moved back from where they were standing, but not shooting, their guns at their sides. But their eyes are cold and locked on all of us. Searching for where the shots are coming from, out from the side, a local crew called the T-Darts come at us guns blazing. One shot after another barely missing us as the pings of the bullets hit the bikes guarding us.

Stepping slightly out from behind a large tree, Paine, the President of the T-Darts, aims at us hard. His void eyes are focused and controlled. This is serious shit. "We gotta get the fuck out of here!" I yell to all the guys trying to motion them to the cage.

"Get behind us!" Dagger yells to Diamond, but he doesn't fucking listen, the damn stubborn ol' man. Instead, he starts moving with the rest of us guns still blazing.

"Pops behind me!" I yell, but he is just as bullheaded as Diamond and continues to move with us.

Diamond barks, "Get to the cage! Now!"

Shot after shot hit the dirt and our bikes ringing off into the distance. Trying to keep an accurate account on where all the shots are coming from is getting fucking difficult. We move quickly and keep pace with each other. Diamond is moving right in front of me as I try to position my body in front of him.

Loud grunts. Fuck. Diamond. Blood pours out of his body. Using every bit of strength I have, I push him hard to the cage and watch him fall to the ground. Rushing to him, a sharp, searing pain flows through my body. Instantly, my legs give out, crashing me to the ground.

Fuck! I clutch my gun tightly in my hand continuously shooting even though the pain is raging. Cruz grabs underneath my arms, dragging me towards the cage. Reaching it, my arms fall to the side, my body no longer having the energy to hold them up. I can hear words, but everything is so fucking muffled it's as if I'm underwater floating. More noises and some movement, but I am useless, nothing wants to work on my body. I try, but everything is still. I feel my eyes slowly begin to shut. I will them to stay open, but it's too much and I give in. The last thing I see is Casey's beautiful face before everything goes dark.

"WAKE UP YOU DICK!" Princess' voice is so fucking loud, like she's got one of those bull horns up against my ear. My head is fucking pounding and my body almost completely numb. Trying to roll over, my body is instantly halted by something big and strong. My body is too weak and numb to fight it off. I can't do anything but lay there.

"G.T. wake your fucking ass up now!" Princess barks louder this time. I want to answer her and tell her to shut the fuck up, but my mouth is dry and I'm finding it difficult to open it. Trying to open my eyes, I fight to get just one lid open, but nothing. Then darkness finds me again and Princess' voice fades in the distance.

"Doc, I gave him the meds like you said, but he isn't waking up. Ma's been here non-stop and hasn't seen anything. And I only saw him move that first day and then pass out. What the fuck is going on?" Princess' voice is coming in much clearer than before and I'm actually able to process the words she is saying.

I try opening my eyes again, but the fuckers feel like they have duct tape keeping them shut to my face. Searing pain is moving through my chest and shoulder and when I try moving it, again, nothing happens. Panic hits me. *What the fuck is wrong with me?*

"Calm your ass down young lady." Doc scolds Princess. "He lost a lot of blood. I pumped him full, but it'll take some time to get him back on track. And the morphine knocks him out. Let's cut back half on the morphine and see if he wakes up."

Morphine. Meds. That's why I can't move my fucking body. That answer I can handle. At least I'm not fucking dead.

"Fine." Princess clips. I can feel a presence at my side. "Come on asshole. Wake up so I can be pissed at you."

"Princess!" Ma yells out. "Don't!" Fucking great, they're both here.

"Come on Ma. You know he's not gonna respond to me breathing sweet nothings in his damn ear. I need to get Casey's ass here. She'd be able to wake him up." Her name. Casey. God I want to see her, smell her, and feel her.

"Yeah, she would alright." Ma mutters. "You two need to knock this shit off now. He wakes up, you fix whatever this is."

"Me fix it? He's the one that got pissed at me Ma. How the hell can I?"

"Figure it out!" Ma said, as I feel her squeeze my hand.

"He'll get through this Ma." Princess says.

"He'd damn well better."

I tune them out and thoughts of my beautiful girl drift me back off to sleep.

HER BLONDE HAIR whips in the wind as I see her sitting on a picnic table. I've seen her there so many damn times and she's always wearing barely anything. If I didn't know better I'd think she was trying to fit in with the momma's, but she would never. This is just her.

I walk slowly up to her, her eyes widen in surprise as I grip her in my arms slamming my lips to hers. It only takes her a moment and she is there with me, kissing every inch of me back.

The entire world disappears and there is only the two of us in the middle of the courtyard, nothing else exists. I kiss down her neck, licking as I go, tasting the sun and sweat on her skin. Her moans and whimpers push my drive.

I pull the small scrap of fabric she calls a shirt over hear head, pull her tits out of her bra and suck hard. Her body arches off of the table and she screams my name.

"Please" she begs. I rip her shorts off along with my jeans,

sliding into her in one thrust. In and out, I set the rhythm and she meets me move for move...

I STARTLE to the sound of Pop's voice. "What's the latest?" He bellows a distance away from me, pulling me out of my dream.

"He's been moving a bit more and moaning something, but hasn't opened his eyes." Princess replies her voice sounding tired.

My eyes feel laced with sand, scratchy gritty sand, dry as a desert. But I so badly want to open them, but my fucking body will not listen. If I'm not dead, I sure as hell don't want to lay here listening to Princess bellow day in and day out for the rest of my life. Trying with everything I have, I slowly pry one eye open, the grittiness from the sand making it difficult to see.

"Shit." Pops voice says coming closer to me. "Boy... Boy can you hear me?"

My throat is raw and stuck. Trying to clear it, I make some unusual sounds and grunts. Finally, I open both my eyes and blink repeatedly trying to focus them on the blurry figures in front of me. I know who they are by their voices, but they are one big grainy blob. As they slowly come into focus, Pops stands next to me, arms crossed over his chest, his breathing heavy. Looking into his eyes, pain is ripping through them. "Diamond," I croak out my voice nothing like its normal self.

"He's gone brother." The pain in Pops voice is deep.

"Shit." I groan. The weight of what happened begins to crush me. I didn't push him out of the way quick enough. I didn't fucking save him. It's my fucking fault.

"How are you feeling?" Ma asks standing on the other side of me, knocking me out of my thoughts. Her hand sweeps the hair away from my eyes.

"Like shit." I croak out like a damn frog.

"You scared the shit out of us!" Princess yells from the end of the bed, but I'm unable to lift my head to see her.

"Nice to see you too sis." Fighting with her is not on the top of my to-do list at the moment, but knowing her, she won't give me much of a choice.

Glancing over at Pops and ignoring Princess, "What's the plan?"

"You get better then we'll talk." He dismisses.

"You Prez?" Pops nods his head but doesn't say a word. I grunt turning away mumbling to whoever would listen and answer. "How long am I down?"

Princess cuts in. "Don't know yet you stubborn asshole. But you mark my fucking words, while you're lying here; we talk and get this shit taken care of." I close my eyes silently wishing for Princess to disappear. "No getting out of talking this time." The finality in her words is annoying as hell because there is no fucking way I'm telling her shit, especially while I'm lying here and can't get the fuck away from her.

CHAPTER SIX
Casey

"I'M PROUD OF YOU." BELLA'S STORMY EYES FOCUS ON MINE and I stare blankly back wondering what the hell she's talking about. Since my baby died, I've been a walking zombie. "You are an amazing woman."

I chuckled softly. "No. I'm not. If I were *amazing* as you put it, I would have known how to save my baby."

"Babe. There was nothing you could have done. Nothing and it is not your fault." The sincerity in her eyes is too much. I grunt and turn away from her. This past week has sped by so fast, but I did go to class several times and I have gotten caught up on all the assignments that I missed. It's been nice to focus on something other than my baby being gone.

I'm being a total bitch to both Bella and Jace, but I can't seem to help myself. The anger inside of me keeps bubbling over, splashing to the floor like hot lava. I want my baby back. Over this past week, I determined that my baby was a girl and I've named her Mia. When I told Bella and Jace, they turned and looked at each other, but neither of them said a word to me about it.

Mia was a person, she was my person and I refuse to sweep her under the rug as if she never existed.

Bella places a hand on my shoulder, my body tenses. "Casey. You are an unbelievably strong woman. You've made choices that I don't know if I could have made, to make your life better with your baby. Life dealt you a shit blow, but your strength will get you through this."

Tears brim my eyes, I turn into Bella's arms and silently cry. Wishing the pain to go away, I release her, head to my room and pull the covers over my head.

When I awake, the sun is beginning to lower, casting shadows out on the world, exactly like I'm feeling, dark and shadowed. I walk into the kitchen the smell of basil invades my nose. Bella is moving around the kitchen, moving from place to place quickly grabbing utensils and ingredients out of the cabinet like a well-oiled machine. I breathe in deep again this time the smell of tomatoes or sauce flowing through me, my stomach growling reminding me that it's been a long time since I've really eaten. "How ya doing?" She asks stirring something in a pot.

"Alright. Sorry about earlier."

Bella comes over and wraps her arms around me tightly. "No need. That's what I'm here for. We will get through this together." I nod and embrace her tightly.

"Whatcha making? I'm hungry." Bella pulls away from me, looking into my face questioningly.

"Really? I think that's the first time you've said that in weeks." She smiles. "Spaghetti."

"Sounds good." I slide up to the kitchen island grabbing a napkin. I begin tearing it into very small pieces without even thinking about it. My appetite is slowly coming back, but I can only handle small bits of food or I feel like I'll puke.

"Your phone over there has been going off like crazy. I put it on silent 'cause I didn't want it to wake you." She points over to my pre-pay and only one person calls me on it.

My stomach hits the floor. There is no way that I want to talk to Harlow right now. Just hearing about her family, guts me. I want to be happy for her. She deserves it. But just hearing about how perfect Cooper and Cruz are kills me on the inside. I don't want to be jealous of my best friend, but I can't help it. She has everything that I've ever wanted and I'm totally alone, again. But if I don't call her soon, Harlow will send out the cavalry to hunt me down.

"What's wrong?" Bella asks, looking away from her pot.

"I just don't know if I can talk to Harlow. Does it make me a horrible person to not want to hear about how perfect her family is?"

Bella puts the spoon down and sits next to me at the island. "You need to tell her what happened Casey." I gasp and she reaches for my hand squeezing it softly. "No, really. You need to tell her. She's been your best friend for years and from what you've told me she sounds like an understanding woman. You also need to tell the baby's father."

"I had every intention of telling them both. I wanted

to wait until I knew if it was a boy or a girl. Harlow was just going through so much I didn't want to add to her problems. And G.T., he wanted nothing to do with me." I look down at the shredded napkin in front of me. "I've known him my whole life and part of me was so terrified that he'd reject the baby, now it just doesn't matter." Bella squeezes harder.

"It does matter."

"He sees me as just another piece of ass and I can't do that to myself. It kills me. I've been in love with him for so long that the thought of having a part of him growing inside of me made me stronger. How pathetic is that?" I shake my head.

"It's not pathetic. You are strong with or without the baby. You have to know that."

I give her a small smile, not totally believing her words. "I came to school to make something of myself for Mia and me. Now, I don't know what I need to do. I'm kinda lost."

"It's okay to not know. You put one foot in front of the other and move. That's all you can do right now."

I look over at the phone. "How many times did it go off?" I ask.

"Probably ten or more."

I jump from my seat. There is no way that Harlow would call that many times in a row unless something is wrong. Grabbing the phone, I look and there are thirteen missed calls and the voicemail button is flashing. I don't bother checking the messages, I just call her back.

Harlow answers on the first ring.

"What's wrong?" I ask immediately.

"Get your shit and get home now." Harlow's voice is panicked.

"What's going on Low?" I ask using the nickname I gave her when we were kids.

"Diamond's dead." Everything stops. I grab the closest chair I can find and sit down, hard on it. The air in my body gushes out of me while I try to process the words that just came out of her mouth. He was getting up there in age, but he was still so full of life.

"How?" I whisper into the phone as my trembling hand tried to hold it steady.

"Shot."

"Oh. God." I clutch my chest the ache coming hard and fast. Diamond has always kept his eye on me since Bam died. He'd come to the shop and ask me how I was doing, but never in that overprotective sort of way. Just in a casual grandfather way.

They're all gone. Dad, Mia and Diamond. The dark cloud of sadness I've felt over the last couple of weeks gets darker and I feel myself getting more lost in it.

"There's more." Her voice cracks at her words.

"Shit. Who else?" I ask not knowing if I can handle the answer, but needing to know.

"G.T." All-encompassing panic floods through my body eating every cell it can find. Somehow my body left the chair, falling to the floor with a loud thunk, the phone in my hand begins to shake and I clutch it trying not to drop it. Immediately, Bella comes rushing to my side.

"Are you okay?" Bella asks and I shake my head, but can't move from this spot.

"Casey!" I hear Harlow scream into the phone, but I

cannot seem to formulate words. "Casey! Answer me dammit. He's not dead!" She screams louder.

Not dead. She just said not dead, right? "What?" My voice mutters.

"Shit. Don't fucking do that! Do you know how much shit I'm under and you not answering scared the living hell out of me."

"What about G.T., Harlow?" I bite out quickly.

"He was shot twice. Once in the shoulder and once in the chest. Doc sewed him up, said he's gonna be okay. He was out of it for a couple of days. Still pretty out of it."

"So this happened two days ago and you're just now calling me?" I yell, my anger peaks. How in the hell could she keep this from me for so long?

"It was really touch and go. I was taking care of him around the clock and when I wasn't I had my boys. It's just been crazy. And I wanted to make sure he was okay."

"And what if he wouldn't have been? Don't you think I would have wanted to say goodbye, Harlow!" I bark even louder into the phone unable to control my anger. I rise from the floor and begin pacing quickly.

"I didn't think about that." The sheepishness in her voice normally would have me calming down, but I am not in a forgiving mood.

"No! You didn't. Is he awake and talking?" My body tenses not knowing if she's about to totally shatter me.

"Yeah. He's his stubborn ass self. Look, you need to get your shit and get home."

"When's the service?" I know I'm being rude, but I don't give a damn. How dare she not tell me?

"End of the week they're thinking. But it's more. All the guys got shot at. They're not talking about it only to say that someone is gunning for them. We're on lock-down and that includes you."

"No. I can't. I have my life here. I'll come to the services, but I'm not doing lockdown." I will hold my ground on this one. I mean nothing to any of them except Harlow. I will not subject myself to a lockdown or to be in a confined space with all of them.

"You don't have a fucking choice. Buzz is on his way up there now to help you with your shit and follow you back since I know you won't leave your car. Start packing and plan on staying for a while."

"No. I'm not coming Harlow. Like I said, I'll be there for Diamond, but I will not do a lockdown." I argue.

Harlow screams in the phone, forcing me to pull the phone away from my ear. "Fuck you! Yes, you will! You're part of this fucking family and so help me God if I have to leave here right now to come and drag your ass here, I fucking will. My head's in a lot of different places right now Casey and I will not be worrying about your fucking ass! Pack and be ready when Buzz gets there!"

While Harlow definitely has a temper, she's never really gone off on me like this before. And even though I'm still pissed at her, the desperation in her voice has me tap down my hurt and all the swirling emotions plaguing me. She is scared shitless and has no control over anything. This is her way of getting some control, even if it is bossing me around. I know what I have to do even if I don't want to.

"I've gotta talk to my professors. I'll try for two weeks, after that I can't promise anything."

"Thank you." She blew out an exasperated breath into the phone. "I'm sorry." She whispers. I'm not sure if it's about her blow up or not calling about G.T., but I'm not ready to forgive yet.

"I know, but you should have called me as soon as it happened." I'm not stupid and know I have no claim to G.T., but Harlow knows better. I decide to change the subject. "Pops move up?"

"Yeah."

"G.T.?"

"Nothing's official there yet." She knew exactly what I was asking. I want to know if G.T. moved to VP. When Bam was alive, he used to tell me that one day Pops and G.T. would run Ravage. He'd always say 'that'll be the day.' I never understood those words. That is, until today.

"I'll need a day or so to get everything together."

"Buzz should be there in about thirty minutes." I sigh in defeat.

"Okay... I love you Low."

Surprisingly, sniffles come from the other end of the line, "Love you too. Get home."

"I'll be there soon." With that, we end the call.

Turning, Bella is at my side. "What was that?"

I pull the chairs up to the table, since they seemed to have moved across the room, motioning for her to come and sit. I explain what is going on and the tears leak from my eyes.

"So you're leaving?" She asks reaching out and squeezing my hand, the lone reassurance helpful.

"For a while."

"What the hell is a lockdown?" She asks quirking her eye. I haven't really given her the Biker 101 yet.

"Exactly that. All the brothers and their families go to the clubhouse and that is where they stay for however long the President says. Normally it's 'till everything is safe."

"Can you leave at all?"

"Sure. When a brother or a Prospect is with you. You just can't go alone." Bella may or may not know that she is providing a wonderful distraction from all the grief I feel in my heart by asking all these questions.

"So let me get this right... You get to be locked up indefinitely with all of those hunks of hotness?"

"Pretty much." I shrug. "Not that any of that matters." I look down sheepishly.

"Can I come? Seriously, those pictures on your phone... damn girl." If I were in a better mood, I'd probably laugh at that, but I'm not so I didn't.

"No."

"Are you going to be okay?"

"No." I answer honestly. I will have to tell them about Mia and I'm scared to death. This is much sooner than I ever thought, but I will not be able to hold myself together the whole time I'm there. I'm barely doing it here.

"Why you? Your dad's gone. How does that work?"

"I'm the daughter of a very well respected brother. Harlow says I'm considered family. They protect their family."

"Damn. What happens on lockdown?"

"Well, aren't you a vat of questions." I grumble.

"Girl, we haven't really talked in weeks and if this gets you to talk, I'll ask everything I can possibly think of."

I give her a short smile. "I'll answer, but I've gotta get packed and call my professors. Considering I've already missed so much, I have no clue how that will go. Oh...

Buzz is on his way here. You'll be foaming at the mouth for him."

I explain to her about lockdowns and procedures, which are pretty cut and dry.

"Tell me more about Harlow." She questions as I throw my stuff in bags. I'd already called my professors who stated that as long as I kept up to date on the work, I'd be fine. They even offered to let me watch the lectures through Skype, which I thought was pretty cool. There is no need for me to call my boss. After I had lost Mia, I stopped going and quit without telling him. I'm sure my boss is pissed. I just don't care.

"Harlow. Let's see. She goes by Princess in the club."

"Yeah, you said that. Why?"

"She's always been the club Princess, the Vice President's daughter and all. She's been called that since she was young, but what really earned her the title of Princess is she's the furthest thing from it." I keep packing as I talk and Bella sits on the bed listening. "She's a badass bitch and thank God she's my friend, if not I'd be scared shitless of her."

"Why?" She asks grabbing the shirt I just placed on the bed and folds it for me.

"She's a fighter. And I'm not talking those girly fights where hair gets pulled and women scream. Oh no. Harlow can fight. As in she gets in the boxing ring with the brothers and goes blow for blow with them. It's actually how she became an ol' lady. Fought her man. It was a tie."

"She actually fought her man?"

Grabbing my phone, I pull up a picture of Harlow with Cruz and Cooper. My heart gives a small ache, but I push it away. I hold it up to Bella, "this is Harlow and her ol' man. The one she fought."

"Holy fucking shit! Are you kidding me? No way." Her head shakes in disbelief.

"Yeah. Seriously."

"She's not that big and well... He's a monster. And a hot one to boot!"

"Yeah. But believe it. She's something else."

A very loud banging comes from the front door shaking the walls. "Damn Buzz." I say moving to the door, Bella hot on my heels.

"What? You didn't think I'd miss this did you?" Rolling my eyes we head to the door, just about reaching it when the pounding commences for the second time.

Looking in the peep hole, a very handsome Buzz stands before me looking either very agitated or angry, I can't tell which.

Before I open the door, Bella grabs my arm and I turn to her. "You gonna be okay?" she asks.

"I don't know. It won't be easy, but I don't have much choice." I give her a small smile and turn to the door.

"You can do this." She reassures me. I reach down and grab her hand, squeezing it.

I turn and swing the door open, "Damn. You knocked shit off my walls." I bark.

He doesn't answer instead he wraps his arms around me tight and begins to squeeze the living shit out of me, burying my face in his chest to the point where I cannot breathe. "Miss me, Buzz?" I mumble.

"Glad you're comin' home." His deep raspy voice reminds me of a hot bedroom voice right after sex. As I pull away, I stare up into his sky blue eyes, eyes that definitely hypnotize the female race. His blonde hair has grown since the last time I saw him, but it wasn't the only thing. He must have been working out as his body is more defined with his white t-shirt stretching over his broad shoulders and his arms bulging out of the sleeves, tattoos lining his arms. With his leather rag and jeans, he looks good enough to eat.

He pulls away and eyes me up and down. "What's wrong with you? Are you not eating?" He questions and my heart sinks at the realization that it will be known right off the bat that something is wrong. Shit.

"Haven't been feeling well, but I'm getting better. Where you been? Harlow said you'd be here in a half hour." I move away from the door hoping he doesn't press with my change in subject.

"Had shit to do." Is his only response, his eyes land on Bella behind me. His breath catches making me chuckle for the first time in a long time. I knew the guys wouldn't last long around her.

"Buzz this is my friend Bella. Bella, Buzz." My hand waves back and forth to each of them.

"Holy Shit." Bella grumbles under her breath. "Hi." Her hand motions a small wave.

"And there are two of them." Her eyes widen and her lips part ever so slightly. I grab my phone and pull up a picture of the two of them showing it to her. "Yep, his twin Breaker's a brother too."

"God help me." She whispers shaking her head clutching the phone.

"I'm sure we could show you a hell of a good time beautiful lady." Bella's knees begin to wobble. I lean over and grab her arm not wanting her to pass out on the floor.

"I'm sure you could." She turns to me. "Take me with you."

"No. You have class. And you have to get me notes." Bella huffs, coming out of her Buzz induced haze. "Buzz, don't we need to go?" I ask his eyes locked on Bella.

"Yeah. We gotta roll. Too much shit going down." His confidence in his words comes through loud and clear.

"How's everyone doing?" I question hesitantly.

"It's a mess, Casey. A fucking mess. Get your shit and let's go." I nod pulling a practically frozen Bella with me in the bedroom, her eyes not leaving Buzz once.

"Oh my God, Casey... I never... God." I throw the last of my things inside my bags.

"I know. It's hard to take sometimes."

She sat there for a while, not saying anything as I ramble on about how Buzz is a Prospect and not a brother yet. How he has to earn his spot as a brother and some of what that entails.

"Why don't you have a nickname?"

"Huh?" I ask tossing the last of my toiletries in the bag.

"Princess, Cruz, Buzz, Bam, and G.T. and then there's you... Casey. Doesn't seem right."

Bella didn't know that this fact in my life hurt a bit. It's as if I have been pushed aside, no one having the time to come up with my name. My real name is Cassandra and Casey is short for that. But in the club, everyone has a club name. Princess got hers before she could walk. And me? Nothing. Another reason why I don't feel like part of their family, but rather an outsider.

"Don't know. Never asked. Can you help me carry this shit?" I do not have time to open that can of worms.

"Yeah. Are you sure you're gonna be okay?" Her hand reaches out to my arm holding me softly.

I let out a deep breath. "No. I don't know, but I'll find out soon." I give her a small smile.

After a teary goodbye and one last sweep through the apartment, I lock up the door, Buzz on my heels.

"Casey, wait!" Jace's voice booms from the hallway. Buzz stiffens beside me.

"It's fine, Buzz. No worries." I reassure him, but he doesn't relax.

"Where are you going?" Concern laces his voice.

"I've gotta go home for a while. There was a death at the club."

"Oh my God, Casey. I'm so sorry." Jace reaches out pulling me into a hug which I reciprocate.

"Get off her." Buzz growls and Jace's body tenses. I let go and turn to Buzz.

"Buzz, stop it. Jace is my friend." I try to reassure, but the tension radiates off of Buzz.

"Don't like it and don't care." I roll my eyes turning back to Jace, who has let go of me and is now standing in front of me.

"You gonna be okay?" He asks, his eyes darting from me to Buzz.

"We shall see." I give him a soft smile. "I have to go. Bella has keys to my place."

"Call me if you need anything."

"I will." I turn leaving the building.

Buzz follows very close behind my car as we weave down the road.

During the drive, I do not have Bella to distract me, so I let the bottled up tears fall for Diamond and Mia. I am smart enough to have thrown a box of tissues in the front seat, guess subconsciously I knew I'd need them. Then my thoughts drift to G.T., I can't wait to see him, hug him and make sure he's alright. But I'm also terrified to see him. I'm terrified that when I tell him about Mia, he'll be relieved and I can't handle that. If I thought his words cut deep, his relief would break me, shatter me.

Pulling up to the steel doors of the clubhouse, a man I'd never seen is manning the controls. Looking in my rearview, Buzz gives the man a head nod and the doors slowly open. Everything looks exactly the same as it did three months ago. Cars and bikes line both sides of the long driveway. Tables and chairs grace the courtyard. Men and women mingle throughout. As I park my baby, I glance over at the shop and part of me itches to go there, a feeling I haven't had in weeks. But I need to find Harlow first.

I look in my rearview mirror and cringe at my eyes. I rub them trying to give some resemblance that I'm alright. I blow out a deep breath, not getting very far with that and grab my lip gloss and apply it quickly to my lips giving a smack. Ready as I'll ever be.

"Open the trunk and we'll take it all in. Princess has you set up in a room downstairs." Buzz says and calls over another man I'd never seen before wearing a Prospect rag.

"Well hello there." The guy eye-fucks me up and down. His long shaggy hair hangs down low, reminding me of the hair trim we gave Rocky all those months ago. This guy's hair looks like it could use a good wash along with the wayward beard that hangs haphazardly down his face. It needs a really good trim too. His chocolate brown eyes sparkle as his smile widens.

"Hi."

"Who are you and where have you been all my life?"

Fucking seriously? But before words escape my mouth Buzz cuts in, "Skeezer, enough. Off limits." His bark is controlled yet demanding.

"Fuck. Whose is she?" He groans as if it pains him deeply.

Cutting in, "She... is standing right here and is nobody's. Sorry buddy, I don't fuck brothers. I'm a waste of time." Turning to Buzz, "Thank you." I move away quickly and head directly for the clubhouse.

My stomach clenches. This is it. I straighten my back and hold my head up high. I can do this.

I need to find Harlow. It seems like forever since she hugged me in Cruz's room and told me goodbye. That night was unbelievably crazy and I learned some things about myself that I didn't know existed. When Princess suggested we lock Rocky in a room and shave him, I thought she was fucking nuts. I mean shit; did she want to be ostracized from the club?

But after Harlow told me how Rocky used to make her screw him, regularly, to get the tools and information to take care of the bitches the club needed taken out, my opinion of the situation changed dramatically. Fuck him. We had to find out for sure if this ass was the officer from prison. If we were wrong, we'd suffer the consequences. Thinking back, shivers flow up my body.

As we had Rocky tied and gagged in the chair, Harlow shaved his hair off revealing it was truly the officer from prison. It was like Harlow turned into someone else and I did too. Almost like we were on autopilot, giving this man every bit of pain we could come up with. The gruesome scene was a necessary evil. Broomsticks, tasers, dildos and other random objects lay scattered on the floor next to a very out of it man who was bleeding and covered with hair cut from his head. It helped Harlow get over what happened to her, and I'd do it all over again. Just for her.

I need Harlow to wrap her arms around me right now. Even if she doesn't know why, I need her comfort more than anything.

Opening up the door to the clubhouse, a small bit of fear rushes through me at the thought of seeing G.T. again after all this time. Can I handle seeing him with his women? How will he react to Mia? I need to get my shit together. I can do this. He is safe and not my responsibility.

"Holy Shit! Look who the cat dragged in!" Dagger's voice bellows as he walks up, quickly sweeping me in his arms, my arms wrapping around his neck. His tight hug continues and I am grateful he is keeping his hands away from my ass. Dagger loves the ladies and makes no qualms about it. His long blond hair is braided neatly, falling down his back with his signature red, white and blue bandana covering the top of his head. His arms are incredibly strong as he picks me up as if I weigh nothing. The smell of smokes and booze radiates off of him.

"Hey Dagger. Good to see ya." I squeeze back as he sets me down on the floor looking me up and down.

"Damn girl." He says licking his lips and raising his eyebrows.

"Stop it, Dagger." I flirt in the sweetest voice I can muster and give him a soft smile. Two can play at this game.

"Get over here!" Becs calls from the end of the walkway.

Leaving Dagger, I fall into Becs' warm arms hugging him as tight as I can, trying to hold back the tears that want to fall from my eyes. Whenever I'm around Becs, I feel very close to Bam. They were best friends and I was always drawn to Becs because of that. They had so many similar characteristics, even the way they both held their coffee cup with their pinky wrapping around the bottom of the cup. Little things that I'm sure no one else noticed, but I did. I love seeing those things, but it hurt at the same time.

"Hey Becs." I whisper in his ear as he pulls me back looking at me.

"College girl, huh? I'm so proud of you." I close my eyes and smile, he didn't know but I felt as if my dad said those words to me right along with him.

"Yeah. It's going okay. Tough at times." But really not because of school.

"Anybody bothering you up there?" Becs eyes turn menacing in a flash and I want to immediately wipe the look away.

"Nope. No one. Just classes are a little tough. But I'll get it."

No sooner did I finish the last word when I heard, "Where the hell is she!" being screamed by Harlow. Looking around Becs, sure enough Harlow is barreling down the hall heading right towards me. When her eyes lock on mine, she takes off in a dead sprint pushing through the people standing in her way.

Stepping around Becs, I smile wide and steady my stance as she full out collides with me, almost knocking me down to the ground. Her grip is unbelievably tight on me as she whispers, "I'm so glad you're home. I need you."

I need you too. "I'm here babe. We'll get through this." She clutches me like she's afraid that if she let go, I'd disappear. I relish in the feeling, biting back the tears that want to escape. "Hey, it's okay. I'll help you with whatever you need done."

"Thank you." Her voice is so quiet which is not like Harlow. She's always in your face demanding. Not this time.

"No place would I rather be. None. Love you." The anger I had for her earlier dissipates from my body.

"Love you."

We stay in this exact position for a long time, with our arms wrapped tight around each other and our heads buried in each other's shoulders, just enjoying each other's closeness. God I missed this woman and this is exactly what I need. I feel small bits of weight leaving my shoulders just by this small, simple embrace.

"We'll get through this." I slowly pull away from Harlow whose tight smile is forced on her face. Grabbing my hand, she leads me to the bar where Breaker is pouring drinks.

"Glad you're home. What do ya want?" His gruff voice reverberates.

"Sprite, please." My genuine smile flashes at him.

"Well... well... well. What do we have here? A club

momma disguised as a biker brat." I jerk abruptly to the piercing voice behind me, my body tenses and heat flushes through my body. The woman standing before me is about five foot two on a good day, has beautiful brown hair and a very pretty face. But her stance and attitude scream bitch. And it's one I've never seen before.

Before words leave my mouth, Harlow takes over pushing me behind her quickly. I grasp on to the bar trying not to fall on my ass.

"What the fuck did you just say?" Harlow wails, her finger pointing in the woman's face. The brunette stops abruptly looking at Harlow, the slight quiver of her lip showing the fear rising. "Biker brat? Are you fucking kidding me?"

Quickly the room electrifies and the tension becomes thick. Cruz, Becs and Dagger rush up to Harlow and me, taking in the situation. "What the fuck is going on here?" Cruz pushes Harlow behind him, unknowingly pushing me too.

"It's..." I try to speak but get nothing out. Princess is now on a rampage and cuts me off.

She begins talking into Cruz's back. "This fucking bitch called Casey a fucking club momma and biker brat. So now I'm gonna fucking destroy her." Princess grips the back of Cruz's back balling her hands into fists.

"Who the fuck do you think you are bitch?" Dagger busts out of the pack behind us, grabbing the woman's arm.

"I... I didn't think..." She stammers out.

"That's right bitch. You didn't fucking think. Casey is fucking family. You're not!" Becs walks up to the other side of the woman who is now visibly shaking. I would be too if I had both Dagger and Becs holding my arms with death piercing in their eyes.

It's sick to say, but at that moment a small part of me feels wanted, loved.

"Now you've given yourself a one-way-fucking ticket to get the fuck out of here and never think about returning." Cruz retorts nodding to Dagger and Becs.

"Really, I'm sor..." The men pick the woman up and carry her out of the club, her words lost to me.

"I'm so sorry, Casey. You should never have to deal with that shit when you're home." Cruz turns to me his eyes brimming with sympathy. I can see why Harlow loves him so.

"It's okay. Everything's fine." I try to reassure and bring the tension down in the room a notch.

"Don't brush that shit off, Casey. If one of those bitches tries that shit again, you fucking stand up for yourself. She's just a fucking club momma. She has no right." She fumes.

Sad thing is, what the bitch said is partially true. I am a club momma where G.T. is concerned. I breathe in deep. "Babe. I didn't have a chance to. You jumped right in. Remember?" I give a short smile.

"That bitch... No bitch talks to you that way. I'll fucking kill 'em." Her face is red and her body is shaking a bit.

"I know. Calm down babe." I wrap my arms around Harlow and try to hug all the tightness in her body out. After a bit, she wraps her arms around me too and melts into me, all the tension leaving. Cruz nods walking back to the other side of the room giving us a minute.

"It's just been hard and... I just... Lost it." She whispers so quietly in my ear that I can barely hear her. *Hard.* I know the feeling.

"I know babe. I know." I hug her tight, warmth spreading throughout my body.

"Now I want some of that." Tug's rough voice comes from the side of me. I slowly pull away and look over at him giving him a small smile.

He is a very handsome man with brown hair that hangs below his ears and the richest chocolate brown eyes I've ever seen. But the thing I love about Tug is that he talks and listens to me. Back when I lived here, Tug would come by the shop, talk to me and overall help me out, being the friend I needed. He's a great listener and I feel unbelievably comfortable with him. I can tell him just about anything and he doesn't bat an eye. Thoughts of Mia invade me and I quickly push them to the side. I couldn't tell him about the baby, he would have told G.T. Some things are just not kept from the brotherhood.

He knows about G.T. and me, which I'm sure most of the guys do because we were not quiet. But he didn't badger me; he listened and even let me cry on his shoulder when things got bad. The really sad part is I haven't talked to him since I left and I damn well missed him. I actually hope he isn't pissed about that fact.

He pulls me tight to his strong body and locks his arms around my waist as I reached up linking mine around his neck. "I missed you." I whisper.

"You could have called me." He mumbles into my shoulder.

"I know. Sorry." A low grumbling sound comes from the left of me, almost sounding like a growl, but I didn't think that was possible, but when the hair on the back of my neck and tops of my arms begins to stand, I know who entered the room.

Pulling away slowly, my eyes instantly lock on the sharp, crystal ocean blue eyes of G.T. Those same eyes pull me like a thousand invisible ropes and my body is impossible to stop. No matter what words he said to me or the loss of Mia, I cannot stay away.

Without thinking, I move directly to G.T., leaving Tug and everyone else in the dust. All I can see and all I can hear is G.T. His straight, silky, honey blonde hair hangs low to his neck, but the sides tuck behind his ears. His broad shoulders are now covered with a brace that holds his arm and shoulder immobile on one side. As his sexier than sin smirk graces his face around the scruff of his blonde beard, my heart squeezes.

I need to feel him, need to feel his warmth and know he is alive. Even if he doesn't need me, I need him, more than he can ever know. The invisible strings continue to pull me towards G.T. and before I know it, I am standing face to face with this gorgeous man. Not wasting any time, I latch on to him hard, wrapping my arms around his waist being careful not to touch his arm and bury my face in his neck. I suck in deep breaths, taking in his all too familiar scent of leather and the erotic smell of his body. I swear he never wore cologne or anything, but there is something about his skin that always draws me in and turns me into a sex crazed lunatic.

G.T.'s good arm reaches around my shoulders pulling me as close to him as I can possibly get. As his face falls into the crook of my neck, the tickle of his breath falls on my skin, but I don't move. At this moment, I am lost and I'll stay for as long as he'll let me... Maybe even forever.

We stand unmoving and uncaring about what was going on around us, even with the rustle of people, we ignore it all. G.T. whispers, "I missed you" into my neck.

"I missed you, too."

Suddenly, something in the embrace changes and G.T.'s body slumps into mine. His weight is too much too hold on to. "G.T." I call to him, but he doesn't answer. "G.T.!" I yell trying to pull back to see his face, but I can't move much or he will plummet to the ground.

"Harlow! Help!" I yell with everything I have. I will not let him fall; I'll let him crush me to the ground before that happens.

"Shit! He passed out. Cruz, Boys!" Harlow calls out as commotion begins to happen around me and everyone barks orders. Before I can catch a grasp of the situation, I let go of G.T. as Cruz picks him up and lays him on the couch. G.T.'s eyes are closed, but the small rise and fall of his chest tells me he is alive. I blow out a small sigh of relief.

"What happened?" I ask barreling my way through the crowd gathered around him to get close.

"You knocked him on his ass." Harlow answers smiling with a slight chuckle.

"Funny. Seriously, what's wrong?" I stare at him lying unconscious.

"You know I'm right. Anyway, his body's been through a lot and technically, he's not supposed to be out of bed. But the stubborn ass overheard Cruz coming in to tell me you were here and this is what happened." She waves her arms to G.T. dramatically.

"Shit. I would have come to him." I bend down and

reach out moving the hair away from his eyes feeling the stares from everyone around me.

"Man thing." Harlow shrugs as if none of this is a big deal and I'm sure to her it's not. She's seen more of this life than I have. She is this life. I am not. "I'll have Cruz move him to his bed and call Doc, but he looks fine. Color's good."

"I want to go with him." I say my eyes not leaving G.T.

"I know." She wraps one arm around my shoulder and gives me a side hug. My eyes never leave G.T.

As Cruz and Dagger lift him, my heart plummets. Cruz grabs the top half of his body under his arms while Dagger grabs his feet. The way his body lays there limp, mimicking and swaying with every movement they make sends shivers of fear down my body. If I didn't know 100% that he is alive, I would have screamed.

Harlow begins fussing all around G.T., giving him shots and checking this and that after they lay him down. Ma barrels into the room, her eyes wide with fear. "What happened?"

"One look at Casey had him passing out." Harlow laughs and I blush. Bitch.

I stand in the corner of his room and watch, feeling like a spectator more than an actual participant. Ma holds her hands out to me as she walks and embraces me tightly. "I'm sorry you had to come home to this, but girl, I'm so glad you're home."

I never had a mom, never knew what it was like to have one. Ma is the closest I've ever gotten. She always had a way of making me feel loved even when I didn't. I latch on tight feeling her warmth. "Thanks."

"He's okay, just not supposed to be moving too much

right now." She says answering the question that has been worrying me since he went down.

"When will he wake up?" I muffle into Ma, but my eyes lock on G.T. lying in his bed appearing to be peaceful.

"Soon, he just needs some sleep. Doc will be here in a bit to check him out."

"Can I stay with him?" I ask, feeling like I need her permission. Scratch that, like I *want* her permission.

She pulls away from me and my eyes meet hers. Ma is a beautiful woman. Her blonde hair dances around her face in layered curls and her light gray eyes sparkle as if she likes what I just asked her. "Absolutely. You can stay with him as long as you like." Her eyes penetrate mine as her words sink in, unbelievable meaning dripping from them. And as much as I want to tell her that I'd love too, some part deep down, one that I wasn't acknowledging at the moment, knows that once he gets better I am gone.

I shake off the small thought not wanting to acknowledge it and lock it down deep.

"Thanks." I pull away and walk over to the bed. I grab a chair and sit next to him, afraid to actually touch him.

"He just needs sleep. You can touch him, you won't hurt him. He'll actually like it. I gave him a small bit of morphine so he'll be a bit out of it. I'll make sure no one comes in." Harlow says, squeezing my shoulders behind me. Everyone in the room files out, leaving me with a very unconscious hot man. I sigh. If only.

I grab his warm, rough hand looking at all the lines and scars that grace it. Each one, I'm sure with some kind of story. His fingernails are clean and cut short, the clean part must be Harlow's doing because G.T. did not primp at all. He is all rugged and likes getting his hands dirty.

I rub my hands up and down his feeling the rough but soft palms. I lace my fingers with his and bring them up to my lips kissing them softly. "I'm so sorry babe." I whisper.

Everything from that moment, his hurtful words spewed out of his mouth, to losing Mia burst through me. Tears roll uncontrollably down my face and I grip G.T.'s hand tighter feeling his warmth. I lay my head next to his hand on the bed, close my eyes and let myself feel the pain.

"This is all your fault, G.T. Do you even realize that?" I whisper into the bed. "If you could just be with me. If I could just be enough for you, we could have had everything." I let the tears take over.

"Casey?" G.T.'s groggy voice sputters. I jump quickly, wiping my face to wash the tears away. I instantly miss the warmth of his hand in mine.

"Hey." I say softly brushing his silky hair away from his face.

"You're really here?" he asks, his eyes glassy, must be from the meds.

"Right here." Placing my hand on his bearded cheek, I relish the feeling of his coarse hair under my palm. His hand reaches up and covers mine.

"Don't leave me. Please." His words almost a plea, but being heavily medicated I will not read anything more into his words, even if deep inside I wish it to be true.

"I'm right here."

"Tired. Come lay with me." I shouldn't. It will only cause me more pain, but I can't help my damn self. His pleading eyes suck me in and damn if I can crawl out from their spell. And to be completely honest, I need this.

I smile. "Yeah." I kick off my shoes and crawl into bed under the covers feeling his body heat even though we are not touching. Laying my head on the empty pillow, I keep my body far away from his.

"Get over here." His words are demanding and send fire through my body. Dammit if I don't love his forceful-ness, but don't budge. I can't make myself move.

"I don't want to hurt you. I'll just lay here." I stare at his handsome profile. His nose with a slight bend from the fight he had when he was younger, it just never set right, his strong jaw angled just perfectly.

"Now." The intensity in his words makes my body move on its own accord. I can never turn my body's reac-tion to him off and part of me craves him. I move close and he reaches out, his good arm pulling me even closer to his body. My head rests on his arm as I lay on my side, hand on his rock hard chest and my legs next to his. I itch to move them over his, but keep them where they are. His arm holds me tight against his body as I wiggle to get comfortable and it doesn't take much.

I sink into the comfort that he is providing me. I'll only lay here for a little bit, I tell myself. But his warmth is too much and my eyes begin to get heavy.

CHAPTER SEVEN
GT

THE CREAK OF THE DOOR AS IT OPENS ROUSES ME FROM THE most peaceful sleep I've had in months. Opening my eyes slowly, my Angel is draped over my body, her arm close to her as if she knew instinctively not to touch my wounds. Her legs entwine with mine and her chest slowly rises and falls telling me she is in a deep sleep. Casey's beautiful face rests on my arm. Her blonde and now black hair sweeps across the bed in a huge curtain. Cherries. Damn woman always smells like damn cherries, and I fucking love it.

My eyes jet to the noise at the door and see Doc standing there, waiting.

"I heard she was back." Doc says quietly staring at my girl. I want to gouge his fucking eyes out for even looking at her, string him up and beat the ever-loving shit out of him.

"What do you need?" I growl wanting him to leave, shut the door and allow me to forget the outside fucking world.

"Ma called. Said you passed out. Now I can see why." He smiles reaching into his bag.

"Stop fucking looking at her." I warn his eyes shooting to mine.

"Down there, big boy. I don't want your girl. Just nice to see you a bit more alert." He places the stethoscope in his ears and begins to place it on my body listening to me.

"Don't wake her up." I glare in his eyes.

"Wouldn't dream of it." He says smiling only causing my anger to turn red hot. Who the fuck does he think he is?

He checks my bandages and dressings thoroughly and I watch my beautiful Angel sleep peacefully in my arms without even a stir as Doc works. Her porcelain skin is so light against my tan and the little bit of freckles across the bridge of her nose is the only color gracing her face. I love those fucking things; it's where I came up with Angel for her. Her freckles are Angel kisses and she is my Angel.

Casey's tiny frame is pressed up against mine and I relish in the soft curves of her body. Never have I wanted a woman to lay with me like this. Never. Casey is the only one. Ever. And dammit if I didn't want to stay like this forever. Damn sap.

"No infection. Keep taking the antibiotics. You need to rest." Doc says pulling my eyes to his. He looks down at Angel and I glare. "I mean it. If you just rest a day, I guarantee, you'll feel a shit ton better and will be able to get up and move without passing out. Your blood's trying to replenish itself. You need to stay still to accomplish this."

"Fine. You can go now. Thanks." I grunt needing him out of my fucking room and away from my girl.

"Maybe *she* can keep you in line." Before I can fire off a retort, Angel's body moves slightly as she begins to wake. I grip her body tight, expecting she will want to bolt especially if she knows someone is in the room and I'm not letting her go.

"Hey Angel." Her eyes slowly flutter open and widen as she looks at me. Her green eyes utterly pull me under and she doesn't even know it.

"Hey. How ya feeling?" She says trying to pull out of my grasp.

"Don't. Move." I demand feeling her body tense then relax into me. She's always been so in tune to my commands, her body instantly following them and I'm banking on that shit now.

"I was just telling your man here that he needs to stay in bed and rest." Casey gasps turning her head quickly to the man standing at the door. She tries again to get out of my grasp, but I hold tight.

"I told you not to move." I say again to her, my arms flexing around her. She lays her head on my chest, but the stiffness in her body doesn't leave this time. Every muscle in her body is on high alert. Thanks a-fucking-lot Doc.

Casey's soft voice questions the man causing her tension. "Doc. Is he okay?" Concern pours from her voice as my arm pulls her as tight to me as possible. I bend giving her a kiss on top of her head feeling her soft hair on my lips. As soon as my lips touch her head, her body freezes and I'd give anything to wipe away what I've done to this woman.

"He will be *if* he rests. He's gotta stay in this bed for twenty-four hours so his body can get his blood supply back up to where it needs to be. He needs to take his antibiotics, pain meds and rub this salve on his wounds so they don't get infected. Princess has been doing that for him thank God."

"What happens after the twenty-four hours?" Her words come out muffled from lying on my chest.

"Reevaluate. See where he is. Right now, his wounds are healing wonderfully. The salve I gave him is some ancient Native American stuff I got while working with a colleague of mine. It works wonders, *if* the patient rests."

"He will. I'll make sure of it." The confidence swarms her voice.

"You will... Will you? How you gonna do that Angel?" I ask looking down at her as her eyes lift to mine.

"I have my ways." Her smile is as bright as the sun shining as she bites her bottom lip making my dick rise to the occasion. She must have felt it as her leg slowly moves away from my growing dick. I need her to stay with me and not run. I know if I push that'd be the first thing she'll do as soon as she can. Bolt and she has every right to.

"Make you a deal, Angel. You stay with me, in this room, for the next twenty-four hours and I'll stay put. Promise." I grin, waiting for her response, but she surprises the shit out of me at how quick she gives in.

"Done. See Doc. I have my ways." She smirks laying her head back down on my chest.

"Princess has everything. Talk to her. And Casey?"

"Yeah?" She answers Doc.

"Good luck." He turns finally leaving my fucking room, closing the door behind him. I need to lock it, but fuck I am not moving an inch with this hot body next to me.

"So, you're gonna take care of me huh?"

"Yep. Now let me get up so I can get to work." She tries for the third time to pull away.

I retighten my arm. "No. You stay right here."

"Come on. I can't take care of you when I'm lying down." There are so many things she can do for me lying down. My thoughts race to her riding my dick, sucking it, her pussy in my face, but I keep it all to myself. I am not scaring her off this time.

I've hurt her, bad. I watched at that moment as the entire spark left her beautiful eyes and I kick myself every damn day for doing it. I keep telling myself it was for the best, that she deserved better.

And she does. But I'm a selfish fucking prick and almost dying has put a few things in perspective. I don't deserve her, but I need her. I need her like air. And this time, I am not fucking up. I can't.

"You're keeping me in bed. That's all you've gotta do right now." I need to feel her and her warmth, just having her here with me is already making every bit of pain evaporate. Whatever voodoo spell she has going on is sucking me in like a vise and I do not want to get the fuck out of it.

"You wanna watch TV?" She asks making me wonder why.

"Nope."

"Okay." She sighs.

"What's wrong, Angel?" My hand rubs her boney hip absently. Her shorts are so damn short that my finger grazes her skin and even though she doesn't say a word about it, the shudder of her body each time tells me she feels it too. The once plush body Casey had is now replaced with skin and bones. I'm almost afraid to squeeze too hard, afraid I may just break her. She is a shell of what she was the last time I saw her. But I just got her in my arms I'll keep my mouth shut, for now.

"You scared me." She mutters quietly.

"I'm good, Angel."

She turns her head and rests her chin on my chest. Her eyes gaze up at me full of worry and concern. "I thought you died with Diamond. When Low told me what happened, there was a moment when I thought it was you. That you were gone." Pain etches in her eyes and it kills me. I want to wipe it away and never see her hurt again.

"I'm here, Angel." My arm glides up her back, hooking her arm, pulling her face to face with me. Lifting my head from the pillow, my lips connect with her soft cherry ones. Thinking she will hesitate, I'm surprised that she meets me move for move. My hand entangles in her hair, gripping it as I deepen the kiss. If I could crawl inside of her at this moment, I would. And I'd stay there, live there forever. Our kiss is passionate but lazy and I take my time. The intensity is there, but behind it is so much more. I pour everything I can into it, telling her without words how I feel for her and she meets me at every turn.

Her hand presses against the side of my face, while the other threads through my hair. I love her hands pulling me exactly where she wants me. Our tongues do some sort of rhythmic dance and I savor every second of it.

"Well, that didn't take long." Princess scoffs as she pushes the door open. Casey flies off the bed covering her mouth with her hand so fast I can't catch her. The panic that spreads in her eyes is painful to watch. But I did that shit to her. I'm the one who created it. Now it is time to fix it.

"Don't you know how to fucking knock?" I snarl at my sister.

"Nope. Time for your meds, brat." She hands me a small cup as I sit up taking the pills and swallowing quickly. "Good to see you're playing nice."

"Mind your own fucking business." I growl loudly making Angel jump. Instinctively I want to comfort her, but just sitting up causes my head to spin a bit. I wouldn't make it over to her without falling.

"I have to go." Casey says grabbing her bag.

"Where the hell are you going? You made a deal!" I bark out, thoroughly irritated with her.

"To my room. I have to get a few things." She says hurriedly.

"When you come back, bring all your shit so you don't have to leave again." I demand.

"I'll be back in a minute." She breezes past Princess not looking her in the face. Fuck.

"What was that about?" Princess asks coming to the bed.

"What the fuck, Princess?" I growl.

"Down big guy."

"Don't you down me. You need to think before you do shit!" I yell.

"I just came to give you your meds. How the hell would I know you were lip locked with her?" She shrugs.

"You realize that I'm gonna flatten you out in the ring right?"

"Hard to do with one arm." She smarts back radiating confidence.

"Fuck you."

"No thanks."

"Look, you need to tell me what the fuck is going on. I can't take this shit anymore G.T. You've gotta talk to me."

"There's nothing to talk about."

"Bullshit. We fought. You remember that shit and then you still don't talk to me. Explain that shit to me 'cause I don't get it."

The night that Princess challenged me to fight, I couldn't back down. I had to meet her inside the ring. I had mixed emotions about it. I needed to let off steam, but I really didn't want to do it with my sister. But with each blow that she and I landed on each other, I felt a bit of relief. In no way did it help me forget Casey, but for those few minutes, I had something else to focus on.

"I was pissed at myself. Still am. Sorry, alright." Looking away from her, I do not want her to see inside me. I hate that shit and she's always been able to see inside of me, knowing there is more to it than I let on.

"Why are you pissed at yourself?"

"I'm not talking about it." I stare at her determined to not answer.

"You know she loves you right." My eyes shoot to Princess.

"What?"

"Casey. She loves you. She's loved you since we were kids. Now this shit's in your corner. If you fuck this up this time, she'll never be yours."

I hurt her before, allowing the club momma to kiss me. *Fuck.* Closing my eyes, I let the words seep into my body and down to my soul. I cut her deep. Deeper than I even thought I had the power to do. Shit.

"She never told me what happened between you two. I'm guessing you fucked around on her, by what little she did say."

Growling I jump jerking my body towards her, "I didn't fucking cheat on her." I pause as Princess waited. "I just let her think I did."

"Why the fuck would you do that?" Princess' anger lets loose, her face turning bright red.

Rubbing my one good hand across my face, "It's what needed to be done."

"For who? Casey? Because I know, that's a bunch of shit."

"She deserves better." She deserves so much better than my fucked up shit.

Princess got in my face. "You really are a fucking idiot." Her words cut deep, but my anger took over, all-consuming rage burrowed through me.

"I'm not a fucking idiot!" I yell as Princess jumps back eyeing me warily. She didn't say a word for the longest time just standing there staring.

"So that's the reason. You don't think you're good enough for her because you don't have some fancy degree, bullshit. Let me tell you something. Casey doesn't give two shits about your education or lack thereof. She doesn't care that you don't sit in some office with a fucking suit on making millions of dollars. You know what she fucking wants. Loyalty. Honesty. Trust. She wants a man who only sees her and not the other millions of women in the world. She wants a man who treats her with respect and one she trusts to go out and not sleep with the entire female population. She wants you G.T. Now it's up to you, to pull your head out of your ass and make it happen. Because I know. She's the only one you want."

"You fucking tell anyone about this conversation and I'll pound your ass into the ground."

Princess laughs. "Aww... Big bad biker doesn't want anyone knowing he has a heart."

"Shut. The. Fuck. Up." I snarl. Princess' laughter over-taking the room. I need her to fucking leave. Now.

"Decide what you want brother and figure it out. What's this deal you made?"

"She has to stay with me for twenty-four hours and I promised to rest."

"Good. Then use the time to your advantage." Princess gave me a slight wave and leaves the room.

Use it to my advantage. The words ring in my ears and penetrated my head. I'd never had to seduce a woman or charm them. But with Casey, I'd be doing a lot of that. How? I have no fucking clue.

CHAPTER EIGHT
Casey

Rummaging through all of my things, I need a distraction and escape from the guilt that is consuming me and eating me alive. Not even a day home with him and I'm kissing him like some hormonal teenager. I need to tell him, but shit, he can't even freaking stand without passing out. How the hell is he going to react to having a child that I lost?

My stomach hurts the ache inside rising.

It's only a kiss, right? Who am I fucking kidding? Not only was it a kiss, I want so much more out of it. As soon as his lips touched mine, fire seeped in my body, setting it ablaze. Everything with him feels so intense and knocks me on my ass every damn time. Shit.

I turn to the door as a loud knock comes upon it. Opening the door, a smiling Harlow stands there and I want to rip her damn eyes out. Not that I could, but I want to... badly. She knows too much.

"You love him. It's what's meant to happen."

"I can't be with him, Harlow. I knew coming home would be a mistake." I shake my head, tired of repeating myself over and over again.

Harlow slams the door shut as she sits on the bed. I join her and wring my hands together. Looking down at my hands, I want to disappear. I want to tell her, I need to tell her. "Coming home was what was supposed to happen. Needed to happen. Fucking sucks it had to be like this, but we can't change that. You and G.T. need to work this shit out."

"What's to work out, Harlow? He wants a variety of women and I can't deal with that. It's all or none with me." And once I tell him about Mia, it will all be over.

Harlow grabs my leg steadying it when I don't realize it is bouncing uncontrollably. "You need to talk to G.T., you may be surprised. Second, he's going to kiss you again. You know this and next time, I may not be there to interrupt." I nod. "I know my brother's an ass, but you gotta know Casey, he loves you. He won't admit it because he's stubborn, but he does."

"If a man loves you, he won't want anyone else but you."

"You need to talk to him about that, Casey."

"What do you know?" I question, raising my brow.

"Not my place. Talk to him while you're in there. None of this other petty bullshit. Fucking talk. And get this shit sorted out."

"He told you?" She nods. "What was I thinking?" I say

shaking my head frustrated with myself. This is such a bad idea, being locked in a room with him.

"Oh, I can only imagine. Doc said something about him staying put and he grabbed you, pulling you in." She laughs. "He's a smart man. Knew you would help him."

I give her a small knowing smile because she is right and I went for it hook-line-and-sinker.

"I know that coming back to all this is a lot, but are you okay?" I look down at my hands. This is the time. My opening. I shake my head no.

"What's wrong Casey? School not working out for ya?" I can't hold it in any longer. The tears I've been doing such a good job of holding back fall from my face and splash onto my hands, my shoulders begin to shake. Everything in my body hurts and aches and my stomach twists in knots.

"Shit. Casey. What's wrong?" The words will not leave my mouth, it's like they're lodged in my throat and I so desperately need them to come out. She wraps her arms around me and that's when I really lose it. I've craved her since I found out about Mia. And now she's here.

"Tell me what's going on babe. I can help you." She whispers into my neck, her hand glides up and down my body.

"I was pregnant, Low." I sniffle into her neck, close enough to feel her entire body stiffen.

"Was?"

"I lost her about two weeks ago." I sob uncontrollably.

"Oh God, Casey. Why didn't you tell me? I would have been right there by your side."

"I couldn't. Everything with Babs happened and Cooper. Then Rocky... Everything was a mess. I couldn't add to it." I squeeze tighter not wanting to let go, needing her now more than ever.

"It was G.T.'s baby." I nod my head in agreement. "And he doesn't know anything about it." Her words come out as statements of fact rather than being accusatory. "And you've been dealing with this all by yourself. You should have fucking told me."

"No. I have two friends in Cherry Vale."

Harlow pulls away from me. "You told them and not me?" She accuses, hurt lacing her eyes.

"No. I didn't tell anyone. Not until the pain started and I needed help. I called my neighbor Jace who came and took me to the hospital. I had to tell him. There was so much blood, Low." My voice trails off as thoughts of that day plague me. The ache in my gut rises to my chest, I rub my heart. "I was so scared and when they told me Mia was gone, I couldn't take it. I still can't take it."

Lows arms clutch me tight as I weep into them. "It's alright. We'll get through this." Her hand grabs my head and she coddles me, like an infant. I relish in the embrace. I need it.

"You said Mia. Do you know it was a girl?"

"No, but in my gut she's a girl and I named her, Mia Low Gavelson."

"You named her after me?" the shock in her voice would have made me smile at any other time, but not now.

"Of course."

"Were you going to tell us about the baby?" I hate that she is skeptical of this fact, but part of me knew it would come up.

"Yes. I'd never keep either of you away from her. G.T.

may not want me, but I'd hope he'd want to know his kid."

"He would never have let you leave if he'd have known."

"I know. That's why I didn't tell anyone. I needed to get my life in order. I needed my degree and a job. I wanted to be able to support myself and my baby. And I didn't want to trap him into something he didn't want." I pull away and look down at the floor. "And I didn't want to be my mother. Now... It just doesn't matter."

"Everything matters. You are nothing like your mother. You have to know that." I shrug not feeling her words. "You have to tell G.T. Now." She holds me by my shoulders, her eyes bore into mine and the seriousness in her voice is compelling.

I stare into her eyes. "I can't."

"Why the hell not?" She barks with anger.

"He can barely freaking stand, Low. What do you think this will do to him? Give me a couple of days and I'll talk to him, alright?"

"You can't leave here without telling him, Casey. I mean it. Or I will tell him myself."

"Gee, thanks for the vote of confidence." My eyes close and I breathe in deep. This is exactly why I couldn't tell her in the first place.

"Bullshit. You know I believe in you. I just need your word that you will tell my brother. This is too big, Casey."

"I know. I will."

A loud bang rattles the door and walls. "Who is it?" Harlow yells.

"Me." Cruz's gruff voice says from the other side of the door. Harlow jumps from the bed opening the door quickly. Cruz wraps his arms around Harlow pulling her up to his awaiting lips. My stomach lurches and I turn away quickly. I'm happy for them. I am. But right now seeing it is too much.

"Casey, G.T.'s callin' for ya." I turn to face the man standing with his arms wrapped around my best friend. He hasn't changed a bit from the last time I was here. Same brown disheveled hair, jeans and rag. Now though, he looks happy, truly happy.

I sigh. "I'll be there in a minute. Low, go ahead and go."

"You sure?"

"Yeah." I whisper needing just a few minutes to get myself together before going back up to face him.

"Alright, you need anything, find me."

"I will." I wave softly as they leave the room, shutting the door behind them. Burying my face in the pillow, I let go. Tears, screams and a few blows to the defenseless pillow occur hard and fast. By the time my body stops, my breathing is hard, labored and my face feels raw from the wetness.

I somehow pry myself out of the bed and to the bathroom, quickly washing my face and press a cool cloth to my eyes. My breathing is now calm, but the ache is ever present.

"Casey?" I look in the mirror quickly seeing the red puffs around my eyes; there is nothing I can do to hide it. I blow out a long deep breath. What the hell is this, Grand Central Station?

"Hey Tug. Be out in a minute." I open the door and give Tug a small smile.

"Hey. What's up?"

"Heard you were down here. Wanted to come see you." He says in the doorway.

He steps further inside the room making his way to the bed. The room is incredibly small just a bed, dresser and small bath off the corner. But it is much better than the bunks with all the others. With him inside, it suddenly feels even smaller. With not having anywhere else to sit, I motion to the bed. "Have a seat."

"How have you been?"

Looking into his brown eyes, I feel warmth and comfort. Trust. "Good. School's going good. Some classes are a bit rough, but for the most part good."

"Wanna tell me why your eyes are red?"

"No. How have things been here?" I look away not wanting him to see inside. Back when everything went to hell in a hand basket with G.T., Tug was there, talking, laughing and being the shoulder I desperately needed.

"Fucking shitty... What do you think?" He shakes his head. "You like it up there?"

"It's alright." Before I loved it up there, now it just reminds me of Mia and the sadness is too raw.

"Just alright. What's going on? You need to tell me now." His voice becomes forceful but still very caring. He only wants to help, but I cannot tell him before G.T. That just feels all kinds of wrong.

Before I can speak, I am saved by another pounding on the door. Jumping up quickly, I pull the door open wide.

I am surprised to see a very disheveled G.T. standing there, his smile instantly falls when his eyes look inside the room and lock on Tug. I close my eyes, sighing. I'm not G.T.'s but the predatory look on his face is indicating a confrontation.

"What the fuck are you doing in here?" He growls loudly at Tug, making me jump.

"Just talking." Tug says standing up and walking behind me. Not the best move.

"Get out!" G.T. booms his face so menacing the vein in the side of his neck twitches. This is going to go bad quick.

I place my hand on G.T.'s chest causing his body to tremble. As his eyes meet mine, they soften a touch. "He was just saying hi. I was just getting ready to come up and see you." I smile sweetly. Knowing the fire that is about to be set ablaze, I do not see it as a lie because I am going back up to see him, eventually. "Bye Tug. I'll see ya later." I say my eyes not leaving G.T.'s.

"Later." Tug says moving to the door. G.T. barely moves an inch as Tug's large body squeezes through. Damn men.

"You're not supposed to be out of bed." I say my hand still on G.T.'s chest. I can feel the strength under his t-shirt.

"You're supposed to be with me. I came to find you." He rumbles unapologetically.

"I'm here." I want to move my eyes away from his, but they captivate mine into submission and suck me in.

His hand rests on mine squeezing gently. G.T. bends down slowly giving me a chaste kiss on the lips. My heart jumps. "I'll have a Prospect move your stuff to my room."

I freeze and think quickly. "Nah. That's okay. I'll bring what I need for the twenty-four hours." I try to pull away from him, but he grips me tighter. I think I can break away with him only having one arm on me, but I don't want to hurt him.

"You think after our time is up, I'm gonna give you up?" He shakes his head. "Angel, you know me better than that." That I do.

"G.T. I..." my words are cut off by his.

"We'll talk. Get your stuff. I need to lie down." He pulls my hand up to his lips kissing me softly; my stomach falls to my knees at the sweetness of his gesture. He releases me and I grab a small bag I brought, throwing extra clothes, pajamas and my toothbrush inside along with my laptop and phone.

"Ready?" I ask, but as I turn around G.T. is opening and closing his eyes rapidly, his body leans to the side and he struggles to get his balance. "Oh no you don't big guy." Dropping my bag, I race around him and grab a chair from the game room. Just as I place it behind him, he falls with a thunk into it. Damn it. But as soon as he goes out he comes to again. "G.T?"

"I'm alright. Just tired." He tries to open his eyes to me, but from the pained look on his face, it's not working.

"Rest for a minute. Let me see if I can find Cruz." He nods, which surprises me. He must really feel like shit to take help so damn willingly. Racing through the clubhouse, people are everywhere, but I ignore all of them searching for Cruz. I finally find him over at the table, coloring with Cooper. "Cruz! I need your help, please." I call over to him. He stands instantly striding towards me.

"What's wrong?" His eyebrows pull together in concern.

"G.T. got out of bed to come find me. Now he's downstairs almost passed out in a chair. I need your help bringing him up to his room, please." I beg and have no shame in that at all.

"Buzz, Breaker, follow me." He calls out as he heads to the stairs with me on their heels. "He'd be alright if he would just fucking rest."

After the guys lug G.T back to bed, Harlow pumps him full of more drugs and he's out like a light.

"ANGEL?" G.T. calls from the bed. My eyes instantly lift to the man lying on the bed. I move quickly to his side. My insides turn at his name for me. He started calling me Angel a few years ago and I never questioned it.

"Right here. How ya feeling?" He smiles a devilish grin, the color back in his face.

"Better that I know you're here. What are ya doing?" He questions and I sit next to him on the bed facing him.

"Homework. I don't want to get too far behind." I don't know if he really wanted to know about school. Nowadays, I don't feel like I know much of anything.

"Tell me about it." He says, as I look into his crystal eyes. I can see in them that he genuinely wants to know. And so I tell him about the entire thing from start to finish and he listens attentively to every word coming out of my mouth, leaving out everything to do with Mia. I do not know how long I spoke, but he continues listening till the very end. "Wow. Sounds like a lot of work."

"It is." I smile, lifting my shoulder knowing if I don't get my shit together soon, everything will be much harder.

"I'm proud of you."

I am taken aback a bit by his statement. Of all people, I didn't know if he would care one way or the other. "Thanks." I look down at my hands, not embarrassed but almost shy.

"Come here." He calls from the bed. I quickly get up needing distance.

"I need to get your meds. Harlow said as soon as you get up." I scurry over to the table where Harlow laid everything out for me with notes. My eyes search for the needed meds.

"You trying to avoid me?" He chuckles.

"Nope. I'm here aren't I?" I respond not looking up. Damn he's got several bottles. I find the one I need and take two capsules out placing them on a napkin.

"I missed you, Angel." My hands stop what they are doing. I close my eyes and breathe in deep taking a moment to love the words he just spoke.

"I missed you too, G.T." I grab a bottle of water and the pills quickly bringing them to him. His eyes focus on me, eating away at what resolve I have with this man. I hand him the bottle and pills, he takes them his eyes never wavering from mine.

He hands the bottle back, I quickly turn and put everything away. Great! Now what the hell am I going to do for the next twenty hours? My stomach tenses and I instantly feel very thirsty. With G.T.'s water bottle in hand, I twist the cap and gulp down the water, but it does little to quench my thirst. I want to tell him about Mia, but I need to wait until this twenty-four hour thing is over, when he's stronger. I can do that. I can hold it in. I can. I must.

"You gonna come lay with me?" He grumbles expectantly.

"No. I'm gonna do some work. You just lay in bed and rest."

"That wasn't the deal."

"The deal was to stay with you, not that I was going to lay in bed with you. Now get some rest." I say moving back towards the desk and sitting in the chair. I can feel his eyes peering through me, trying to coerce me to look at him, but I do my damnedest to resist. Shivers rack my body and I desperately try to turn them off.

"Angel." His words come out a caress over my skin. "Why don't you put a movie on and come lay with me."

"I really need to get this done."

"Angel." The sweetness from his voice evaporates and is replaced with his demanding one. I turn and eye him. His lower body is covered with a thin white sheet, arm splayed on the bed while the other is wrapped up in his brace. His heated eyes are solely focused on mine causing my body to quiver. I need to not give in, but my body does not listen.

I rise from the chair grabbing the remotes off of the table and handing them to him. "What do you want to watch?" I ask tentatively, my hands beginning to sweat.

"Action." I smirk; he's always loved action movies. Even as a kid, he loved to watch them.

I head over to the bookshelf filled with all of his favorites and settle for a Vin Diesel flick, no reason why I can't have some eye candy. I place the movie in and walk over to the chair by the desk, pulling it to the side of the bed.

"So that's how you're gonna play this, huh?" G.T. says from the bed.

"I'm not playing anything. I'm going to sit here and watch a movie with you. That's what you wanted." He smirks and turns his head to the movie.

Vin Diesel is hot and all, but after about an hour, my eyes begin to get heavy. It's been a hell of a few weeks, and my body is giving out on me. I rest my head on the back of the chair and my eyes droop heavily, lulling me into sleep.

"Angel?" My name being called wakes me from sleep, but the grogginess is pulling me back under. "Come here, babe." My arm is being tugged. I open my eyes slightly to see G.T. pulling me towards his body. I have no will to fight, sleep is all I need. I climb into bed and rest my head on his arm. He places a cover over my body and pulls me tight to him. I instantly fall back to sleep.

I'M HOT, really really hot. My body is on fire and I need reprieve now. My eyes open to see the source of the heat melting my body into the bed. G.T.'s arm is pulling me too tight to his side and his body heat radiates off of him. Looking up at his face, his face has lost all the tension in it making him look younger and relaxed, more like the boy that I fell in love with all those years ago.

I wish things were different between us. I wish this could work. It kills me that I'm not enough for him and it kills me more that I lost the only part of him that I had left. Tears spring to my eyes. My hand reaches for my stomach and rubs gently remembering the day I found out about her and I smile. I'd never been so happy in my life as the day I got that positive pregnancy result and that day is tarnished because of G.T.'s actions. I shake my head and pull G.T.'s tight grip off of my waist.

He mumbles and grunts but his eyes don't open. I slide out of bed and look at the clock. 10:17pm, damn I slept a long time. My stomach growls and I realize I haven't eaten since early morning. Looking back over at a peaceful G.T., I head out of the room in search of food.

The music blares through the clubhouse and I'm surprised I didn't hear it back in G.T.'s room. Entering the main room, brothers, ol' ladies and women are scattered around, most with drinks in their hands and dancing to the beat. On top of a couple of tables are women with barely there clothes dancing their asses off. Since the club is on lockdown, I know it's a club party and not a brother one.

A club party is all the members of the club, their ol' ladies and the entertainment of strippers. A brother party is a no holds barred party that ol' ladies and significant others are banned from.

Cruz sits on a stool at the bar nursing a beer as I walk up to him. "Hey." He turns on the stool.

"Hey Case. How's the patient?" He smirks like he knows something I don't.

I eye him. "Stubborn and sleeping."

He chuckles which makes me smirk seeing a big guy like him chuckle. "You did good, girl."

"I haven't done much Cruz. Pretty much just slept the day away." I shrug my shoulder.

"Woman. That man wouldn't sit still for five minutes. You come along and he's sleeping like a baby."

"Cruz. He just likes a warm body to keep him company, and I'm just the closest thing he's got right now. I'm sure the next one will come along in a day or so and I'll be long forgotten."

"You need to talk to Princess about this shit. And for the record, you're full of shit." He grabs his beer and leaves me at the bar.

Looking around, Becs nods his head to me and I nod back. I search for Harlow, but see her nowhere. She must be with Cooper. The thought is a double edged sword. I want to see him, but I know it will hurt to see the little guy running around, when my little one didn't have a chance.

Shaking my head, I move to the kitchen where Ma is standing preparing food with Legs and Bubbles. "Hi." I give a slight wave as all eyes turn to me. Ma rushes to me wrapping her arms tight around my body as I do the same.

"Man, I missed you baby girl. I'm so glad you're home." My insides turn warm, wanted, loved. I feel the red blush creeping up my cheeks. Ma pulls away, "Look at you! You are skin and bones, you need food, now." She shakes her head disapprovingly.

"I eat Ma. I've just been under a bit of stress with school, but it'll get better." I reassure her not knowing if it will ever get better.

"You'll eat now while you're here. If I have to watch every bite you put in your mouth, I will young lady." I grin. "And you need strength to take care of my boy." My lips fall and my eyes close.

"Ma, it's only for a few more hours and then he'll be on his own, but thanks."

"Sweetheart, my boy is a stubborn man like his daddy. You don't give up on him, you hear me."

I nod and the tightness in my chest returns. I give a slight cough to clear my throat. "I need to get some food for G.T. he hasn't eaten in a while."

"I'll get it sweetheart." She releases her hold on me, moving quickly throughout the kitchen.

Legs approaches, "You are so beautiful Casey and smart to boot. Your daddy is so proud of you right now."

One small mention of Bam and I'm fighting back tears that I thought had dried up. "Thank you." I choke out trying to hold back.

"We were all so worried when you left. We still are. I know that Bam wanted you to go to school, but can't you do that online or something so you're home?" I stand there shocked at her words. Never once has anyone really said anything about my leaving. Never once have any of them said they wanted me to stay here. "I mean, we all know you are smart and can do it, we just miss you here." She smiles pulling away.

"I never thought about online school." In fact, when I found out I was pregnant I couldn't get out of here quick enough.

"Just something to think about." She winks moving back to the counter of food.

Bubbles giggles as she walks over and wraps her arms around me tight. "I agree with everything they said. But I want to add, G.T. needs you. He just hasn't been himself since you left."

I pull away from her, hurt by her words. "He doesn't

want me, Bubbles. He made it perfectly clear and I'll be going right back to school when Diamond's funeral is over." Something inside of me strengthened. I just don't care that he isn't the same. It's his own damn fault. Not mine. He did this, not me.

"I'm sad to hear that." She shakes her head back and forth. "We sure do miss you."

"I really need to get G.T.'s food and get back. He'll be waking up soon and if I'm not there, he'll get out of bed." She nods, moving away.

I turn to Ma, who holds out two plates of heaping with food. "Thanks." Ma doesn't say a word as I leave the kitchen heading back to G.T.'s room.

Entering the room, G.T.'s eyes bore into mine as I enter. "I got food." I hold up the plates showing him.

"You weren't supposed to leave." His voice is tense and strained.

"I was only gone for a minute." I walk to the side table setting the food down.

"That's what the phone is for. You could have called it in." He demands.

"I needed some air. I'm here. Calm down." I place my plate on the desk and walk back over to the bed, grabbing the small bed tray to set his food on.

G.T. slowly moves up and I place the tray on his lap along with the food. "You need to stay here with me. Alright?" His voice pleads catching me off guard. I pause and stare at him, his face showing every bit of the plea.

"I'm here. No worries. Let's eat." I move to the desk and bring my plate to G.T's side table. We eat in companionable silence. I can only get a little down, my appetite still not up to normal.

"That all you're gonna eat, Angel?" He asks swallowing his food.

"I'm finished."

"You hardly ate anything. Here." He holds his fork out with turkey and mashed potatoes on it to my mouth expectantly. I roll my eyes, but open my mouth to take a bite. "See now that's not so hard."

"The ol' ladies are good cooks."

For the next fifteen minutes, G.T. takes two bites and then feeds one to me. Warmth floods my body at his sweet and kind gesture. My heart flutters threatening to fly out of my chest. I try not reading more into this than it is, but he is making it difficult.

After we are done, I clear the plates setting them on the desk after G.T. refuses to let me leave to take them back to the kitchen. I give G.T. his meds and he takes them without complaint.

"Harlow said I need to change your bandage. You alright with that."

"Better question is, are you?" My spine stiffens and my face shows resolve.

"Of course I am. I can handle just about anything."

I remove the bandages, seeing for the first time the wounds that could have ended his life. My gut clenches at the thought of losing him. It's one thing to not be with him, it's another to lose him forever. I clean and add the salve from Doc and bandage him all back up.

"Why don't you go back to sleep. I'm gonna work on some homework." I move around the bed to the desk sitting in the chair.

"I think we need to talk." My blood runs cold; there is

no way Harlow had the chance to talk to him without me around. I continue looking at the desk.

"About?"

"Angel, come sit down." I blow out a deep breath the coldness in my veins heating fast, nerves begin to rack me.

I get up slowly and sit on the edge of the bed. He grips my hand tight and the most unexpected words fall from his lips.

"I lied." I stare at him having no idea what he's talking about. "I didn't fuck that woman who came out of my room that day. I lied about that."

I gasp and jump out of his grip moving quickly away from the bed. "Why would you do that?" I try my damnedest to hold back.

"I'm a fucking dumbass." He grumbles and I wait. "Bam wanted you to go to school, get your degree." He pauses. "And you need someone better. Someone who doesn't live this fucked up life."

Anger rises in my gut. Strength I thought I'd lost when I lost Mia comes back in full force. I move quickly to the other side of the room needing some space. "Fuck you! I needed you! I wanted you and only you! And I'm sure you fucked anything that came in front of you."

"No."

I stare at him. "So this whole fucking time, I thought you cheated on me. That I wasn't enough for you! That my pussy didn't satisfy you." I turn away not wanting to give him the satisfaction of seeing the welled up tears. He does not deserve them.

"Not good enough?" G.T.'s voice reverberates through the room making me jolt. "You're too good, Angel. Too perfect. With you, I don't want anyone else. I don't need anyone else." I hear movement over by the bed.

"Do not get out of that bed." I demand between clenched teeth. "You pass out again, I'm leaving your ass on the floor."

"Angel. Look at me."

"No." I am not falling for this shit. "I saw you kiss her G.T. Don't tell me that was a figment of my imagination."

"That was a thank you peck. It wasn't a kiss. She cleaned my room, Angel. That's all."

"So you're telling me you never fucked her." I bat the tears away focusing on the anger bubbling inside of me.

"I didn't say that. It was before we got together." He did this. If he wouldn't have lied, I would have told him about Mia and I wouldn't have lost her. It's all his fault. "Look, I fucked up. I know it. Please come here."

"It's your fault. It's all your fucking fault!" I scream so loud I think the walls will shudder. Fury races through my body and I cannot control anything, especially my mouth. My hands shake and my vision becomes hazy. "You're the reason she's gone. If you wouldn't have lied and told me the truth, none of this would have happened!" I clench my fists wanting to punch something, mainly G.T.'s face.

"Who is she?"

"Mia!"

"Who in the hell is Mia? You've got me lost." I don't even register the confused look on his face because I don't care. I don't care about anything. Nothing.

"The day you told me I wasn't good enough, you remember that? Well, it was the day I was coming to tell you I was pregnant!" His eyes widen. "Yeah. Your baby growing inside of me, but no, that happy moment got crushed because you were a fucking prick!" I scream.

"You're carrying my baby?" His eyes move to my stomach, my very flat stomach, his forehead wrinkles. I hold on to the fury and grab it with both hands because if I break now, I'll be in a pile on the floor. Fury is the only thing that can get me through this right now.

"*Had* G.T., had your baby growing inside of me."

I turn to him and he straightens on the bed standing up to his full height, well over six feet. His face turns menacing and if I were anyone else, I'd probably be shitting myself right about now. But I'm not. I stand my ground.

"You mean to tell me you aborted my baby?" Each word comes out in rage, a small amount of spittle with each word. His words make me snap and lose all sense of reality.

"No, you fucking prick! No! I would never kill *my* baby!" I point to my chest to punctuate the word my. "I miscarried, you fucking asshole!"

He crosses his arms over his chest, wrinkles forming around his eyes like he's in deep thought. My body is breathing so hard I'm beginning to feel light headed, but keep my head up. "You weren't going to tell me. You fucking left here, carrying my baby and weren't going to fucking tell me, Casey? What the hell is wrong with you?" He seethes.

I laugh not a happy one but a what-the-fuck-am-I-doing one. "I was coming back to tell you, even if you didn't deserve to know. I was waiting until I found out if it was a boy or a girl!"

"You fucking said it was a girl."

"I don't know for sure. It's what I think she was. I lost her before I could find out." My grasp on the anger is beginning to slip, but I hold on by my fingertips.

"So if I wouldn't have gotten hurt and Diamond wouldn't have gotten killed, would you have even fucking told me? Or would you have just gone on living your happy little college life up north?"

"Fuck off. I'm done explaining myself to you. You know about her and your twenty-four hours is officially up in my book. Stay the hell away from me while I'm here."

I walk to the door and grab the handle. "How do I even know the baby's mine?" He questions from behind me snidely.

The knife that he just stabbed me with had become encased in my heart. Anything left inside of it shrivels into nothingness. "You don't. Guess you have nothing to be upset about." I turn the handle of the door and slam it behind me. I turn to go to my room, but stop. If I go there, I will cry myself into oblivion. I need to be around people, it will be the only way to hold myself together.

Walking into the main room, I head directly to the bar where Buzz is standing with a smile as he sees me, but it falls. "What's wrong girl?" He asks innocently enough.

"Nothing. I need a bottle of Jim and a glass, please." I motion to the bottle on the wall.

Buzz gets them and pours my first shot, the burning seeps through my body and I can feel the exact moment it hits my stomach. I close my eyes at the fire, but open them quickly pouring another one. I don't normally drink, but screw it. Screw it all. I pour another and another, shooting them both back quickly.

"You might want to slow down there sunshine." Tug says from behind the bar next to Buzz.

I wave him off and pour my next shot. My head is already fuzzy, but I can't stop myself. The music and the commotion around me does nothing to deter my interest in the golden amber liquid in front of me. If only I can forget, just for a while. I gulp another and the bottle is snatched away from me.

I turn my head to the culprit and sigh. Becs. "What are you doing, girl?" The little girl inside wants to shrivel up in his arms, just to feel some closeness with Bam, but I refrain.

"Just having a drink. That's what we do around here, Becs. Drink, screw and drink some more."

"You're done." He says with authority, I roll my eyes.

"I am not done! Give me a bottle and I'll take it to my room." I yell looking into his eyes that are laced with deep concern.

"No, care to tell me what the hell is going on?"

"Guilt!" is boomed from across the room and all movement in the clubhouse seizes. I blow out a breath, wishing I was back up in Cherry Vale, even if it reminds me of Mia, it's better than this.

I ignore him and turn to Becs. "Just give me one more, please." I plead, but it falls on deaf ears.

"Guilt from what, Casey?" I shake my head at Becs question.

"From not telling me she was pregnant with my baby and leaving like a fucking coward!" G.T. yells. The audible gasps around the room make my stomach constrict, even if what he's saying is a lie, it hurts.

"Go to hell!" I yell over my shoulder.

"You're pregnant, Casey?" Becs asks gripping the bottle in his hand so tight, his knuckles turn white. I thought for sure he'd crush the bottle.

I look him in the eyes. "I lost her." I whisper softly only to him, but no doubt everyone in the room heard it.

"Yeah. She says she fucking lost it. How do I know she didn't kill it herself?"

I jump off the bar stool fast and aim straight for G.T., my head a bit foggy. "I fucking did not kill *my* baby! I loved her more than I loved anything in this world. *I'm* the one who carried her for thirteen weeks and two days. *I'm* the one who felt her growing inside of me. *I'm* the one who took care of her as if she was the most precious thing in this world. *Me!*" I seethe not caring if the entire club hears my business because more than likely they'd all know by morning anyway, may as well let them to know the truth.

"Because you didn't give me a chance!" He bites back.

"But remember what you said? You don't know if she was even yours. Considering I'm a whore who sleeps around with all your brothers. Whose do you think it could have been?" I tap my finger on my chin pretending to be in deep thought. "Hmm... Oh, I bet you think it's Tug's right?" His face lights up with red fury. "Don't worry, we never had sex. You're the only asshole I let touch me!" I shake my head. "God, I was so fucking wrong about you."

"And I was about you! How could you keep our baby a secret?"

"Because you'd just told me that you wanted to fuck other women and that I wasn't good enough. How did I know you'd be happy we were having a baby? You'd just told me you didn't want me. So what was I supposed to say? 'Hey G.T. now I've got your baby. You're stuck with me.'" I shake my head. "I wouldn't do that. I left to build a life for myself and my baby. You were going to know her, but I'd have a life for her with or without you."

"That's so big and noble of you." He coughs. "Problem. You should have fucking told me from the start."

"Well, I didn't. And if I could do it all over again, I'd do the same damn thing. You're the one who fucking lied. You set all of this in motion. You, G.T.! One lie was all it took to set this big ball in motion. You are just as guilty in this as I am." I turn and head straight for Becs.

"I want a bottle." I demand.

"Baby, you don't have to go through this on your own." He says quietly.

"I don't belong here. This is Bam's family, not mine. I've never belonged here."

"That's bullshit and you damn well know it." Becs nods to the side to someone, but I don't turn to look.

"Bullshit. Let's see. I don't fit in. I don't live the life. I don't ride. I don't fight. Do I need to continue?"

"You think all that shit matters, Casey? You being Bam's daughter *makes* you family." Becs' voice is calm and I want to scream at him.

"No. It makes me an obligation." Tears form in my eyes but, I blink them back. I'm so damn tired of tears.

"What the fuck are you talking about?" Harlow bellows from behind me, I breathe out deep holding back the roll of my eyes.

"I'm going to my room!" I say moving away from Becs and meeting a very pissed off Harlow.

"Not part of this family. Are you fucking kidding me right now, Casey?" Her face is mere inches away from mine and I can smell the peppermint on her breath. I go to move around her, but she stops me. "Oh no, you don't." She sidesteps and grabs my arms. "You are not a fucking obligation. If you were, we'd all be considered that. These men and women love you Casey. They'd lay down their fucking life for you. How do you not know that?"

I shrug not knowing what to say. My whole life I've felt like an outsider looking in, never really being part of it.

"Bullshit. Don't you remember graduation? The party all of these people threw for you?"

"That was for you, Harlow."

She eyes me and tilts her head. "You really believe that don't you?" I nod.

"What about when you and Bam finished your car? You remember that night?"

"That was for Bam."

"Holy shit. You really don't see it." I hang my head letting the humiliation course through me.

Harlow begins pointing to the member's one at a time around the room. "See them. See?" I shake my head. "Babe. This entire club loves you. Those parties were for you, too."

"Then why don't I have a club name, *Princess*?"

Harlow looks behind me and I turn to see Becs standing right behind me. "Bam never wanted you to have a club name. He asked us not to."

"Why would he do that?"

He clears his throat repeatedly and comes to sit next to me. "Bam was a bit more traditional with the club. He told all of us that your ol' man would give you a club name if you chose to be part of this life. It's not easy. You know that and Bam wanted to make sure that it was your choice."

"If that's the case, I'll always be Casey." I mumble. Becs and Princess look at each other and I roll my eyes. "I need to lie down." I say to Harlow. "I have to or you're going to be carrying me." I look around and see G.T. is no longer around and sag in relief. I cannot do this anymore. The fight is leaving me fast.

"Come on. I'll get you settled."

CHAPTER NINE
GT

CRUZ PULLS ME OUT OF THE MAIN ROOM BY BARKING HIS fucking order to go. Any other time, I'd be able to kick his fucking ass, but not this time.

I hear Princess and Casey screaming, something about her not being family or some stupid shit. Fucking women.

The glass on the table flies across the room, my arm feeling incredibly strong at the moment. Adrenaline courses through my body, no longer feeling weak. Pregnant. And didn't fucking tell me. Fuck!

"Calm your ass down." Cruz says from the doorway. I turn and clench my fist. I'd love nothing more than a fight right now, even if my body can't take it. He'd pound me though and I don't want to live with that shit the rest of my damn life.

"Fuck off brother."

"No, thanks. I have your sister for that." He smirks; my breathing hitches and my teeth grind together. "This is a shit deal, at least from what I heard about it. You're gonna pass the fuck out and I'm tired of carrying your ass everywhere."

"Then leave."

"Can't do that." He walks over and takes a seat in the desk chair, propping his feet on the desk and crossing his legs seeming to make himself right at home. "Talk."

"I'm not fucking talking about it. You already heard it!" I bark moving to the window. Looking out, cars go up and down the road one after another reminding me that the world always continues even if everything you thought just went to shit.

"Is it true what you told her? That she wasn't good enough and you wanted different pussy?"

I continue to stare out the window the fury bubbling now to a small boil. "I never said she wasn't good enough. She made that shit up herself. I did tell her that I needed a variety of pussy and I did kiss the club momma coming out of my room. I lied to her, saying that I fucked her."

"That was fucking stupid. We all know she means something to you."

My shoulders sag a bit, but not much. "No shit?" I shake my head. Casey's right. If only I hadn't let the lie spew out of my mouth. I'd already regretted it, now quite a bit more.

"Why'd ya do it?"

"Fuck if I know."

"I call bullshit."

"Call it whatever the fuck you want. You can leave now." I turn and face my brother, his eyebrow quirks.

"You don't wanna talk about it, fine. It's your shit deal, not mine. But Princess will be all over you like a fly on shit and then I'm gonna hear her bitch. Therefore, this shit storm affects me. So, brother what the hell are you going to do about it now?"

I stare into his eyes, knowing he's doing his best to help or at least keep himself out of the mess, whichever. "I don't fucking know." I say honestly.

"You need to get your shit together. We have Rabbit, Paine and the T-Darts to deal with after Diamond's funeral. VP will be voted for the day after. You're obviously gonna be out of commission for a while, but you need to get your head in the game, quick. And now this shit, figure it out."

I don't answer him. He's right and I fucking hate that. "Give me some time. Now go." I order. This time he listens and leaves the room.

I collapse on the bed my body feeling the exertion that I just gave it. Mia. I was gonna be a dad. The thought is overwhelming. I never thought I'd be one and now I'm sad I'm not. I can see her little face; she looks just like Casey growing up, so alive and full of spunk. Her long blonde hair flowing down her back, blowing in the wind and the biggest green eyes I've ever seen. My heart aches and I throw my good arm over my eyes to block out the light. I need dark to match the feelings swarming inside of me like bees ready to sting.

My breath catches and my body feels unbelievably heavy all the sudden, but I welcome it. I welcome the pain; it's the least I deserve. A lone tear escapes my eye. I bat it away, my mind wandering, nothing making a lot of sense, but the thoughts flood me.

Diamond, T-Darts, Rabbit... VP... Casey... Mia... What the fuck am I going to do? I close my eyes, just as everything turns black.

"G.T." A voice says from above me. "G.T." The sound is louder. "G.T.!" I jump as Princess' shrill voice comes loud and clear.

"What?"

"Time to take your meds you fucking idiot." She growls handing me a bottle of water and some pills. I sit up slowly and take the offerings.

"Thanks."

She huffs. "What the hell were you thinking?!"

"Did you know?"

"No. Not 'till earlier in the day. She said she was going to tell you after the twenty-four hours was over. She wanted to make sure you were healthy enough to take it."

"I'm not talking to you about it."

"Fine." She crosses her arms over her chest. "Then just listen 'cause I'm only saying this shit once asshole brother of mine."

I lay back down waiting for the blow.

"Her not telling you was shitty, but look at the circumstances surrounding that time. It wasn't all her fault. You pretty much degraded her into her mother, G.T." My stomach churns at the thought. Casey has always despised the way her mother slept around the club and then abandoned her. "And what was her life? Being raised by a single parent. She knew she could do it on her own and that's what she was trying to establish before she talked to you. She was giving you an out, G.T. You may not see this, but she was fucking giving you the freedom you told her you needed. Even in her time of confusion and hurt, she was thinking of your ass. She wanted to have enough to raise this baby on her own if that's what needed to happen."

I pull my arm over my face, not blocking out what my sister is saying, more like trying to process it all. I didn't want to think I did that to her so I latch on to the only thing I can. "So why didn't she tell you then?" I clip.

"Cause I would have told you. She didn't tell anyone G.T., except for her doctor. She carried it around on her own for months. And the only reason she told her friends Jace and Bella up there was because she was bleeding so bad she needed help."

"Where the hell you hear all this?"

"Where the hell you think I've been for the past four and a half hours brother? I've been downstairs trying to console an inconsolable woman. She finally passed out, so I made my way up here."

How in the hell can everything turn to shit so fast? A few hours ago, I'm ready to make Casey mine and now I'm so fucking angry with her and hurt, I don't know what end is fucking up. It has to be all these damn drugs I'm on. I've got to get off of them.

"I'm not sure what's running through that thick skull of yours, but you need to figure it out. If you truly love Casey now is the time to show it. She's a shell of a woman G.T., losing Mia killed a part of her and now she believes you are gone as well. She's empty and broken. You need to decide what you want and quick. She's leaving right after Diamond's funeral and this time she vows no matter what happens, she won't be back."

Princess didn't give me time to respond, the click of the door tells me she's gone.

I roll off the bed, needing a drink, now. I don't give a shit about the meds. I need alcohol. Walking out into the main clubhouse guys line the walls and stop to say hi or pat me on my good shoulder. Everyone except for Pops whose eyes glare at me. I walk up to him and the vein in his neck twitches.

"Church, you and me now!" Pops brushes past me and I follow, closing the doors behind me.

Pops looks out the window not bothering to turn and look at me when he begins talking. "Boy, this shit ends now. We've got too much going down. The club is at stake and we're taking out our problems very soon. I need your fucking head in the game and not stuck up Casey's pussy."

I nod. "I'm ready."

"Bullshit you're ready. You're still out for another few weeks Doc says, which means, you stay behind."

"Fuck that! I'll be fine. You can't tell me that I have to stay back."

"Can and did." He turns and looks me in the eye. "You'll handle shit inside, but not outside. We will take care of all that."

"What the fuck Pops?"

"Don't go getting your pretty panties in a bunch." He smirks. "Got info from Ransom. Rabbit's got a hushed meeting coming up here in a few days. Fucker's trying to be quick and under the radar, but Ransom's got people." I nod for him to continue. "All his members in one building and that's our chance."

"Bomb it?" He nods. "Buzz needs in on this and so does Tug. They're real good at that shit."

"Yeah. After Diamond's funeral, we have church and it all gets set up. You'll work from here. Got it?"

"Yeah." I grumble not happy about it.

"We'll be picking VP too." My ears perk a bit.

"Am I up for it?"

"Yeah. You and Becs." I stare for a moment and process it. I never once thought that I wouldn't be sitting next to Pops at the table and hearing the other man's name stuns me for a moment. "Yeah. You're still young. Remember that." He says opening the door.

Fuck. All those damn tests they put me through and to not get voted in. I follow Pops out of the room and stop dead in my tracks. Casey is standing behind the bar, her back to me. Tug pauses when he sees me but then continues his conversation with her smiling softly, but keeping one eye on me. Smart man.

Casey's shoulders sag and she turns around, her eyes landing directly on mine, so many thoughts pouring out of them. She abruptly turns back, Tug nods and she walks out the front door of the clubhouse.

Tug wipes his hands, walking up to me. "Brother, she wants me to take her somewhere. I'm gonna go."

It isn't a request for permission, but it is a plea for understanding.

"Where?" I ask abruptly.

"To see Bam." Fuck. I rub my hand over my face, nod and turn away. He takes his cue and leaves.

CHAPTER TEN
Casey

THE ENTIRE MORNING I SPENT HELPING HARLOW AND TEN other women get all the food ready for after the funeral today. We made enough food to feed an army, but that's what we were feeding. An army of brothers. I do anything and everything to keep my mind off of the swirling inside my head, even if only for a moment.

After getting back from seeing Bam yesterday, I stayed locked in my room. Harlow brought me food and tried to coerce me out, but I needed to be alone. Which is totally ironic considering all I wanted before was her comfort before.

I didn't truly know how G.T. would react to Mia and even though he is pissed as shit, I'm happy about it. I'm happy he cares. It means she mattered to him. Even if he can't stand to be in the same room as me, at least he cares enough about her to be upset. That's all that matters.

"You're riding in the limo." Harlow says rushing into my room. I'd just gotten the last of my makeup on. I'd decided to go with a simple black dress that hugs my body, but flowed at the bottom. Simple yet cute.

"Okay."

"You'll be with G.T." I turn abruptly.

"You think that's a good idea? Having us in a confined space."

"You're family. You ride in the limo. He can't ride yet, so he's with you in the cage."

"Fine." I grumble. This is so a bad idea.

"Come on. We gotta get upstairs." Harlow is wearing her leathers which is to be expected. All the brothers and their ol' ladies will be riding today in honor of Diamond.

"You riding or riding with Cruz?" I ask climbing the stairs to the main room.

"Riding next to Cruz." She answers quickly.

Scanning the room, G.T.'s eyes instantly find mine and suck me in. I turn away quickly not wanting to get pulled into the hurt right now. It's too difficult of a day and I cannot add to it right now.

A commotion from the door commands our attention and all eyes of the club swing that way. A little pixie of a woman stands waving her finger at everyone and no one in particular. I move closer to get a better view. She is dressed in a sleek black dress that shows off her hourglass figure. Her long chestnut hair flows straight down her back. As she turns, I know instantly who she is.

"Shaina?" G.T asks from the far couch. My eyes flicker towards him. He looks good enough to eat. His black pants hug his legs, tight black t-shirt hugs his chest and his rag sets it all off. I shake my head and turn back to Shaina.

Shaina makes eye contact with him. "Well, if it isn't the MC golden boy, born and bred to run this shithole. Too bad my dad had to die for it to happen."

"Nice to see you too. Didn't think you'd make it." None of us thought she would show her face for it, guess we were wrong… Her relationship with her dad was not the greatest, at least what we knew of it.

"Now come on G.T. what kind of daughter would I be if I didn't come say goodbye to my daddy?" The tone in her voice pisses me off. It's smug and arrogant and totally disrespectful to Diamond.

"You didn't want to fucking say hi to him when he was alive. I doubt it would fucking matter if you say goodbye." G.T. barks loudly.

"Such a fierce, loyal man you are G.T. Don't worry, after today I'll be gone for good. That is after you give me my money."

G.T. rises from the couch. "What fucking money?"

"I know there is a shit ton of rules in this place. Isn't there one for a brother killing another brother?" She walks in and stops in front of G.T., turning cold as she says the last three words. My body stills and part of me wants to run to his defense, but I stop myself.

"You fucking bitch. You fucking think I killed him?" G.T. roars.

"You should leave." Harlow calls from beside me. Shaina's eyes snap quickly to hers.

"Oh and look who it is, Miss Princess. Don't you look pretty in all your leather?" She chastises Princess, who walks toe to toe with her.

"You need to shut the fuck up quickly or all these men here will throw your ass out."

She smirks and turns back to G.T. "What would you call not protecting my dad?"

"I tried to fucking save him." G.T. clips his vein starts to pulsate.

"Didn't do a very good job, did ya?" G.T. lunges for the woman just as Harlow grabs her around the throat.

"You are not welcome here. You want to come to the funeral, fine, but don't fucking step foot back here." G.T. growls. "Buzz, make sure she leaves. Now." He nods, grabs Shaina and takes her out of the clubhouse.

"Nothing like getting started early." Harlow says brushing her hands down her clothes to smooth them out.

"It's time." Pops calls out to the club, not acknowledging the outburst and everyone files out.

"I'll see you there." Harlow says as I enter the limo.

"Yep. No worries." I don't know if I am reassuring her or myself. She nods and takes off leaving the door wide open. I move as far over in the seat as I can, not wanting to touch G.T. I stare out the window waiting to hear the rumble of all the bikes that will follow us. I love that noise.

My body vibrates, sensing him before I feel the movement on the seat. I do not turn to him or talk. I don't even think I can breathe. This is the closest I've been to him since I told him about Mia and while he said some horrible things, I know they were in a moment of hurt. I can't say I wouldn't have done the same.

His breathing is the only sound I hear until all the bikes behind us roar to life and we move. The seat begins to shake repeatedly. I look over to see G.T.'s leg bouncing uncontrollably as he looks back at the bikes, his face twisting. He's hurt and crushed he can't be on his bike, riding for this. My insides twist.

My hand instinctively reaches out and grabs his leg making him jump and I quickly pull away. "Sorry." I mumble turning back to the window. Heat flushes through my body. He grunts, no words escaping his lips.

It's strange that in the course of one day, G.T. and I can crush everything we built over the years. Words. They cut deep, deeper than actions. Each one that spewed out of our mouths came from hurt and in my head, I know that, but my heart is another story.

Anger radiates off of G.T. and if I sat any closer to him, I might just go up in flames. Today though, I don't have it in me to confront him. When I woke up this morning, I grabbed every bit of strength I could, but now at this moment with the cemetery getting closer, the strength oozes out of me, leaving the grief to strangle me like a vise.

Everything is exactly the same as when Bam died, the limo, the brothers and sisters behind it, and all the chapter members behind them, making one endless stream of bikes. I breathe in deep, I can do this and I will.

The limo comes to a stop and I clutch my tissues in my hand, willing myself to get out. "It's time." G.T.'s deep voice bounces off the walls of the car. I nod pulling the door open. The warm air caresses my skin as I turn to look at all the bikes. I breathe in and out deep to stop the tears, but the ache in my heart is so strong, I fear it will bring me down.

Heat envelops my back and I inhale G.T. as his hand

rests on my shoulder giving it a gentle squeeze. The kindness is almost too much to bear, but I take it, even if for a moment.

I spot Harlow right away. She parks her bike along with the rest of the club, grabs Cruz's hand and makes her way to the limo. She eyes her brother behind me and I can feel the daggers in her penetrating stare. "You alright?"

I cough to clear the lump in my throat. "Yeah."

"Come on." She grabs my hand pulling it with her and Cruz. I keep my eyes straight not wanting to turn around and see G.T. standing there.

The service is long, which is to be expected and standing this entire time is beginning to wear on me. I glance over at G.T. who is only about ten feet from me, his head is bowed down and I want to go over and wrap my arms around him. Love just doesn't disappear when you're pissed at someone. It's always on the forefront. Always looming.

And I know that Shaina's words cut him deep.

I lace my hands together in front of me and stare at the man talking in front of this massive group. He's the same man who talked at my father's; when his eyes find mine he gives a slight nod in recognition. I let my head fall to my chest and don't bother to stop the tears from trailing down my face. Thoughts of Bam, Mia and Diamond, swirl so fast in my head that everything begins to get hazy.

I register a hand on my arm, but it doesn't stop the spinning in my head. "Casey," is whispered in my ear but I can't answer. My mouth is dry like I haven't drunk anything for days. My body begins to feel light. "Casey."

The words are stronger now, but I still can't answer. I feel the water leaking from my eyes, but none of it matters.

"Cruz, something's wrong." I hear. Harlow and I want to answer her and tell her I'm alright, but the words won't come out. My knees buckle and slam into the dirt, but I don't feel any pain. I only feel numb.

STANDING HERE, I feel a huge weight on my shoulders pushing me down to the ground. Shaina's words still bounce around in my head. Deep down, I know I did everything I could to protect Diamond at that moment, but I can't stop the guilt of not saving him.

I look to my left at the beautiful blonde standing next to my sister. I'm so fucking pissed, she didn't tell me about the baby. I want to be rational and tell her I understand, but I can't and it's because of her. The thought of my child growing inside of her flips all these damn feelings inside and I like it, a lot.

I said some pretty shitty things to her. I knew she'd never abort the baby, but I said it anyway. I knew the baby was mine, I never had a doubt. But my damn anger kept shit falling out of my mouth.

Turning back to the ground, I stare at the same blade of grass and think about my life. I love my club. I will protect it and the people in it. She's what's missing. Casey my Angel. She is who I need.

A commotion from my left catches my eye. Harlow and Cruz are reaching out to grab a collapsing Casey, but they aren't fast enough, her knees crash to the ground. My legs move quick, pushing my way through the crowd.

"What the fuck happened?" I growl at my sister who is helping Cruz get Casey up to a chair.

"Shit. I don't know. She just started swaying back and forth. I called her name, but she didn't respond and then went down for the count. I tried to catch her." She bends down climbing in between Casey's legs. Casey's eyes are open, but they are glazed over. "Casey? Answer me dammit." Harlow yells, snapping her fingers in front of her.

"It's too much for her. Cruz, pick her up." He does so and I sit in the chair as he places her in my lap. "It's fine. Please continue on." I grip Angel as tight as I can; her body lying limp across mine.

After the service is over, I announce, "I'm taking her back to the limo. We'll ride in the processional back, and then I'm putting her to bed." I try to rise from the chair, but my grip on Angel isn't good with one arm. "Cruz, fucking help me." Anger surges through me that I can't fucking pick up my girl, but it's not the place or time for this shit.

"You got it." Cruz lifts her effortlessly and I can't help the small bit of envy.

"Take care of her." Princess says as she grabs my arm tight.

I look down at my sister, "Always." A smile adorns her face as she lets go.

The ride back to the clubhouse is quiet. Angel's head rests on my lap and her eyes have now shut. I don't believe for a minute she is sleeping though and when she speaks, I know she's been awake the whole time. "I'm sorry. I didn't mean to make a spectacle."

My hand sweeps in and out of her hair, feeling the silkiness brush through my fingers. "You didn't. I knew it was too much for you. I should have been by your side."

"You don't need to be anywhere you don't want to be."

"You're always where I want to be, darlin.'"

"I'm so sorry. I should have told you." I swipe my thumb across the tear that escapes the corner of her eye.

"Yeah, you should have and I shouldn't have lied about shit either. We both fucked up." She opens her eyes and stares at me, the lines around her eyes laced with worry. "It's gonna be alright."

"You don't know that. I don't think it will ever be alright." No, I didn't but I'd do my damnedest to make it that way.

"We'll get through it together." Her eyes widened and she gaped. When she tries to move, I lock her down with my arm. "Stay."

Her body stays down, but the tension inside of it is strung tight. "You don't mean that." She sighs and looks away.

"Look at me." Her eyes slowly come to mine. "I was angry when I said that shit. I didn't mean it. You're my girl, Angel. You've been for a long fucking time and I'm done with all this other bull shit. From this moment on, we figure this shit out together. Got me?"

She stares at me and blinks her eyes. "Are you able to forgive me for not telling you about Mia sooner?"

I can't lie. "I want to, but right now it's too raw. We gotta work through that shit. And it's the same with you and what I did. But Angel, this time I'm not walking away, I'm not making up some bullshit excuse, and I'm not giving you up. You're with me; the rest of it will find its way."

"You really believe that?"

"Fuck yeah. I lost you once, it won't happen again." Angel's body shivered

We were the first ones in the clubhouse as I pull Angel through to my room. After slowly taking her clothes off and putting her into one of my t-shirts, I lay her down on the bed and cover her up. I kick off my shoes and pants, climbing in behind her. "Sleep." I tell her and brush her hair softly until her breathing evens out.

I slide slowly out of bed. I don't want to leave her, but there is a big party in Diamond's honor that I can't miss.

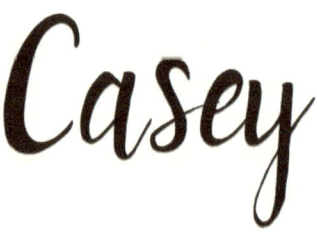

WAKING UP WITH A START, I quickly look around the room. *G.T.'s.* I sigh and feel the sheets next to me, they are ice cold. He's more than likely at the party for Diamond and that's where he should be. I get up and get my purse off the desk. I open it pulling out three black and white pictures. The only pictures I have of Mia and look at each one, each only a small peanut on the paper.

"I love you, baby girl." I whisper, but this time I don't feel the twinge of tears that threaten every time I've look at them. Instead, a smile graces my lips remembering the feeling of having her grow inside of me.

The door opens and I jump. I look into the blue eyes of the man who has captivated me for most of my life. "You scared me." I say quietly.

"Whatcha got there?" He points to my hands.

"Pictures of Mia." His face twists as he steps closer.

"Can I see them?"

I smile. "Of course." I hand them to him, his eyes graze the paper.

"She's a little peanut." I chuckle.

"That's what I called her." He hands the pictures back to me and sits on the bed. "What are we doing here?"

"Not exactly sure, never done it before. But I meant what I said in the limo, I'm not letting you go."

My body pulsates with his words. So long I've waited to hear them. "I'm supposed to leave tomorrow." I say quietly.

"I know, but you can't. It's too dangerous. Not right now. I know how important school is to you. We'll get you set up with shit online or something. You will graduate, I promise you that, but you can't be up there by yourself."

"I don't want to go back." I whisper. "It's where Mia was. That apartment is where I lost her."

"Come here." His arm splays open and I wrap my arms around his waist and hold on.

"Then you don't go back." He says matter-of-factly.

"I wish everything could be that simple."

"Look at me." I raise my head resting my chin on his hard chest. "It is that simple. We will figure out a way for you to get your degree and keep you safe. And because I'm selfish, keep you here with me."

I smile up at him. "Selfish, huh?"

"Damn right." I lift up on my tiptoes and bring my lips directly in line with his. His breath hitches and my hands snake down his thighs. "You want this?" he growls.

"Always." I whisper on his lips. He doesn't give me time to think. His hand reaches up behind my head pulling me to his lips, our lips performing a wonderful dance. He pulls me down on top of him and I straddle his hips feeling his growing length beneath my panties, along with the wetness that's always there, always for him. He breaks away and stares into my eyes.

"You, Angel. Only you." His nose dips down and grazes mine making me look up again. He kisses me again, but this kiss is full of promise, of hope, of love. I can feel it in every fiber of my body and I want to believe it. More than anything. I want this... him. Being as careful as I can not to touch his arm and shoulder, I place my arms on each side of his neck and begin rocking back and forth on his body.

Our lips do a magical dance that is sweet and caring, not like the other times. This is different, almost as if we are now on a different level. One thing I always love about G.T. is his intensity, but this... This is squeezing my heart.

I continue to rock my body against his, massaging him and feeling him grow hard as stone. Reaching up he weaves his fingers through my hair, pulling me exactly where he wants me, into a deep kiss, skyrocketing the already intense connection growing inside my body.

I pull away slowly needing to come up for air, my breath coming in small pants. I rest my forehead on his. "I need you, Angel." My entire body ignites at his words, pulsating and throbbing. "Take your shirt off." He orders and I eagerly comply, throwing it to the floor.

HER PERKY PINK nipples stand at attention and beg me to taste them. "Give them to me." Casey rises up on her knees and places her hands on her tits giving them to my mouth. I love the way she listens during sex; it is such a fucking turn on. With my tongue and my teeth, I assault those beautiful buds. Putting one in my mouth, I suck hard feeling it elongate as I work it. Casey's moans and mews spur me on. I love the noises she makes during sex.

Popping her nipple out of my mouth, I move to the second and give it the same treatment as the first. I have never met a woman before that could come just from getting her nipples sucked and bit, but to hell if my Angel can't. Her breaths get shorter and shorter. She is close. I pull away. "Play with your clit." Her hands drift down to her panties and her right hand slides right inside. One small graze and she set off like a lightning bolt. Her head falls back as she clamps her mouth closed muffling the sounds coming out. Fuck that.

Watching her fly off is the hottest fucking thing I've ever seen. Her breathing slows and she lowers back down to my lap as her glazed eyes focus on mine. "Next time, I hear you. Got it?" She nods her head. "Can't hear you."

"Yes."

"Angel. I'm gonna need your help here. Take off your panties." She moves quickly and stands next to the bed as I lay down flat careful not to bump this damn arm. "Top drawer." She smiles and reaches for the drawer pulling out a condom. I pull my pants down quickly using my feet to push them off completely. My dick springs free, she takes the condom and places it over my engorged head and rolls it down my shaft. Just the slight touch of her hand and I am ready to shoot off.

"Good?"

"Yeah, Angel. Climb up." She positions herself above my dick and painfully slow, lowers herself inch by inch. I want to push up hard, but I hold back, at least for now. She begins riding up and down, her hair flings back and forth. The sight alone makes me fucking grow harder inside of her.

With her feet planted on either side of my hips, the

only part of her body touching mine is her sweet pussy as she slides up and down. Her legs are strong as she rides harder and harder. My hips piston up hard, I use my legs to give me the strength my arm has taken away. Angel's hands land on my abs and my hand on her hip.

I dig into her flesh and push her down hard with each thrust. "G.T." She yells as her moans become louder and push me on.

"Touch yourself, now." I bark. Her hand slowly descends down to her sweet pussy. She rubs as I watch my dick pump in and out of her tight wetness. It's the best sight I've ever seen. "Come Angel."

As if waiting for my command, she detonates screaming my name loud enough I knew every fucker in this place could hear her. Three more hard thrusts inside of her, I come hard shooting myself in the damn rubber. I hate these damn things, but they are a necessity. Angel is the only woman I have fucked without one, but with everything being so hard with Mia, it's not the time.

Angel collapses on my good shoulder side careful not to touch the other. Her breathing is unbelievably labored as she tries catching her breath. I notice I am doing the same, but grip her tight not wanting to let go.

THIS FIRST HOUR of church is in remembrance of Diamond. In here, the stories told involved club business that we didn't need prying ears to hear. When the discussion turns to the day he died, I clam up inside. I wait for the judgment from my brothers, but it never comes. I can't say I am relieved, because no amount of hatred anyone feels for me about the situation, can compare to how I feel about it.

Shaking myself off, I take in my surroundings. Pops sits at the head of the table. To his right is Dagger and to the left is an empty chair. My stomach twists knowing what is coming.

"Alright, next. G.T. glad to have you back, son." Pops says pleased. "Tell the brothers how you're feeling."

"Thanks. I'm doing good. Arm and chest are healing up."

"We had a discussion while you were on your back." Here it came. "The vote for VP is between you and Becs." I nod looking at Becs, who's been here for as long as Pops. Even though Diamond and Pops have been preparing me for this role since I was thirteen years old, something inside of me says that it isn't my time. And I feel okay with that. I actually feel a weight being lifted off of my shoulders at the realization.

"I nominate Becs. He's the man for the job." Immediately all eyes turn to me, even Pops. "I pull my name out of the running. Becs is the guy for the job."

"You sure about that son?" Pop questions.

"Damn sure." I turn looking at Becs and light a cigarette inhaling it deeply.

"We vote then."

The vote goes quick and Becs is our new Vice President and I'm actually relieved. Even though I can damn well do the job, it's not my time. I don't feel it yet. It's better for the club this way, letting the older generation continue the legacy that they started. I'll have my time.

"We need to fill G.T. in on what's been going on. Dagger, you're up." Pops says.

"Paine needs to die." I am in total agreement with that. "He contacted me the day after Diamond was killed. Said one down and more to go. Fucker." My blood boils. He will not pluck my brothers off. I will not allow it. "It's all about that land. Pops, you may need to help me here because I joined about a year after this happened, but this is what I got on it. About fifteen years back, Zane, Paine's father, owned the land. We needed access to it because it was a direct pipeline down to Florida. Zane wouldn't allow it. War broke out, we took it. Gunfire and blood was everywhere, but Ravage won and took over the land. Zane was pissed and wanted revenge. Diamond suggested a hand to hand fight."

"Becs and I were there. It was rough." Zed chimes in. Becs nods.

Dagger continues. "Zane agreed and played it dirty. Somehow Ravage came out on top, getting the land fair and square. Zane left shit alone. Zane died about a year ago and his oldest son Paine took over. Paine wants it back, by any means necessary."

"Alright, what's he offering?" I ask snuffing out my smoke.

"He's not offering shit. He said, he's going to take it, like we took it from his father. And if we don't give it up, he's going to pluck us off one at a time." Fury courses through my veins. Dagger is absolutely right. This fucker will die.

"The hell he is. Where is he?" I demand.

"Underground. Can't find him. Dropped off the radar after the phone call. He's like a fucking ghost." Cruz cut in running his hands through his hair in frustration. "Last time he was seen was at a diner. After that, gone."

"You asked all of our contacts?" I direct to Cruz. I may not be VP, but damn if I needed to catch the hell up from my little impromptu vacation.

"Yeah. All but Ransom have gotten back to me. I expect to hear from him by the end of the day with his little tidbit after he gets confirmation. Other than that, nothing. No trace of the fucker."

"Where's his money coming from?" I ask. No one could run themselves underground that good without money.

"His crew is still running. Just Paine seems to be gone. But I'm sure he has a few guys with him." Dagger answers.

"So, we find some of his crew and make them talk." Seriousness drips off my words.

"Agree and on it. We'll take them out to the small house in the woods. It's quiet there." Dagger smiles, sadistic fucker.

"Good, let's do it!" I say and slam my hand down on the table actually excited to get back in the groove again.

"We go, you stay." Pops says, halting my thoughts.

"What?" I growl remembering his words the other day and not liking them one fucking bit.

"It's not something new. You stay back 'til you're 100%. Can't have you going in there with one fucking hand." Pops growls back.

"Bullshit. I'm fine, I'll drive a cage." I counter knowing one of the reasons is that I can't ride yet.

"No. End of discussion." Pops says, slamming down the gavel.

"What am I supposed to do then? Sit here with my thumb up my ass?" I ask thoroughly pissed now.

"Why don't you go fuck Casey? Relieve some of your tension." Rhys says with a laugh.

"You're just fucking jealous she's not in your bed." I say getting up from the table and walking out of the room, to do just that.

"WHERE ARE YOU GOING?" I bark entering my room. Angel is pulling her dress on from the night before and gathering all of her things.

"I've gotta get downstairs and pack. Breaker is going to follow me back." Angel says without looking at me.

"Didn't we just have this fucking conversation last night?"

"Relax big guy. I need to talk to my professors and get some things. I'll be back in a couple of days. No worries."

"No."

She stops in her tracks, turns and glares at me. "What do you mean no?"

"You're not going without me." I say matter-of-factly. "I'm driving you up there."

"You are not driving my car, one handed." She demands. A small smile plays on her lips.

I step close. "Hurry up. We leave in a couple of hours." Her eyes lift up to meet mine. They flare and her breathing picks up.

"Getting back to the old G.T. I see." She smiles catching her bottom lip in her teeth.

"Damn right. Those fucking drugs were messing my shit up. Doc gave me some different ones that don't mess with me so much."

"You sure you're okay to drive?"

"What do you think?" She didn't say a word, just scoots around me towards the door. "I'll be downstairs."

"WHAT THE FUCK WAS THAT BOY?" Pops billows in my room as I'm putting a couple of shirts in a bag.

"What?"

"Why the fuck did you bow out of VP?" The vein in his neck ticks showing his rapid heartbeat.

I sit on the bed and rub my hand over my face. "I love this club. I am this club Pops. But it's Becs' time. Mine will come later."

"After I'm fucking dead." He growls. "This better not have anything to do with Casey."

My anger peaks at the sound of her name in such a demeaning way. "No, it has nothing to do with her. It's on me, just like every other fucking thing."

"What's that supposed to mean?"

"Nothing. Look Pops, for once it was the right thing to do. Let's just let it lay."

Pops clenches his fists but nods his head.

"I've gotta take Angel up to get her shit. She's coming home and this time she's not leaving." I say as I put jeans in my bag.

"Good. Then maybe you can get your head out of

your ass." He says pushing the door open and slamming it shut.

Some decisions you make are good, some not. Deep down, in my gut, not being VP right now is what needs to happen for me.

CHAPTER ELEVEN
GT

I LOOK OVER TO THE PASSENGER SEAT TO A FIDGETY ANGEL, her hands are in front of her and not one finger has stopped moving since the car left the clubhouse. "You nervous, Angel?"

She looks up, a soft smile graces her lips. "A little." She swallows and looks out the window. "We're going to the place where I thought I'd have Mia and where I lost her. Just hard going back."

A lump forms in my throat, but a slight cough helps it melt away. I want to reach out to her and hold her hand, but with only one arm, that's not going to happen. "I'm here Angel. We'll get through this." I try to reassure her.

I can't say I'm happy about coming up here and that the anger isn't there. It is. It's not burning me like it did at first. Now, it's more about the fact that I didn't get to be a part of it. Regret. Even though, I know deep down it's not my doing, it still doesn't sit well. If I hadn't lied, maybe just maybe baby Mia would be here. We could have been a family. I stop the car at the light and rake my hand over my face trying to clear my head.

Pulling up to the building, Angel gives a small sigh and reaches for the door handle. I follow and move around the car swiftly and wrap my arm around her body. I nuzzle my nose in her neck and pull her tight to me. "It's okay." She nods.

I release her waist and grab her hand, making it to the elevator.

I give her hand a gentle squeeze before releasing it for her to unlock the door.

"Casey!" A deep voice calls from my left and I quickly turn putting Angel behind me. A guy in shorts and a fancy shirt walks towards us. Angel goes to talk, but I interrupt.

"Who the fuck are you?" The guy flinches and Angel's hand falls on my arm and she peeks around my body.

"G.T. calm down. This is Jace." She whispers.

"And that means shit to me." My anger spikes. My eyes lock on the guy coming down the hall towards my girl. Dude's got fucking balls to keep coming; his eyes show a small amount of fear, but not enough.

"He took me to the hospital and stayed with me. He's a friend of mine." She rubs my arm up and down sending shocks to my dick. Not the time to be getting hard. And it dawns on me the name Jace is one that Princess said to me. Shit.

"You took care of my girls." I state as I look him square in the eye. "Appreciate it." That is the closest to a thank you he'll ever get, I don't trust him.

Casey moves around me, "Hey, Jace. This is G.T."

"I caught that." His eyes do not waver from mine and I can't help but feel this is a standoff of some sort. Whatever the fuck it is, I'll end him.

I grunt. Angel wraps her arms around my waist and leans into me slightly, my body instantly warming from hers and calm flows over me.

"We just came to pick up a few things and get school sorted out. I'm going back home." Jace's eyes snap to Casey's and glare at her, a slight redness creeps up his neck.

"What?" He asks her and I keep to myself for the time being.

"I'm going back home, Jace."

He balls his fists up like he's gonna swing and I move Angel fast behind me. The instant I do, Jace blows out a deep breath and unclenches his fists. But his eyes are cold and hard. "A couple days home and you're gonna throw everything away." The annoyance is perfectly clear.

"G.T. he won't hurt me." She moves to the side of me, but I keep her tight against my body. "Jace. I'm not throwing anything away. I'm gonna finish school, but I'm doing it online. I need to be home."

"I thought you were starting over. I thought..." He trails off and I fill in the blanks.

"You thought she'd be on your dick. Nope. Not happenin'."

"G.T.!" Angel scolds, but I ignore it and she growls. "When the two of you are done with your pissing contest, I'll be inside packing." She unlocks the door and storms through.

"Stay the fuck away from her or I'll fucking pound you into the ground. She's mine." I clench my fists tight.

"She's not some property you can claim." He barks back crossing his arms over his chest. The glint of fear I saw earlier has dissipated and is replaced with defiance.

"She will be my property soon enough and wearing my leather. Stay away." I glare, turn into the apartment and shut the door in his face. No way this little piss-ant is gonna weasel his way in. I'll crush him.

Walking into the space, everything around me screams Casey, from the color on the walls to the engine magazines thrown across the table. I make my way down a small hallway and look in the first room. Angel is working on getting clothes put together.

She looks up and sighs. "You didn't have to be that way with him."

"Yeah. I did. He wants in your pants and it's not happenin'" I grind out and lean against the door jam.

"I don't want him. I've always made sure that he knew we were just friends and never gave him any indication of more. My heart is yours G.T., it always has been." She smiles walking over and gripping my shirt.

My heart constricts. "Damn right your heart's mine but babe, you need to open your eyes cause that man wants you." She stops and looks at me then goes back to her clothes.

"He may want me, but I don't want him." I nod and

walk in the room. "Have a seat." She says pointing to the edge of the bed.

"You need to talk to the landlord about this place. Get out of the lease. You want me to do it for you?"

"I have a year contract. I'll have to pay it."

I crack my knuckles. "I'll work it out."

"Don't hurt the poor guy." She smirks.

"Me? Never." I lean on the bed resting on my good arm.

"I need to get a new place first so I can get my stuff there, so give me a month or so."

"I'll have the brothers move ya and you're moving in with me."

"What? No. We've got too much to work out."

"Yeah. We do. Until lockdown's done, we stay at the club. When it's lifted we go to my house. You want a different one; I'll buy it for ya. But under no circumstances will you be moving anywhere besides with me. We'll work it out, but I will not go another night without you in my bed and in my arms."

Angel went to protest, but a screech stopped her words.

"Holy fucking shit!" I spring out of bed and stand in front of Angel. The woman's voice is smooth like honey and shit if she wasn't pretty, but nothing like my Angel.

"Bella!" Angel moves so quick I'm not able to catch her and she lunges into Bella's arms. She's told me a little about her.

Angel releases Bella, her eyes widen as they make contact with me. "Hey." I say and sit down on the corner of the bed.

"Well hello, G.T." Bella's sultry voice is intoxicating.

"I see you know me." I smirk.

"Pictures. Casey showed me. But damn you're so much bigger in person."

"That's what they all say." I smile and Angel huffs rolling her eyes.

"And a dimple to go with it. Shit girl. You have got to take me to the club!" Bella turns grabbing Casey's shoulders and my spine stiffens, eyes narrowing.

When Casey's beautiful laugh echoes through the room, I allow myself to relax a bit. It's been a long time since I've heard an actual carefree laugh from her. I love it.

"They'd eat you alive and no offense, but I'm not gonna be the one responsible for feeding you to the wolves." Casey says coming back to her clothes.

"I don't want all the wolves, just Buzz. And maybe his brother."

"That can be arranged." I move and perch myself at the head of the bed, resting my back on the headboard.

"Oh, I like him." Bella says looking at Casey. "He's a man who makes things happen. Love it!"

"Baby, you haven't seen nothing yet. You come to the club and I promise a wild time."

Casey clears her throat and glares at me. I hold my hand up in mock surrender giving her a full smile. "Not me babe."

"Yeah. Right." She mumbles going back to the closet. I am not letting that pass.

"Angel!" I yell sternly and she stops in her tracks and turns putting her hand on her hip. "There is no one but you, got it?" She nods her head, but she doesn't believe it as she huffs back into the closet, and I know I'll have to make her believe it.

Casey

I LAY in bed reliving the conversation about us moving in together. I know it will happen again someday, but there is no way I will put myself in a position to rely on him. Not yet. Moving in with him is just not an option. He is going to fight me and it's one thing that I'll have to stay solid on. For both of us.

He has yet to fully understand and feel everything he needs to about Mia and what I did to him. When his feelings about Mia blow, I need to make sure I have a place that is mine. But I need to go home. Not just because of the lockdown and the club, but for me.

Would I feel different if Mia were here with me? Maybe. But she's not and everything changed in the blink of an eye. Life shattered so fast and relying on G.T. to rebuild it, won't happen. I can do this myself.

But I need to do it in Sumner, not here. Considering how my grades have slipped these past few weeks and I'm hanging on by a thread, online classes at home would be better. Maybe G.T. and I can work through everything and come out stronger on the other end. A woman can hope.

Rolling over to my side, I watch the slight rise and fall of G.T.'s bare chest, the sheet barely covering his lower body. I want to lick every single tattoo on this man's body. From the tribal to the Ravage Club symbols lining his arms and chest. But I won't wake him. He needs to heal and get his arm moving again. I slide out of bed quietly and head to the bathroom.

After finishing, I throw on a t-shirt and shorts and head to the kitchen. I need coffee. I wait for it to brew and grab my phone turning it on. It beeps instantly and I swipe the screen. A text from Jace pops up. *I need to talk to you, please come to my place.*

I reply. *What's going on?*

The response is immediate. *Come over please, I really need to talk to you.*

I sigh. He's been a really good friend since I've been here and helping me with Mia. I really do not want to fight.

I'll be there in a couple minutes.

:) He replies.

I quietly go to the bedroom and put on some jeans and a bra to go with my t-shirt. G.T. is soundly snoring on the bed. Just the sight of him makes me smile.

I quickly scroll a note telling him where I am and leave it on the counter, then head out the door locking it behind me. The short walk to Jace's apartment does nothing to ease my tension. I want him to be happy for me and not upset.

I quietly knock on the door and it flies open quickly startling me. He must have been waiting.

"Hey." He smiles.

"Hey. What's going on?" I question looking up into his eyes, they have a bit of a spark in them and I'm not sure what it means.

"Come on in."

I step through the doorway and the click of the door sends chills up my spine. I've never been in his place before. He's always come to mine and I never thought twice about it. His apartment is simple with the bare minimum of furniture. The kitchen is laced with pizza boxes and beer bottles, sort of reminding me of the club.

I stop in the living room. "Jace, what's so important that I needed to come right over. I don't want to fight with you."

"I don't want to either. I was just shocked when you said you were leaving." He motions to the couch. "Please sit." I do.

For some reason, I feel like I need to justify myself. "This is the best thing for me. I'll finish school and I'll work at the shop. It'll help me work through all the emotions of losing Mia."

"You can work through them here. You can't just leave because of him." His body language changes before my eyes. His body stiffens and his hands clutch his knees as if he's trying to keep them in place. A chill runs up my spine, and I know me coming up here was not a good idea. Something is not right.

"I'm not leaving just because of G.T. I'm doing it for me. My family is there." I begin to judge my distance to the door.

"How do you know what you need?" He barks and the hairs on my arms stand to attention. In all the time that I've spent with him, not once has he ever talked to me this way. I need to get out of here. Now.

I slowly rise from the couch and without looking away from Jace, I begin to back to the door. "Jace, you've been great and helped me so much. I'll keep in touch with you. I promise."

"You need to stop moving towards the door." His eyes turn menacing, my heart pumps so fast it may just explode from my body. My chest constricts as fear washes through me.

"I'm going to leave, Jace. I'll talk to you soon." My feet move soundly to the door I reach back and turn the knob and nothing happens. Jace stands up from the couch and prowls towards me. Sweat begins to bead on my head, panic setting in.

"You'll have to pull the lock on the top of the door and you'll need two hands for it." He smirks, but it's not a comforting one.

His hands grip my shoulders quickly and I jump. "Why are you doing this?" I ask, my breathing labored the tightness in my chest constricting into pain.

"I spent weeks holding you when you lost that baby. Before that, months trying to show you what a great pair we'd make. Then suddenly one phone call with a trip home and you're leaving? I can't have that Casey. We are meant to be together."

I breathe in deep, a feeling of dread laces me; this is not going to end well. My first response is to try to run, but I stop myself knowing he would be able to out run me and not only that, I can't run inside his apartment, there is no way out and I need out. Thinking quickly to what Harlow would do, I lift my knee hard making contact with his nuts.

He grunts and releases me grabbing his junk and backing away. I quickly spin looking for the lock blocking the door. Jace's hard body crushes me against the door as I reach up for the lock. I whimper at the impact, but begin elbowing him with everything I have, hitting him in the side of his body. I back up but he wraps his arm around my body pulling me to the couch, throwing me onto it.

His eyes are feral and nothing like the Jace I know, or knew. I move quickly, roll off the couch and get up to my feet to move away from him. Being on the third floor, a window escape is barely an option, but I will if I have to.

I search around for something hard to grab, but see nothing. He lunges for me and I move quickly out of the way, but my hair does not move with me as quickly. He grabs it pulling it tight to him. His grip is so tight and tears spring to my eyes.

I move my arms trying to hit him in any way that I can, but he wraps his arm around my entire body trapping them tight.

"You are mine, Casey. Not some stupidass biker that doesn't give two shits about you. You're coming with me."

"No. I'm not yours! I'm going back to my apartment, Jace. Let me go." I struggle again to get out of his grasp.

The laugh that escapes his lips is laced with evil rage. His body is wound so tight, I need to get out of here and come up with something, quick. I stomp hard on his foot with my heel using every bit of power I can muster. His grip loosens enough and I elbow him hard in the ribs. He lets go and I quickly move away.

"Casey, I don't want to hurt you, but you're leaving me no choice." He growls and comes at me, but not with as much force as before and I'm able to side step him but stumble over one of his side tables. A small ceramic coaster falls to the ground smashing into a bunch of pieces. Thinking quick, I grab a shard of it that has a very sharp edge. Just as Jace comes at me I swing slashing him across the face.

I stumble up quickly; reach the door and a hand grips my arm hard. Without thinking, I swing the shard as hard as I can, landing it in his chest. With every bit of muscle I have, I turn and kick him in the stomach sending him stumbling back. I drop the shard and unlock the door throwing it open.

I run out the door fumbling for my keys, so I have them out and ready. I unlock the door as I keep looking back behind me to make sure he's not following and thank God he's not. I throw open the door, lock it and run into the bedroom faster than I ever thought I could run before. "G.T!" I scream with the last bit of wind I can muster out of my body. He jumps up out of bed and looks around quickly.

I throw myself into his arms, tears stream down my face. "What the fuck is wrong, Angel?" His arm holds me tight.

"Jace. He sent me a text and I went to see him. He..."

He pulls me away from the comfort I desperately need. "He what, Angel?" His voice is now menacing sending a shiver down my spine.

"He... told me that I was his and he was gonna take

me away. He..." I lifted up the arms on my shirt showing him huge red marks that no doubt will be huge bruises tomorrow and my hands covered in blood. He moves quickly almost knocking me to the floor.

"Where the fuck is he?" He asks as he opens his bag. He reaches in and pulls out his gun, cocking it using his bum arm, even though he's not supposed to.

"His apartment. Please don't leave me!" I beg him.

He turns, looking me in the eye. "Angel. I need to take care of this. Are you hurt anywhere else?" His hand traces my bruises and I shake my head no. "He won't hurt you again." He hands me the gun. "He comes in here. You shoot. Don't reason. Don't ask questions. You fucking shoot him, Angel." I nod. "I'll be back."

G.T. throws clothes on fast and leaves the room grabbing another gun and cocking it ready. I climb into my closet and shut the door. I fall as far as I can into the back corner and clutch the gun in my hand and wait.

I GRAB Angel's cell off the counter as I walk past, dialing as I move.

"What's up, Casey?" Cruz answers on the second ring.

"It's G.T. Get up here now. Bring all the brothers."

"On it. Details?"

"Guy that helped when Mia died tried to kidnap Casey. Going into his apartment now. Make it fast."

"Got it."

I place the cell in my pocket and move the gun to my good hand. I slip on my boots, open the door slowly and look all around the hallway, not seeing anything or anyone. I move to the door the asshole came out of earlier and try the handle first, it's locked. I should pick it and make this clean, but fuck it. Standing in front of the door with my gun up, I kick in the door and it buckles at the top. Fucker must have some type of bar up there. I keep kicking until the door splits and enter looking quickly around.

The room is empty. "Hey asshole!" I yell. Looking around, the room is in disarray. A table is knocked over and blood is all over the carpet. She showed me that she wasn't bleeding, so I'm glad it's the fuckers blood that's spilled. Pride surges through me at her strength.

I scope the room and listen, but hear nothing. I move without making a sound through the apartment checking every room. Nothing except blood trails from the living room, bedroom to the bathroom. Fucker is gone. But how the hell did he get out and put that fucking bar in place? I need to hurry. The cops have probably already been called, but we are lucky that none of the nosy ass neighbors have come running in.

I run to the windows. The one in the bedroom has a fire escape staring at me. I look down seeing nothing. If the fucker went out like this, he's gone. "Shit!"

I look around quickly for items that are of use. On his desk sits a laptop, I grab it. Looking through the drawers, there are several flash drives and CDs and I swipe them too putting them in my pockets. A couple of spiral notebooks sit there and I grab them too, setting all of this on the kitchen counter. I open and shut all his drawers quickly and look through his closet. Nothing stands out.

The kitchen is the same, nothing flashing at me. Needing to get the fuck out of here, I gather all the shit and make my way back to Angel's. I slip into the door and lock it behind me, sitting all the goods on the counter top.

I head to the bedroom. "Angel?" I ask when I don't see her anywhere. The closet door slowly opens and a gun is pointed at me.

My eyes land on hers, relief fills hers and she lowers the gun. "Are you okay?" She asks walking out.

"Fine. He was gone."

Her eyes widen and a gasp leaves her beautiful lips. "What do you mean? I stabbed him in the chest!"

"You stabbed him?" She rushes into my arms and I hold her tight, kissing the top of her head. She nods. "I'm gonna need you to tell me exactly what happened. Start to finish."

She breathes in deep and everything spills out of her in a rush. My body is humming with murderous rage. My jaw is sore from clenching it so damn tight, but I welcome the pain. I'd do anything right now to take Angel away. I rub up and down her back trying to soothe her. But a huge part of me is pissed at her for fucking leaving this apartment in the first place. But I tap that down for the moment.

We sit on the bed and she crawls into my lap where I

hold her. The sounds of sirens fill the air and her body stiffens. "I'm so sorry, baby." I try reassuring her. "The cops are here. I expected it. You are going to stay locked in this apartment and not go out. You are not going to talk to him until I talk to the brothers. Alright?" She nods slowly. "I need to know everything you know about him, family, friends and work. And if you know where he could have gone?"

"No. His family is from here and his father owns Blankenship Enterprises. That's where he works. He has friends named Alex, Jared, Ella and Joey. He studies business like me. Other than that, I have no idea." Her body stiffens and her breathing picks up. "Bella. We have to get Bella here now. He'll hurt her. He knows how much she means to me. He'll hurt her!" She tries to get out of my grasp, but I hold her tight.

"Calm down. Call her and tell her to come over." I hand her the phone. Her hand shakes, but she's able to call.

When the roar of bikes rattles the walls, she immediately stands.

"You called them?" She asks looking out the window, no doubt seeing the bikes and the cops, one big happy fucking family.

"Hell yeah. Shit's about to get messy babe. I will find him, I promise you that." I kiss her rough on the lips and head out to the door, her soft footsteps following me.

I slip my boots on not bothering to tie them and open the door. "I've gotta go out and get them. Stay here. Do not open this door. Not even for the cops."

"Okay." She clutches on to the gun that she hasn't let go of since I gave it to her.

"Lock this." She nods and I rush out to meet my brothers who made excellent time.

Walking out into the sunlight, I blink my eyes adjusting them. I pass several cops who eye me suspiciously, but I head right to my brothers. Pops, Becs, Cruz, Dagger, Zed, Rhys, Tug and Princess get off their bikes moving towards me. "What are you doing here?" I bark at Princess quiet enough for only her and the small group before me to hear.

"Relax. I came to settle Casey. Not get involved in this shit. What apartment?" I give her the number and watch our large black cage pull up behind them, Buzz and Breaker piling out.

"I'm going up." Princess says, gives Cruz a kiss and leaves.

"What's going on son?" Pops asks.

"Let's go upstairs. We'll talk there, too many eyes." The guys look around, they've drawn an impressive amount of attention, eyes are solely focused on all of us including the cops. They nod and we turn to go in the building.

"G.T.!" is screamed across the parking lot and only one other woman knows I'm here. I turn quickly to see Bella running towards us.

"Who the fuck it is that?" Dagger chokes out.

"Bella, Angel's friend."

"Holy shit." He growls and I can see why. Not only is she pretty fucking hot, her tight shorts and tank top leave little to the imagination.

Bella slows and takes in all the guys staring at her. "Come on." I say breaking the spell.

She shakes her head. "What's going on?" She asks

coming up to me. "And these must be the brothers." She waves her hands at the guys who grin.

"Yes. Brothers. Get in the apartment and I'll tell you all what's going on." Some of the guys take the stairs while others ride the elevator. I put the key in the door and open it wide. I'm met with two guns pointed at my face. "Fuck girls. It's just us." Princess puts hers down and Casey launches in my arm. I pull her tight to me.

"Casey, what the hell is going on here? Why all the cops?" Bella asks stepping around us.

"Oh my God Bella!" She yells and throws herself at her. As the guys pile in, she hugs each and everyone one of them taking more time than needed to hug Becs and Tug. Becs I can handle. Tug needs to keep his fucking hands off my girl.

I pull her tight. "Give me the gun, babe." I say quietly and for the first time since I gave it to her, she releases it to me. I retell the entire story and gasps from Bella continue to roll out of her mouth. Apparently, she didn't see this coming either.

"We need to find him. Now." I growl staring at my brothers.

Pops starts barking orders. "Buzz get on that laptop of yours and start searching. He couldn't have gone too far. Dagger, Rhys, Tug and Becs make sure everything's ready to go. The rest of us stay here with the girls." Everyone leaves quickly to start their tasks.

Angel looks a bit shaken up still, but her color is coming back to her face along with some serious black and blue marks she's going to be facing. The marks send fury through me and all I want to do is find the fucker and end him. And I will end him.

"What am I supposed to do?" Bella asks from the couch.

"When Buzz gets done, he's gonna take you back to your place. You need to appear as if everything is just fine. If the cops pull you aside, you say you saw nothing and you heard nothing. You stick to that shit no matter what. You need to pack enough to be gone for two weeks."

"No. I can't leave for two weeks." She begins to argue, but Angel cuts in.

"Bella. I'm sorry, but this is how it is. I need the guys to protect you right now. I don't know what the hell is wrong with Jace, but he knows how much you mean to me. He will come after you. You're coming with us."

Her face lights up. "Like to the clubhouse?" Angel nods. "I'm in." Bella smiles and Angel tries returning it, but to no avail.

"Here ya go." Buzz hands me some sheets of paper. "Everything on Jace Andrew Blankenship. Down to his last time using his credit card. According to this, it was about thirty minutes ago about an hour away."

I walk over to Angel. "I've gotta go with the guys right now." I hand her back the gun. "He comes here, you shoot. Breaker will stay here with you and Buzz will be back soon." I look at the three girls. "You all do what they say, got it?" I make sure to linger on Princess, who concedes.

"Yeah." I hear in unison.

"Baby. It's gonna be okay. I'm gonna take care of this so he won't do this again. Alright?"

"Be careful." She says quietly. I pull her up from the couch and crash my lips to hers, partially for me and partially to let every bit of feeling I have for this woman pour through. I love her plain and simple.

"Always." I look at Princess. "Take care of my girl."

"You got it." She grins and cocks her gun.

I nod to Pops knowing my sister will protect Casey with everything she has.

"Let's go." He says and we all file out. Unfortunately, I can't fucking ride yet, so I'm stuck in the damn cage with Tug. Not exactly the best place for me, but my adrenaline is pumping so fucking hard, I don't think about it. I focus on finding the fucker and ending him. For good.

CHAPTER TWELVE
Casey

IT'S BEEN OVER SIX HOURS AND STILL NOTHING FROM ANY OF them. I keep pacing unable to stop. I know I'm wearing the carpet thin, but my nerves are so shot. And I don't care. I need to move. Bella's already packed her things and is ready to go back with us to the club. She's even contacted her professors and helped me contact mine about our 'family emergency.' I seem to be having a lot of those lately.

Cops came by when Bella came back in the door. Harlow knew they would come and gave us a cover story she made us repeat several times. We were all listening to loud music and didn't hear a thing. It helped that when Bella walked in we had the music blaring. We even added a bunch of questions about what had happened. One of the female officers eyed my face, but I shrugged it off saying that Harlow and I got into a bit of a fight over a guy. Somehow they bought it and left us alone.

Harlow's tried several times to get me to eat, but I want nothing to do with it. My stomach is in knots and just the thought of food makes me want to throw up. She also insisted that she check me over for injuries, even though I knew I didn't have anything but a few bumps and bruises. It could have been so much worse.

It baffles me that Jace thought we had more than we do. I've never given him the impression otherwise. Or at least I never tried to and I was always straight with him. He never once gave me any indication that he had this other side to him. He was always so damn caring towards me especially after I lost Mia, never once even raising his voice. A twinge of sadness creeps through me as the loss of the Jace I thought I knew envelops me. Why did he change? What the hell happened? So many questions and ones that I will probably never get any answers to.

I turn to Buzz, who's been eyeing Bella since they got back from her apartment, never letting her out of his sight for more than a few minutes. "Anything?"

"Nope. This shit takes time. You gotta settle down. They're fine." He says way too calmly.

"Easy for you to say." I pace... And pace. My mind clouds with so much shit it may just explode. I can't lose him, I just got him back.

"I'm about two seconds away from sitting on you." Harlow calls from the couch. I don't stop, but gladly take the irritation her words make me feel.

"How can you just sit there like this isn't bothering you?"

She waves her hand. "It's not. The guys know what

they're doing and they're not stupid. And it's one guy... Piece of cake."

I huff at her and nibble on my fingernails that are now raw and on the verge of bleeding. How did everything go to shit so fast? What the hell changed?

Buzz's cell rings and I stop dead in my tracks, eyes glued to him and ears peeled to the one sided conversation.

"Yeah."

"Got it."

"Yep. Cops came by. Took care of it. There are three still in the building, but have left us alone."

"Alright."

He shuts off the phone and looks at me, not saying anything for a moment.

"What!" I yell, needing something from him.

"Apparently your boy is smart. He went to his folks' house about thirty minutes from here where there is a huge party going on. Boys are sitting outside... waiting."

"First, he's not *my* boy." I say through clenched teeth. "Second, is everyone ok?"

"Everyone's fine. Action hasn't started yet." He smiles and Bella sighs. I turn and she is staring at Buzz like he is the be-all-and-end-all, but when he looks she snaps her head away.

Whatever, I don't have time for their dramatics right now. "So we wait." I say finally plopping down on the couch for the first time.

"We wait." Harlow says. "So you and my brother finally get shit sorted?" I look over at Buzz not really wanting to talk about this in front of him. Breaker is outside the door guarding it. He must have sensed my hesitation because without a word he gets up and goes out the door for the first time since he got here.

"Yes. No. I don't know." I blow out after he shuts the door.

"Okay... That was fucking clear. Spit it out." Bella starts laughing looking over at Harlow who spoke. I get the distinct impression they will be ganging up on me really soon.

"What?" I ask.

"I like her." Bella points to Harlow. "A lot." Harlow smiles.

"I don't get that much, most want nothing to do with me." Harlow shakes her head turning her glaring eyes back to me. "Spill."

I sigh, lean back on the couch and put my arm over my eyes. That's such a loaded question and every word I say will be evaluated and she will read what she wants to into each of my words. "He wants me to move in with him, but I told him no."

"Why?"

"I don't think he's come to terms fully about Mia and what I did. I think it'll blow up eventually. I agree, now more than ever, that I need to be home, but I need my own place. I need to know that when this whole thing goes south, I have my own space to get away."

"You honestly think he's gonna let you have your own place?" I remove my arm from my head and stare at Harlow. "You've been around just as long as I have. Shit, Cruz demanded I stay with him. You think that after all these years, now that my brother has you, he's going to let you just walk away?" She shakes her head. "You know this life Casey. It's not new to you, at all. He loves you and you love him. Yeah, there's shit you gotta deal with, but that doesn't change anything. My brother is bossy, overbearing, stubborn and possessive, but he has a good heart. He won't let you leave this time."

"I don't want him to hate me." I sound so pathetic I want to kick my own ass, but there is so much truth to my words.

"He doesn't. He'll work through his shit just like he does everything else. You believe in him, right?" I nod. "Then trust that he will take care of you no matter what. He won't make the same mistake twice."

"God... I want one of these men." Bella sighs and I can't stop the small smirk that plays on my lips.

FOUR FUCKING hours now and this damn party is still in full swing. I called Buzz over two hours ago hoping to relieve Angel a bit. Now, I'm just getting fucking pissed this guy is wasting my time. If there weren't a fucking shit ton of people spread throughout the house, we would have gone right in. But here we are waiting in the fucking trees for the asshole to leave. If he's smart, he'll stay, but I'm banking on him not.

Pops comes over and sits next to me. We sit in silence waiting.

Three hours later, we are all getting fucking antsy as shit, mostly hungry and really fucking temperamental. Rhys has to walk off several times to get himself together.

"There he is." I whisper and the guys' eyes snap to the blue four door that Jace just got into. Each one pissed and ready for blood.

"Let him move. Once he gets to a clearing, take him." Pops says with authority. After Jace gets in his car, he turns off the driveway. The guys hop on their bikes and I climb in the cage. We take off, but the bikes stay far enough back because of the roar and we don't need him seeing us quite yet.

My body is pulsating and my good hand is fisted so tight I'm sure my knuckles are white. I want this fucker. Now. No one messes with Ravage and no one fucking messes with my girl.

Pops gives the go ahead signal. "Go!" I bark at Tug, who pulls ahead gunning for the car. We're lucky the fucker took the back roads, clean up should go pretty easy.

Tug moves the cage swiftly, pulling up alongside of the car. Jace looks over and I wave my gun saying hello. His eyes widen and he attempts to pull ahead of us. Tug is smarter though and maneuvers the cage close enough not to hit, but instead Jace veers off the road, the dirt of the ditch stopping his car.

Tug stops and I jump out quickly running to Jace's door and yank it open. His body is hunched over the steering wheel and his moans do nothing to stop my anger. This fucker will pay for putting his hands on Angel. "Get out!" I bark, yanking his shirt and pulling him out of the car. My brothers park their bikes and join me on the side of the road.

"Need to move him into the woods for a few." Dagger says. "And make it quick. It's quiet but not for long." His words piss me off. I'd love nothing more than to take my time ripping this asshole to shreds.

"Get up!" I kick him with my boot and he grunts, but doesn't get up. I nod to Rhys and Dagger to pick the asshole up by his arms and move him further into the darkness. I punch him hard sending his head flying to the side. I hear a faint laugh coming from Jace's lips. "What the fuck are you laughing about?" I punch again his head snapping back.

"You're a stupid bunch of fucking idiots." He says spitting blood out of his mouth. Dagger and Rhys pull on his arms tight, almost yanking them out of the socket.

"What the fuck did you just say?" I lift my leg kicking him hard in the ribs.

"Paine was right. You all are a bunch of fucking sheep, following each other around. Where do you think he is right now? Burning down your clubhouse or fucking your girls?" He laughs. This time I don't stop each punch as I feel his bones break under my knuckles.

"Stop!" Pops barks and it takes every ounce of willpower to do so. "How the fuck do you know Paine?"

"He's going to destroy every single one of you assholes. So, go ahead and kill me, I don't fucking care. I did my part."

My body shudders and my breathing is rapid. I pull away from them and grab my phone dialing Angel.

On the second ring, my mind believes the worst and I yell for her to pick up the damn phone. On the fourth ring, she finally does. "G.T.?" her voice is soft.

"Baby. Are you girls okay? What's going on there?"

"We're fine. Just fell asleep. Are you okay?" Her voice picks up as if the fog from sleep lifted.

"Good. I'll be back in about an hour. Alright?"

"Alright. Love you." She says.

"Love you too. Go to sleep Angel." She hangs up the phone quickly and my breath catches imagining something happening to her. I pull the phone away from my ear and quickly dial Buzz.

"Bolt that fucking door. You and Breaker inside with the girls keep them in the same room. No one leaves. Got it?"

"Got it."

Jace is hanging from Dagger and Rhys. I want to kill him. End this. But now that he knows Paine, Pops will not allow it. We'll need to find out what the fucking connection is. Shit.

I look at Pops. "Son, he's gotta come with us." He digs in his pocket grabbing his phone. "Gotta call the club-house see if what this asshole said is right?" He walks off.

Becs steps forward. "You wanna do this or you want me?" I simply nod at him. "Tug, get the tape. Dagger and Rhys, make sure he doesn't move, doesn't talk. Search him and the car, then light the car up."

I nod standing there. None of this is turning out like I fucking wanted. Pops comes up. "You tell the girls nothing. We'll take him to the old warehouse and see what we can get out of him." He sighs. "I know you want to end him. You will when the timing is right." I nod, knowing the brothers wouldn't take that pleasure away from me. "Clubhouse is fine. Brothers from Clayton are there and have everything under control. Everyone is on guard and nothing out of the ordinary. He's feeding us a line of shit. But the fact he even knows about Paine says something and we need to figure it out."

"He has to stay away from Angel." The words escape my mouth without thinking, caught up in my worry.

"You think we'd let that fucker anywhere near the compound?"

"Nah. I know." He lifts his chin and moves to the guys.

The ride back with the fucker in the back of the cage is daunting. Tug and I do not speak. The fact that we are driving this asshole back to Angel's apartment is not lost to me, but he will be leaving as soon as they drop, me, Cruz and Becs off.

As I walk into the apartment, Angel gasps and runs into my body. I catch her and squeeze her tight. She begins patting my body frantically and under other circumstances, I'd have some smart comment, but now is not the time. "Are you okay?" She says breathlessly.

"Yeah babe. I'm good. Have a seat we gotta talk." She moves away sitting next to Princess on the couch, Bella next to her. "Breaker you need to ride with Tug." He nods and heads off. "Buzz you're with us, but we're all riding home together." He crosses his arms over his chest.

"What's going on, G.T.?" Princess asks grabbing Angel's hand. I kneel down in front of Angel and look her in her lost eyes. "

"Club business. You done packing?"

"Yeah. Pretty much everything but a few things that mean nothing. Buzz loaded the car."

I pat her leg. "Alright. We gotta get home now."

"Okay." She whispers.

"Load up."

ONE WEEK AND THREE DAYS, we have kept this fucker alive and he keeps this fucking goose chase up. We've gone on every fucking lead this asshole has sent us on and nothing. Each one a pile of shit. The shit from his house, Buzz did all his techy stuff and we canvassed every lead, again nothing. The thing that pissed me off most was all the fucking pictures he had of Angel on his fucking laptop. He took pictures of everything from her getting out of her car to shots inside her apartment. No fucking clue how he got those, but he had them.

I want the fucker dead, but Pops keeps saying not yet. It fucking pisses me off, but I stand by my Prez and he keeps telling me to beat the shit out of him, which is not a bad release. We're on the lookout for the fucker's dad. After searching for him, he miraculously disappeared, but Deara, Princess's friend has one lead, her boys are checking out. We just sit and wait.

We have learned that Casey was Paine's target. She is, after all, a brother's kid and he wants blood. It was Jace's job to get in good with her and supposedly that's all he was told. I think it's a bunch of fucking shit that he's spewing.

Angel is back to herself in more ways than one. The

crying has all but halted. I know she misses Mia, fuck I do too, but she is no longer crying every minute of the day. She doesn't think I notice though that she's a bit jumpy. If a brother happens to walk up behind her, she is seriously startled and her face doesn't hide it. I'm hoping that shit clears up soon.

Doc says that now I can start moving my arm and getting it back into action. He's got these fucking exercises that Angel makes me do, but she's usually naked when she makes me, so it's a win-win. I feel it getting stronger by the day. And I get to ride now. It sometimes fucking hurts, but I don't say a damn word about it. I suck that shit up.

Pops got a call from Ransom about the information on Rabbit we've been waiting for, but we have to meet him on his turf. Not that I blame him, last time we were together bullets flew everywhere.

Pulling up to Gizmos, a local bar, I kill my bike, parking it in the very front of the building. Pops, Dagger, Cruz, Becs and Rhys all pulling alongside. We proudly wear our rags as always, but going into another clubs territory is always an iffy situation. We have an understanding with Ransom though, so Pops agreed to a meeting here.

Walking into the bar, all eyes are on us. Dagger is first, then Pops and Becs, followed by myself, Cruz and the rest of the brothers, just to be on the safe side.

"We're here to see Ransom." Pops says to the overly made up bartender with her boobs barely covered in a bikini top.

She points across the room. Darting my eyes there,

Ransom is sitting in a booth with a barely legal blonde straddling his lap, smiling.

Everyone in the bar is focused on us, they move to the side when we walk by. "Sorry to break up the party, but we got shit to discuss." Pops states with authority.

"Dammit Pops. I was just getting to the good part." Ransom looks up smiling, red lipstick covering his lips. "Babe. Make yourself scarce and find me later." The woman crawls off of him and Ransom slaps her ass on the way out. At one time that would have appealed to me, now, nothing.

Sliding into the booth, Pops and Becs sit on one side while us brothers stand behind. "What is it?" Pops asks, as he steeples his fingers in front of him.

Ransom pulls his cut away from his body and his other hand reaches in. We all start to grab our pieces. "Relax. Just gonna grab a piece of paper." I keep my hand on the barrel of my gun as I watch him do exactly as he said. He slides the paper over to Pops.

Pops unfolds it carefully and reads it. He then folds it back together. "This is?"

"Meeting. Rabbit's crew. Some top secret bullshit and every one of those fuckers will be at it. It's mandatory." Ransom smiles. "Told you and this is confirmation."

"And you know this how?" I ask suspiciously.

Ransom eyes me. "I've got guys everywhere searching for this fucker. I even have a guy in his club. He'll be dead before he can say a fucking word, but I got what I needed out of him."

"When is it?" Pops asks.

"Tomorrow night. 8pm."

"What are you gonna do?" Dagger questions beside me.

"Not a fucking thing. Gonna let you have this one. But..." He trails off and smiles. "All I ask is you stop by here after it's done so we can toast it together."

"What proof we got this is right?" Rhys speaks for the first time and catches everyone's attention.

"You got my word that this is what I was told. It's as good as it gets." Ransom doesn't break eye contact from Pops and I believe him. There is no underlying malice to him. I believe that this is what he was told. Whether it is right or not is up for debate still.

I chin lift to Pops, who turns and looks up at me. I've always had a great knack for reading people and this is no different. He's always relied on it. "Good. We'll be here tomorrow around 9." He says and we all stand and shake hands.

Hopping on our bikes, Pops orders, "Church, now. Get there."

"I BELIEVE HIM." I cut in to the argument that has been going on for the past fifteen minutes. These fucking men are making my damn head ache. It needs to stop. "He's got no reason to lie and he wants the fuckers just as much as we do."

"You don't think it's a fucking set up?" Dagger asks his eyes piercing mine.

"Nah. I don't. Saw it in his face."

"I agree." Pops cuts in. "We need to get rid of Rabbit. Get Buzz in here and have him pull it up on his GPS."

Dagger leaves the table and brings Buzz inside. "Buzz, we need to see this place." Pops hands him a piece of paper. Buzz leaves the room coming back seconds later with his laptop. A quick click of the keys and he is pointing to our destination.

Buzz shows the screen to all of us. An old warehouse stands in the center with a large number of trees surrounding it.

Sure enough, there are tons of spots for people to hide, so getting in and out undetected isn't an option. "We need to do it remotely." I say looking at Buzz and then Pops who nods. "Can you rig up explosives and detonate them from your computer?"

"Fuck yeah." Buzz's huge smile reminds me how much he gets off on this shit.

Looking over at Pops, "It's our only option. There will be a shit ton of guys and with such short notice, we'll barely have enough time to get in, rig it and get out."

"It'd be cleaner too, but fuck I want Rabbit." The fire in his eyes burns bright. We all want Rabbit, but doing this remotely will be the best thing for the club and that is what matters.

"I know. Buzz, we'd need cameras to see who goes in and out. We need to make sure that fucker is inside before it blows."

"Not a problem. I've got a stash," we all stare at the man. What the fuck. He shrugs and continues, "Of shit that'd be perfect. Got all the equipment to rig it up. I'll just need some cameras."

"Breaker!" Becs calls through the door, he rushes in.

"Yeah?"

"Need cameras to be rigged up remotely. Ask your brother. Get at least ten and pay cash."

"Got it." Breaker nods his head and leaves the room, closing the door behind him.

"Buzz, tell your brother what you need, then you ride with us. We go check out the place, quietly." Pops orders.

It's time to roll, God it's great to be back in the mix.

After scoping out the place, we head back to the clubhouse and make the plan, and head back out to the site after dark. The place is deserted which I find eerie. Either Rabbit doesn't think we know anything about it and isn't afraid or the meeting isn't happening. I am hoping for the first.

After rigging the explosives and the cameras, we meet back at the clubhouse and discuss everything, laying out how we expect everything to play out and hope it does exactly that.

"Hey, Angel." I walk up behind my girl and she jumps. "Sorry, babe. It's just me." I pull her long blonde hair to the side, raking my lips over her neck. Shivers take over her body making me smile. The smell of cherries emanates off of her and I want to lick her from head to toe.

"Hey." She whispers turning around in my arms. I crash my lips to hers and suck her bottom lip. Her moan spurs me. She wraps her arms around my neck diving into the kiss.

"As great as it is that you two got your heads out of your asses, I don't need to watch it." Princess barks.

Angel pulls away and grins. "Come on baby. I need you."

"DID HE GO IN?" I ask Buzz who has been eyeing the three computers he's got set up in Pops office.

"Yeah. Here, I snapped a shot of it so you can confirm it." Buzz pulls up the picture and sure enough, Rabbit and his VP just walked into the building.

"How many inside and out?" Pops asks.

"Inside. 87. Outside. 6." Buzz answers not skipping a beat.

"You counted?" I ask surprised that he thought of it.

"Fuck yeah." Buzz smirks, his finger twitching to push the button.

"Alright. Give it here." Buzz's face falls and Pops laughs.

"Bud, you're not a full member yet and Pops needs to do this shit." I answer holding back my own smile.

He hands over the computer. "Push these." He points to three buttons. "Once you do, it will be thirty seconds before it blows."

Pops stares at the screen. Who the hell knows what is going through his head. When his eyes lock with mine, I nod curtly. He does the same with Becs.

Pops hits the buttons Buzz told him to and we wait staring at the three screens. I never realized how long thirty seconds is until this moment. The small count-down clock on the screen is down to 5... 4... 3... 2... 1.

Nothing happens.

Nothing.

"What the fuck?" Pops roars, standing up so quickly his chair flies to the ground. Buzz scrambles to the computers, pressing all the buttons it seemed like at once.

"Buzz?" I question.

"I don't know what the fuck happened. It should have blown." He scrambles, fingers still flying across the keys. There is now no movement on the screens even the guards have disappeared.

"Get the fuck over there now and find out what the hell happened." Pops yells enraged. Becs puts in a call to the Clayton and Guthree chapters to meet us there. We need bodies and back up, fast. We load up and head to the site.

The tension is so fucking thick you'd need a damn machete to cut through that shit. We all ride in two cages to the site not wanting to make any more noise than needed and park away from the building. There are no people in sight, it looks totally deserted. Four other cages pull up behind us and our brothers from Clayton and Guthree get out with us.

Moving slowly through the edge of the tree line, no one has come out of the building or is guarding it. My phone vibrates in my pocket. It's a blanket text from Becs saying for everyone to surround the building, he will text us to start the countdown to open the doors when the coast is clear.

I scope out everything around us and there is nothing.

I head to the side door with Buzz at my side. We stand and wait. A few moments later, my phone vibrates saying to start the countdown. My adrenaline kicks in and I hold up five fingers to Buzz and count in my head. 5... 4... 3... 2... 1... I nod to Buzz, who kicks the door open which flies with no restraint.

A sudden metallic smell waves into my nose. With my gun drawn, my eyes dart around the building. "What the fuck." I say softly. Dozens of men lay on the linoleum floor, blood seeping from their bodies, not one moving. Bodies lay with heads practically cut off of them; stab wounds straight into hearts and some have limbs chopped off.

I've done some wicked shit in my day, but this... This is a fucking massacre, something I have never witnessed before and never want to again.

"Clear!" is yelled out by several of the guys. I look up into all their stunned faces, not one seeming to put words together at the moment.

Becs reaches for his phone. "Pops. We got a huge fucking problem." He starts and tells him everything that we see, even to the graphic details that I know will be etched into my head for years to come.

I walk around slowly, careful not step in blood or on a body, which makes it very difficult. "Find Rabbit." I say out to anyone and everyone. That fucker needs to be gone.

"Found him, I think." Zed says grimly. "And it ain't fucking pretty." I slowly walk over to Zed with most of the guys close by.

A man is lying in a pool of blood, a large knife is impaled through his skull, but there is a piece of paper covering his face. I grab the paper tearing it off of the body. To my relief the man is Rabbit. When I look at the paper, my heart stops as I read the words.

"What's it fucking say?" I look into Becs' eyes, hopefully conveying my thoughts.

"It says… 'This is how Paine is really done.'"

"Paine did this shit?" Dagger asks pissed off.

"Yeah. It's spelled P-A-I-N-E. He beat us to the fucking punch here." I growl and turn to Becs. "Needs to go up."

Becs nods and turns to his phone. "Pops we need to light it up. It will all land on us. We gotta clean it up." He nods. "Got it."

"Find whatever the fuck you can and get this shit ablaze and fast." Becs orders and we get to work.

ENTERING CHURCH, Pops stands at the front of the table fuming. "That piece of fucking shit!"

"Gotta get rid of him." Dagger speaks.

"No fucking shit. How the hell do we find him? We've got every fucking chapter looking for him and nothing. So you fucking tell me how the hell we're gonna do that?" Pops fires back.

Pops is always so damn even keeled that having his rage show up is a bit unnerving. I knew shit was bad, but having him go off, shit is worse than I even thought.

"We need to see if Buzz can do some of that techy shit and track him. It's a long shot, but it's the only thing we got right now." I say calmer than I feel. I need to keep my head on straight especially if Pops is going to lose his shit.

"Let's assess this." I say motioning towards Pops, who takes his chair so we are all at least now sitting.

"Alright. Positive. Rabbit and his guys are dead." The guys nod.

"Paine could be anywhere. We keep our eyes and ears open, but he won't make it easy."

"We need to get over to Ransom's. How we gonna play this?" Cruz asks.

"Tell him exactly what fucking happened and we question him. We need to know who the fuck his informant was." Pops states, placing his fists on the table.

"You think he's a rat?" Dagger asks.

"Never can be 100%. Eyes and ears open." Pops says, dismissing us. "Son."

"Yeah?"

"And you thought it wasn't your time for VP. Bullshit." He smirks and leaves the room.

Leaving church, my eyes lock with Angel's as she sits at the bar with Princess. Cooper's sitting on her lap looking up at her with wide eyes. I know how he feels. She is beautiful, I can't blame him.

Stalking to her, Angel smiles but it doesn't reach her eyes. "Hey baby. Gotta head out."

"K."

"Uncle G.T.!" Cooper screams catching me off guard. Turning to the little guy, his smile is infectious.

"What's up little man?" I ask ignoring the fact he just called me uncle, but I guess that's to be expected since Princess is now his mom. It just happens to be the first time and by the smirk on Princess's face, she caught it too.

"Casey gonna pay airplane wit me!"

"She is? Sounds fun."

"You wanna pay?" His face turns excited and damn I didn't want to disappoint the little guy, but I have shit to do.

"Can't. Gotta head out." Cooper's face falls and my gut clenches.

"Hey, Buddy. It's alright we'll have lots of fun. Let me talk to your Uncle G.T. for a minute okay?" Angel looks over at Princess. "Take him?"

"Sure." Princess looks at me knowingly. "Be careful," she says as she walks away with Cooper.

Angel's eyes grow wide and I can see in her face she wants to ask, but she refrains. "I gotta head out. Be back in a bit." I pull Angel up from her seat and slam my lips to hers. I need to feel her against me. With all the shit falling apart, I need this woman more than my next breath. She doesn't fucking know it, but she is holding me together. The fact I can come back from all this bullshit and bury myself in her is getting me through it.

"I'll be here." She smiles.

GIZMO'S IS HOPPING. Pops, Cruz, Dagger and I meet up with Ransom sitting in the same spot as before with a different woman on each side of him. After getting rid of them, we are able to get down to business. Pops does the talking. After he had his ride, his head is clearer and his anger slightly dissipated. It is there, just hidden well.

I sit studying Ransom's body language; which is difficult because he gives nothing away. There is only a slight flickering in his eyes that I could have easily missed had I not been paying attention. He says he didn't know shit was going down, but we are all leery of it. Too big of a coincidence.

Ransom already took out the fucker that talked to him, but said he'd investigate and let us know. Pops isn't happy. If Ransom doesn't come up with something, we'll be taking his ass out. And the fact that Ransom took out his informant before we could talk to him is another reason we don't know if we can trust him.

"Drinks." Ransom calls out to the waitress, who brings shots all around. "Didn't go as planned but the fucker Rabbit is gone. Let's drink." We all look at each other and then swallow the drink.

CHAPTER THIRTEEN
Casey

WATCHING COOPER PLAY WITH HARLOW IS PULLING AT emotions that I've been trying to tap down. For the past two weeks, I think I've been doing pretty good. I still think about Mia and what could have been all the time, but also think about what could be now and that helps.

Bella has been staying in the basement and she recently decided that it's time for her to go back to school. I can't stop her and as far as I know Jace is gone. She's been spending a lot of time with Buzz and I know he wouldn't let anything happen to her. It's easier for her to stay here, but I can't force her. I'll just miss her and the selfish part of me wants to beg her to stay. I won't though.

"You alright?" Harlow asks catching my attention.

"Yep. Just thinking." I smile at Cooper as he runs off through the clubhouse; it's like his own little stomping ground.

"How's school going?" I talked to my professors before leaving and they agreed to let me finish out the semester and then I'll begin my online classes. My professors say I can finish here in Sumner and I won't need to go back. So at least that's looking up.

"Good."

"You sure you're alright?" She asks again.

"Yep. I'm good. It's getting late. I'm heading to bed." Harlow grabs my arm.

"You know you can talk to me, about anything. Right?"

I give her a soft smile. "Yeah. I'm good."

"Family sticks together, Casey. If you need me, come find me." I nod heading off to G.T.'s room. He's been out on club business most of the day and as much as I love having him around, I need a break. His protective streak has hit an all-time high and when he's not side by side with me, he's hovering and it's driving me a bit nuts.

I can't blame him though. Not with all the shit that went down. My mind still reels from Jace and what he was going to do. But I learned something from the whole mess. I'm stronger than I thought I was. I survived losing Mia, Diamond and my dad. I survived Jace trying to hurt me. I even survived G.T. for the most part. I've always considered Harlow to be the strong one, and she is. But, so am I and that's a wonderful feeling.

There are days where I collapse and cry, but the kicker is, I pull myself up and continue going. Continue moving. Continue living.

I undress and lay on the bed pulling the covers up to my chin and drift off.

The bed dips and strong arms wrap around my body.

I breathe in deep, smelling G.T. and snuggle into his body. "Hey babe." He whispers kissing the top of my head.

"Hey. You okay?" He sighs and takes in a deep breath. I move and look up at his face and gasp moving quickly to sit up. A large gash is across his eyebrow and it looks as if it's been sewn up.

"What happened?" I ask reaching to touch the cut but then pulling away quickly.

"Club business, Angel." He stares in my eyes. "You are so beautiful." He says stroking his hand down my face sending shivers throughout my body. This is the side of G.T. that I fell in love with; the caring, compassionate, loving man that not everyone gets to see.

G.T. reaches for my arms and pulls me down on top of him. His nose brushes against mine and butterflies start swarming in my stomach. How he does this to me is beyond me, but I wouldn't change it for anything.

His lips leave a trail of fire as he kisses my jaw and neck. My hands move to the sides of his head to hold myself steady. He pulls away and looks deep in my eyes. "You're mine." His words ring in my ears.

"I always have been." I lean down pressing my lips to his. The kiss is passionate, yet unhurried and thoughtful. Each move of G.T.'s mouth feels like he's planning it and thought long and hard about each stroke. Or he just knows how to make me flutter and come undone.

He flips me over on my back so fast a laugh escapes me because of the surprise. "You think that's funny, huh?" He teases.

I smile and bring my hands to thread through his beautiful hair gripping him tight. "Are you sure you want this?" Looking into his eyes, I see my future. I see us together making this work. I need to know that he's in it for real. That he's in it with me. That I'm not losing my mind and seeing things that aren't really there. I want this. I want him.

He leans down to my ear, his voice soft. "I've wanted this from the first time you threw mud in my face. I love you, Angel." He kisses my earlobe and my heart implodes in my chest.

"Say it again." I whisper back wanting it to be real and not a figment of my imagination.

He raises above me his eyes focusing on mine. "I love you, Angel. And only you." A lone tear leaves the corner of my eye and G.T. bends down to kiss it away. "I need to make love to you." My heart soars. *Love.* I nod unable to find any words.

He slowly slips inside of me taking his sweet time and filling me inch by slow inch. His eyes lock with mine and he begins to move. I close my eyes reveling in the feel. "Open your eyes Angel." I open them, his eyes so full of love for me.

He doesn't rush his strokes, he stays steady and calm. Small beads of sweat form on his forehead. I raise my hips and begin meeting him stroke for stroke. I reach around and wrap my arms around his back and link my legs around his waist. "Harder." I whisper, needing more.

"No. Not this time. You're almost there. I feel you."

"I feel you too." I dig my nails in his back no doubt leaving marks on his body. It doesn't take long before his languid strokes cause us both to fall over the edge. Our heavy breathing echoes throughout the room and his smile is going to be the death of me. I want to lick his dimples and go again now.

Bang... Bang... Bang

I groan and roll over away from the seriously warm body that stayed cocooned around me throughout the night.

Bang... Bang... "Open the damn door." Harlow screams from the other side and G.T. sits up. I wasn't aware he was even awake.

"Go the fuck away!" He yells back and I wince. "Get back over here." He reaches for me, pulling me tight against his chest. I love this feeling. I love feeling safe and protected.

Bang... Bang... "Now G.T.! Casey wake up and open the fucking door!"

"What's her deal?" I whisper to G.T.

"Fuck if I know. Ignore her." He nuzzles into my neck kissing me repeatedly.

"If you don't open it, I'm kicking it down!" Harlow yells again. "5... 4..."

"Shit." G.T. mutters both of us knowing that she will definitely do it.

"I'll get it." He groans, but releases me and I wrap the sheet tight around myself heading to the door.

"2..." I swing the door open.

"What's the problem?" I ask looking up and down the hallway, but no one is around.

"You two need to get dressed and I need the keys to your car." I stare at her and I think she may have just grown three heads. No way she's driving my girl. I shake my head, but she cuts me off. "Don't say no. Just do it. Everyone is out here waiting for you."

"Everyone? What's going on Princess?" G.T. growls from the bed and I'm thinking the same damn thing.

"Everyone." She repeats. "Now give me your keys." I walk over to the dresser hesitantly and glance over at G.T. who nods. I hand her my keys and give her a warning look. "Stop it. I'd never hurt your car. You have thirty minutes to get dressed and meet us in the main room." She turns on her heel and strides down the hallway.

I shut the door and turn to G.T. "What's going on?" He shrugs his shoulder.

"No clue. As much as I want to lay with you all damn day, Princess won't give up. Let's see what the hell she's up to." He swings his legs over the bed and strides to the bathroom. I take in his tight ass and the huge Ravage MC logo tattoo covering his back. One day soon I will lick every inch of it. He turns abruptly.

"Keep looking at me like that we won't make it out of this fucking room."

"I don't wanna." I lick my lips.

"Fuck babe." He strides over picking me up cradling me to his body. "Shower now." He growls and my body ignites.

The steam from the shower caresses my body as G.T.'s hands roam up and down it. He pushes me gently under the spray and wets my hair. He adds shampoo then massages my head making my knees weak. My hands land on the wall to hold myself from falling. He rinses my hair and then does the same to himself as the water flows down my back.

His arm wraps around my waist and he pulls me tight

to his body. "This is gonna be fast, hold on." G.T. spins me around, lifting me and my legs instantly wrap around his waist. He plunges into me; I scream from the impact and wrap my arms around his neck, holding on for dear life.

The slow lover I had last night is gone and in his place is the fierce demanding one that I also love. He pounds into me and bends down taking a nipple in his mouth. He sucks and I yell overcome by the surge of feelings racing through me.

He pounds relentlessly and somehow manages not to slip on the tile. He pushes me against the wall and takes one hand rubbing my clit hard. I detonate. G.T. is right behind me with "Angel" falling off his lips. He rests his head on my shoulder as we catch our breath.

WALKING INTO THE MAIN ROOM, G.T.'s hand is in the small of my back, but I stop dead in my tracks at the amount of people surrounding us. Everywhere I look, wall to wall are brothers and their ol' ladies. Harlow steps forward. "What's going on?" I whisper.

"You two are going to have to trust me." She pulls out two pieces of silk.

"What the fuck is that for?" G.T. gnarls.

"Calm down, brother." Cruz steps up behind Harlow. "Just trust her." I turn to look at G.T. The confusion in his eyes must be reflected in mine. I shrug not knowing what the hell is going on, but I do trust Harlow. I nod.

"Fine, but I'm not liking this shit." He rumbles. I put my hand on his arm and rub it up and down.

"It'll be alright." I kiss him quickly on the lips and turn to Harlow. "Alright. So you blindfold us, then what?"

"We go for a ride." Cruz holds up my keys and my nerves flare. I've only let G.T. drive her and even though I do trust both Harlow and Cruz, she's still my baby and if anything happened to her, I'd be crushed.

I take in a deep breath, "Do not hurt my car." I warn and he laughs not saying a word. Deep down, I know he wouldn't, but there is always a part of me that worries.

Harlow comes behind me placing the soft silk over my eyes plunging me into darkness. "Can you see?" She asks softly.

"No. Everything is pitch black."

"Good. I won't let anything happen." She says softly in my ear.

"Now you." G.T. growls at his sister and I smile. At least I'm not alone in whatever this plan is they've got going on.

"Can you see?" Harlow asks G.T.

"No." He grumbles and I move my hand up and down his arm again trying to reassure him.

"Great. Cruz you grab G.T." My arm is touched, assuming by the small hands, it is Harlow. "I've got you. Let's go." She calls out and we are on the move, my hand moving away from G.T. My pulse picks up as we walk and I can only rely on my hearing, but everyone around me is talking so much that it's all one big jumbled mess of words. I want to reach for G.T.'s hand, but I don't know where he is.

The cool breeze hits my cheeks and it's my only sign that we are now outside. My car door opens. "In ya go." Harlow says, I sit down and the door slams shut. The seat next to me moves and I instantly smell him and I reach over quickly and grab his hand. I need comfort desperately.

"It's alright, Angel." He squeezes and pulls my hand up to his lips, kissing each knuckle softly.

"Is Bella still here?" I question remembering that she was supposed to leave today and I don't want to miss telling her bye.

"She's on Buzz's bike. She'll meet us there."

"Where the fuck is *there,* Princess?" G.T. demands.

"Sit back and enjoy the ride. It won't be long." The sounds of lots of bikes roar to life and I jump. G.T.'s thumb rubs the top of my hand reassuringly. It's amazing how I can feel every single bump that is hit, but the only sounds are the motorcycles.

The ride comes to a short stop and the engine cuts. All the bike engines shut down. My door swings open and I squeeze G.T.'s hand. "I'm right here, Angel." I nod and then curse myself remembering he can't see.

"Out ya go." Harlow says and pulls my arm up. I reluctantly release G.T.'s grip. Boot steps surround me and the cool breeze hits me again. The smell of freshly cut grass invades my nose.

"Where are we?" I ask her, but she doesn't respond, she just pulls me. My arm brushes up against something, but I instantly feel it's G.T. I reach out and grab his hand interlocking our fingers.

"Alright Princess. This game needs to end." G.T. cuts off.

"Shut up would ya?" Princess growls.

"Oh no, ya don't brother. Keep the damn thing on.

We're almost there." Cruz says from my right catching me off guard, G.T. must have tried to pull it off.

"We need to walk." Harlow takes my hand, but I still clutch G.T.'s and we walk. I hear mumbling behind me, but cannot make anything out.

We stop abruptly and Harlow lets go of me. I press my body against G.T. seeking comfort that I desperately need right now and he provides by wrapping himself around me.

"Casey and G.T. we brought you here because we love you, because you mean the world to us and because we are your family. And family no matter what takes care of each other." Harlow's words echo through my head. "We needed to do something for you."

I can feel someone behind me and I jump. "It's just me, Casey." Becs words instantly relax me as he unties the blindfold and it falls from my eyes.

I blink my eyes repeatedly trying to adjust from the darkness to the bright sun and look around. Directly in front of me is Bam's headstone, but what catches my attention are the pink balloons and flowers on the stone next to it. I gasp covering my mouth and fall to my knees. G.T. doesn't release my grip, but he stands there unmoving.

Next to Bam is a small heart shaped headstone that reads 'Mia Low Gavelson You will be in our hearts forever. Love, Mommy & Daddy.'

My chest clinches so tight I can't breathe and my throat constricts like a noose. My eyes go blurry from the tears that are unstoppably flowing down my face to the ground. Everything around me is spinning, like I'm falling down Alice's rabbit hole and it's engulfing me.

G.T.'s warmth meets me on the ground and he pulls me into his lap rocking me back and forth.

"Breathe, Angel." He whispers in my ear, but my mind isn't listening. A soft hand lands on my shoulder and squeezes, but I don't dare turn away from the stone in front of me.

The hand on my shoulder doesn't move, but words are said in my ear. "We all wanted you two to have a place to talk to Mia." I turn to Harlow at her words; tears are streaming down her face. I pull out of G.T.'s arms and wrap them around Harlow as tight as I can and pull her down to me.

I sob as she rubs her hand up and down my back. I look over my shoulder at the stone not believing that she did this for me... For us. "Thank you." I choke out as best I can. I look over at G.T. his eyes are red and his hand keeps batting away tears. I release Harlow. "I love you." I whisper looking into her eyes.

"Love you too." She says kissing me on the cheek. I move quickly over to G.T. He's sitting with his knees propped up and his arms resting on them. I wrap my arms around his chest and pull him tight to me. His face plunges into my neck and he silently shakes in my arms, tears rolling down my neck. I rub his back up and down, not knowing what to say. The shock of what just happened is keeping me weighted down.

A throat clearing causes me to look up into the eyes of a man that I hate seeing. Not because of who he is, just for the mere fact that every time I do, someone has died. "I'd like to say a few words if that's okay." The pastor asks and G.T. pulls away from me looking up at him. He wipes his face and turns to me. I give him a small nod.

"That'd be fine." G.T.'s voice strangles to get out. When G.T. tries to stand, the pastor stops him.

"Please, stay where you are." G.T. falls back to the ground and wraps his arms around me pulling me tight.

I sit listening to the words flow out of the pastor's mouth, each one as sweet as the next. He does the sign of the cross and says amen. He steps over to G.T. and sits down in front of us. "Mia will always be in your hearts to love and cherish. Bless you both."

I sit there staring, not knowing what to say and G.T. must feel the same because no words are coming out of this tough guy's mouth and I can't blame him at all. The pastor rests his hands on our shoulders and leaves. I pull away from G.T. "I don't know what to say." I tell him honestly.

"Nothing to say. We love her and our family gave us one of the greatest gifts they could." He picks up my hand and kisses it. He pulls his shirt up from the hem and wipes his face with it, standing up. I follow suit but do it a bit more discreetly. He holds out his hand and for the first time, I turn around.

I heard all the bikes, but nothing prepared me for this sight. Hundreds of brothers and ol' ladies and even friends stand behind us in solidarity. G.T. squeezes my hand and intertwines our fingers. Words are caught in my mouth and I'm relieved when G.T. speaks for the both of us.

"Thank you all. This means more to us than you'll ever know." He looks down at the ground.

Harlow comes up before us. "We wanted Mia to be by her grandpa so he could watch over her." I look down at the ground tears pooling in my eyes and shake my head. "Casey."

I look up at Harlow. "See all of these people here?" I nod. "They love you. We are here because you are our family. We will do anything and everything for you, no matter what." And for the first time in my life, I truly believe it.

CHAPTER FOURTEEN
GT

THE RIDE BACK TO THE CLUBHOUSE IS QUIET AND SOMBER. I kiss Angel's hand and lay it on my lap needing to feel her closeness and comfort. What our family did for us, I can never repay. And for once, I'm actually at a loss for words. Seeing brothers from chapters all around standing in unison with Pops in front, choked me up to say the least and I tried my damnedest not to shed tears, but couldn't stop it. It's times like these that we really remember who has your back. Everyone can be around when shit is good, it's the tough times when you know, who you can depend on. And I... we can depend on our brothers and family.

When Ma hugged me at the cemetery, I clutched on to her for dear life. She's always been my rock no matter what stupid decisions I've made in life. But the words she whispered in my ear ring through my head. *"You *keep this one G.T. This woman is your forever."* Ma's always into that mushy shit, but this time she is completely right. Angel is my forever and I'll show her, every damn day.

"We have a party planned when we get back, but if you two want to take a breather and go lay down for a bit, go ahead." Princess says from the front seat. Angel didn't even balk this time about Cruz driving; she curled up in the backseat without a word resting her head on my shoulder.

"A big one?" Angel asks her voice raspy.

"Yeah. We wanted to celebrate Mia." Princess looks back at Angel. "I hope that's okay." The reluctance in Princess is a fresh change of pace. I love my sister, but hearing the apprehension in her voice tells me that she wants Casey comfortable and to me that means a lot.

"It's fine, but I need to lie down for a bit and get myself together."

"Of course."

"Harlow?" Angel's voice quivers.

"Yeah?"

"Thank you. What you did for us." She stops and breathes. "Dammit, I need to stop crying." She blows some more and I squeeze her hand. "I love you so much, sister."

"Love you too." Princess turns away quickly her hands coming up to her face, my tough ass sister not wanting to show her tears.

"Yo sis." I bellow.

"Yeah." Her voice breaks.

"Love you." I say and her head drops to her chest. Her shoulders move up and down silently. I reach over the chair and squeeze her shoulder. Her hand instantly comes up and covers mine squeezing back.

I WATCH ANGEL SLEEP, her face is still red from the taxing morning we just had. We've been lying in here for the past few hours, but I can't sleep. I tried my damnedest, but just keep pulling my woman closer to feel her warmth and feel her heart beat on my chest.

I lay here thinking about the decisions that Casey made, and while I may not agree, I do forgive her. I love her and it's time to officially let go of the anger and strip it away from me... From us. I'll remember Mia every day and what could have been, but no more anger.

The music is thumping so loud its penetrating the walls. I'm surprised that sleeping beauty here hasn't woken up in my arms yet. It's been going on now for a few hours, but luckily it's still early in the day so when we get there, it won't be out of hand... Yet, it is after all a celebration.

Angel's body moves, her eyes flash up to mine. "Hey." She says her voice hoarse.

"Hey. You alright?" I brush the loose hair away from her eyes and she smiles.

"Yeah. I think I really am. I can't believe they did that for us." She digs her head into my chest pulling me to her.

I sigh and squeeze her, "me either."

"I'm so sorry, G.T." Her head burrows deeper in my chest. "For everything."

"Look at me." I demand and she stills, slowly turning her head to me. "No more. It's done. Understand?" She doesn't move. "Angel, what's done is done. We move on and live." The air I didn't realize she was holding escapes her body.

"How can you say that? After everything I did."

"After everything *we* did Angel. We are in this together. I'm working through it all, but you have to trust that I do forgive you as I hope you forgive me fully and truly."

She sucks in a deep breath. "Okay." She whispers.

"Okay. You ready to go out there?" Her smile radiates the room.

"Yeah, let's celebrate."

"Let's."

I LACE my fingers with Angel's as we step into the main room of the clubhouse. Tables and chairs are everywhere. A DJ is set up in the corner, his large speakers bumping with bass as music flows out of them.

"There you are!" Princess yells from behind the bar, running towards us quickly. Before I can protest, Angel lets go of my hand as Princess picks her up swinging her around. "You okay?" She asks.

"Yeah. I really am." Angel says putting her feet back to the ground.

"Good. There's food. You need to eat." Princess looks at me. "I'm taking her for a while."

Before she can pull her away, I grab Angel and pull

her flush with my body wrapping my arm around her waist, pulling her as close to me as I can. Her eyes widen in surprise. I lower my lips crashing them to hers, my tongue moving in and out of her mouth. She meets me move for move and I grab her ass pressing her body against my hardening dick.

Angel's arms reach up, wrapping around my neck and hold me tight, her body melting into mine. I need to take her back to my room. Now. Whoops and hollers come from the room and they get louder and louder the more we go on. I couldn't give two shits if they watch, but my Angel pulls slightly away. I nip her bottom lip with my teeth and rest my forehead on hers. Her breathing is labored and I take great satisfaction in the fact that I did that to her.

"You done pissing on your territory?" Princess says smiling wide.

"Never. But it'll do for now." Angel smiles and I nip her lip one more time before she reluctantly releases my neck and moves with Princess. I watch her ass sway side to side only making my dick harder. I move my hand down to my jeans, adjusting the hard-on that she will be taking care of soon enough.

"Here brother." Buzz calls handing me a beer and a shot glass full of amber liquid. I shoot the whiskey first and then start on the beer.

I look around in search of Bella knowing she wouldn't leave without saying bye to Angel. "Thanks. Where's Bella?" I know she rode back with Buzz, but looking around I do not see her now. Bella's had quite an education coming here for the past couple of weeks. Even though everything has been pretty calm for the most part, from what I hear, she's been pretty busy getting to know Buzz and Breaker for that matter.

"Asleep. Be out in a bit."

"Been keeping her busy?" I smirk.

"Fuck yeah, brother." He laughs. "She's fucking hot and a wildcat in the bedroom."

"She still leaving?"

"Yep. Tomorrow now. She wouldn't miss this." I nod and head over to the large table with Pops, Dagger, Cruz, Rhys and Becs.

"Brother. Bout time you get your ass out here." Dagger chuckles holding up his beer in salute.

"I'm here." I hold my arms out wide flashing my rag and smirk. I pull out a smoke, roll it between my teeth and light it. Pops kicks the chair next to him in invitation and I sit. Judging by the slew of bottles on the table, this party is in full swing.

"Raise 'em boys." Pops declares. All of us raising whatever concoction is near. "To my beautiful grand-daughter."

"Mia." They say in unison. I smile and take a pull from my beer.

"Princess sure outdid herself this time." She utterly amazes me sometimes. With all the shit being thrown at her, she's stronger than ever.

"Brother, you have no idea. That woman is relentless." Becs says smiling.

"No shit. Try living with her." Cruz laughs. "She's been a fucking basket case. I can only calm her ass by fucking her." He shrugs. "Not that I mind."

"I gave her a lot of leeway with this shit, probably more than I should have, but I knew how much it would mean to you and Casey. And shit, who doesn't like a kick ass party." Pops grins, taking a pull from his beer.

"I just don't even know what to say brothers, besides, thank you." I shake my head and search for my girl. I spot her at a table on the other side of the room, Princess next to her and a big pile of food in front of her. Her eyes lock with mine and she smiles so brightly it lights the entire fucking room. I raise my brows suggestively and she blushes turning back to her food.

"She yours brother, or free game?" Rhys asks. My head jerks to him. I clamp the bottle in my hand so hard I feel the bottle waver a bit but not enough to break. My teeth grind and my pulse picks up, fiery rage spreads through my body.

"No one fucking touches her. Got me?" I grind out through gritted teeth starting directly into his eyes.

"You puttin' colors on her?" Becs stares at me intently and it's as if Bam asked the question and not him. I know that Casey sees Becs as the closest thing she has to a father because of their tight friendship, so his question doesn't piss me off; instead it calms me a bit from Rhys' mouth.

"Absolutely." I answer immediately.

"Good boy. About fucking time." He stands up and stretches.

"I'm gonna head outside, make sure everyone's happy out there." Dagger smirks standing up too. Outside the club doors, the club mommas wait until the party gets really going. Inside is just for family, for now.

"You do that." Pops answers knowingly. We sit for what seems like hours talking and shooting the shit about everything; sports, women, our bikes. Members from other chapters come up, repeatedly patting me on the back and giving condolences along with the ol' ladies who all piled around Casey. She caught my eye several times, giving me her sexy smile and each time, I am tempted to pull her into the bathroom and fuck her senseless, but refrain. Why? Who the fuck knows. But the way the ol' ladies are rallying around her warms my heart. She's feeling the family that she never thought she had.

The party is seriously picking up and club mommas in scraps of fabric come in, some with brothers from other chapters hanging on them, some alone but all looking to party.

The ol' ladies have loosened up and are dancing in front of the DJ shaking their asses, Casey in with them. Currently, she's wedged between Flash and Harlow shaking her body tempting me at every step. The sly looks she keeps sending me are about to send me over the fucking edge. The thing that stands out though is she's the only one that doesn't have a Property of rag on and that will fucking change soon.

I watch as she moves her body back and forth and up and down. Flash, Dagger's ol' lady, grabs her from behind and begins grinding with her. Angel's face turns flush as she pushes her ass right into Flash, her hands hugging her hips tight.

I continue watching, catching her eye often. The sexual tension thickening with every passing minute. Feminine hands land on my shoulder, I glance up seeing DeDe. Back in the day she used to clean my room. "Hey." I smile up at her as she moves around the table resting her almost bare ass on it.

"Hey handsome." She crosses her leg, her skirt rising. "I've missed you." Her hand reaches out touching my shirt.

"How ya been?" I pull out of her reach, her once long nails now look like daggers and the dark brown hair does nothing to appeal to me.

"Alright."

"You been taking care of yourself?"

"Yeah. Some friends of mine wanted to come tonight. Heard about your daughter. Sorry."

"Thanks."

"I was hoping we could catch up." She smiles bashfully.

"Nah. I've got my girl." I look out to the dance floor and eyes are piercing through me. Several ol' ladies are killing me right now in their mind; Angel is nowhere to be seen. Shit. Without a word, I move to get up and DeDe stops me by grabbing on to my arm.

"I won't tell her." She says softly.

"You don't have anything to tell." I growl and move out of her embrace and head to the ol' ladies on the floor. "Where is she?"

"She needed air." Bubbles says, nothing like her happy go lucky self. But I don't need to explain anything to them, they don't matter to me, Angel does. I leave them, quickly heading out the door.

Casey

DANCING WITH THE OL' ladies is more fun than I've had in years. They know how to let loose and from what they told me, they feel safe here knowing their men will protect them. I do too. One difference that hits hard is their rags. Every single one of them proudly wears theirs and I didn't realize how much I truly craved that with G.T.

I've tried my damnedest to keep in contact with G.T. some way the entire night. Partially for selfish reasons. I want him to know that I'm here and I don't want him to have any reason to think he needs any other woman. Ever. I am all he needs.

Glancing over at G.T. a woman approaches him. I blink a couple of times to see more clearly and then it hits me like a thousand sledgehammers all at once.

It's her. After all this time, it's her and she's fucking touching him. A combination of the booze and sweat has flushed my body and on top of seeing her... I need air. Now. "I'm going outside." I yell in Princess' ear. She looks at me then G.T. and shakes her head.

"What is she doing here?" I grumble to myself knowing no one would hear me over the music.

"Don't. It's nothing." She latches my arm.

"I just need some air. I'll be fine." I give her the best

smile I can muster and she releases me. I feel her eyes watching me as I exit the building, the cool air hits me as soon as the door opens and I breathe in deep.

The sight before me is straight out of a porn movie, guess they started early out here. Two women lay on a picnic table, their skirts around their waist while brothers from another chapter have their heads between their thighs. Over against the fence a man has a woman pressed tight against it pounding her relentlessly, his bare ass there for all to see.

Others stand around watching the action unfold before them. Nothing like live porn. I walk towards the garage, the dark night lit up by all of the tall lights the guys have installed.

I breathe in and out. A large boulder sits on the edge of the building. When I worked here we used it as a block from backing into the corner of the building. I sit on it just watching all the people.

Seeing her flooded me with too many memories that I want to keep locked down deep. G.T. says he forgives me about Mia and now it's my turn to forgive him for lying. The heartache is still there, but I need to move away from it.

When I first saw her, I had this strong urge to march over to the bitch, pull her hair and beat the shit out of her. She after all, she was touching my man. Only one thing stopped me. He's not really my man.

Being in the club life, you learn that everything can change in the blink of an eye. Such is life. I'm still not sure that G.T. wants me as his and his only. He knows that I will not sleep with any other brother, ever. But he's never talked about commitment or monogamy, only that

I'm his girl. As far as I know, he could have pieces on the side, but I choose to believe that he doesn't. That he only has eyes for me. But until he puts a ring on my finger or leather on my back, he is not mine and if I demand that, it will turn him off. I've seen it happen to women before.

Grunting from behind me tells me I'm not alone. When a woman screams and a man growls, the noises stop. A few moments later a short little blonde with a very short skirt that she's trying to pull down and not doing successfully, steps from the corner of the building. She smirks at me and keeps going. She tries running her hands through her hair but isn't having much luck.

"Hey." Tug's voice comes from behind me as he's buckling his belt.

"Hey back at ya." I point to the girl. "She's cute."

He shrugs his shoulders and stands next to me, his hair a disheveled mess, but the smile on his face is glowing. "She got the job done." He laughs.

"Whatever. To each their own." I wave my hand.

"What are you doing all the way out here? Where's G.T? The girls?" His eyes narrow a bit. "It's not safe for you to be out here all by yourself girl. You know that."

I wave my hand. "Most of these men know me or Bam and they see me with G.T."

"But no rag babe. Remember that. Always remember that."

The words hit me in the gut. "I know." I whisper.

"You okay?"

"Yeah. Just needed some air, it was getting thick in there." I smile looking out at the courtyard and all the people.

"I imagine it's been a hell of a day for ya." He sits

down on the boulder next to me, I move over a bit to make room.

"Yeah. Very unexpected that's for sure." He places his hand over mine, as mine rests on my knee and squeezes.

"You know you could have called me about Mia." I turn to his face and see the concern in his eyes.

"I wanted to. But you would have told Princess or G.T., and at the time I couldn't risk it. I didn't tell anyone, Tug."

"You should have told me. I would have been there for you."

"No. She should have told *me* and *I* would have been there for her." G.T.'s voice makes me jump.

"Hey." I say looking up at him, his face lined with fury and rage, but he's not looking at me. I follow his line of sight and it's Tug's hand on mine. I pull slightly away, not wanting to cause any trouble and by the look on his face, there is trouble.

His eyes move to Tug. "You and me. Meet me in the ring in thirty minutes."

I jump from the rock stepping in front of G.T. "It was nothing. There is no need to fight, G.T."

His eyes do not meet mine but stay focused on Tug. "Fine." Tug says, reaching for my arm. "You gonna be okay?" He asks causing a deep growl from G.T.

"I'm fine, but no fighting." I say directed to both of them.

"It's a long time coming Casey. Long time." Tug says moving away from us.

I look up at G.T. "You can't fight him. He didn't do anything wrong."

"He's out here alone, with you in the dark, holding

your hand." Rage pours off of him and the vein in his neck begins to pulse and tick.

"Tug saw me sitting here and we were just talking, that's it." For some unknown reason, I feel like I have to defend myself here and plead with him at the same time.

"Everyone here knows you're *my* girl. Mine. No one touches you."

I step toe-to-toe with him and look him dead in the eye. "Guess I could say the same thing for you, huh?"

"I knew this was about her. She means nothing. I've already told you that."

I sigh softly. "I know. It's just not the right day for her to show up, today of all days."

"You have nothing to worry about." I close my eyes and tilt my head up to the sky. Nothing to worry about. Sure. It must be the booze that's given me a kick in the ass, but I start to laugh. Full out laugh at his words. "What the fuck are you laughing about?"

"You're not exactly known for keeping your dick in your pants, G.T."

He pulls me close, our bodies colliding together with an uphf. "I have not had another pussy since you came back in my life. Didn't want it. You are mine, Casey. Mine. That means I will put a ring on your finger and leather on your back. You will come home to me every day and wake up with my arms around you every morning. I allow no man to touch you, especially some Prospect, who is trying to become a brother in this club. Rules Casey. He will learn them tonight."

I stand there speechless staring into his eyes letting all the words he just said seep into my soul. Then the dread of the threat about Tug claws its way through and I can't breathe. I don't want him hurt, but I know this is the way. If there is a dispute, you settle it in the ring, and then hopefully it will be done with and laid to rest.

"You will be front and center for it, Angel. I want to see you the entire time I'm in there." I want to question if he is well enough to get in the ring. I know he's been cleared by Doc, but for fighting, I'm not so sure. But I will not question him, I just nod my head.

His lips collide with mine, not seeking permission, but demanding, taking. G.T.'s tongue swipes my bottom lip and I open instantly for him as he plunges in. He tastes of beer and smokes and I can't get enough. My arms pull his t-shirt urging him closer to me even though the air is having difficulty finding space between us. Our lips move in perfect sync, my body igniting with want and need.

His hand inches to the button and zipper of my jeans, undoing them. His hand slowly drifts down under my panties to my sopping pussy. "I love how wet you are for me, Angel."

I moan as he inserts one finger at a time into my body moving them with total precision, playing my body for all its worth. His lips continue to devour mine and sparks begin to take over my body. G.T.'s lips silence my cries.

My breathing is ragged and difficult to control. I reach down to his pants and massage his fully erect dick through his pants. His hand reaches out and stops my movement. I look up at him in wonder. "After I fight. You're mine." He takes my hand and pulls it around his body.

"You don't want me to relieve you now?" I ask batting my eyes.

"Yeah babe. I do. But, you've wound me up, now I'm ready to get in there." Dread washes over me as he points to the ring. I do not want Tug hurt.

BELLA REACHES OVER and grasps my hand tight. "You okay?"

"No. Not at all." G.T. is in the middle of the ring bouncing up and down, his hands taped up for a fight. His t-shirt and rag are off showing his cut abs and hot as hell back tat. I stand behind him because he's my guy, but it doesn't mean I have to like what these two are about to do.

Tug stands on the other side of the ring, hands taped bouncing just like G.T. There are so many differences between the two men though. Where G.T. is sure, confident and knowing, Tug is slightly unsure and his confidence is waning. G.T.'s size next to Tug is the other variable. Tug has a good four inches in height, but bulk wise they seem to be a good match. I do not want to stand here and watch this. Nothing good can come out of it.

Dagger is center and proclaims he will officiate, which stuns me at first. Normally this is not heard of, but for some reason unknown to me it is being done tonight. Rhys rings the side bell and they join together in the middle. Both of my hands are laced with small female hands, Bella and Harlow on each side of me. I squeeze them, needing some type of reassurance.

G.T. moves side to side. "Come on asshole. Show me how tough a man you really are." G.T. goads.

"Ask your girl how much of a man I am." Tug says back and G.T. charges. I cringe and shut my eyes. Grunts, heavy breathing, flesh hitting flesh, continue for what feels like forever. I open one eye softly only to see blood pouring out of both G.T. and Tugs faces. I close them again. This shouldn't be happening, but I can't stop it. Whatever this shit is, they need to work it out.

A loud thud makes my eyes fly open, both G.T. and Tug are wobbling on their feet, neither giving up and all I want is for this to be over.

"Time!" Dagger calls. G.T. turns looking at me with a huge smile on his face, blood dripping everywhere. He turns back to Tug opening his arms, Tug does the same. They embrace in one of the sexiest man hugs I've ever seen. Both men covered in sweat and blood, who'd have thought.

And just like that, whatever shit they were pissed about is done. Over. Finished. I sigh with relief; at least they are both walking out of there alive.

"Casey, get your ass up here!" Dagger yells loud and I look at Princess with the expression, do I go?

"Go." She says letting go of my hand, Bella squeezes and let's go too. I make my way up the small steps into the ring and stand in front of the two men. I smile softly at them both, but walk over to G.T. The cuts on his face really aren't bad, they look worse because of the sweat rolling down his face mixed with the blood.

"Come here, Angel." He reaches out and pulls me to him, crashing his lips to mine in the middle of the ring. Cheers and hollers are probably being heard for miles, but my body melts into his ignoring everything and everyone around. My arms wrap around his neck, his sweaty body presses to mine. My breathing accelerates as does my heart. He pulls away looking into my eyes.

"Now there's no doubt you are mine." G.T. says and I smile softly.

"I love you." I whisper. He sweeps me off my feet carrying me out of the ring, through the clubhouse and into his room, not saying a word to anyone.

CHAPTER FIFTEEN
GT

I need her, right now. I kick the door shut with my foot quickly reaching down to lock it and stride over to the bed. My lips lock with hers and I move her body so her legs are wrapped around my waist and her hands are now pressed against my face. My hands cup her ass and hold her tight to me.

Her breathing is labored and her heart is pounding through her chest, I can feel it as her heart collides with mine through our shirts. My hunger for her grows to the point of uncontrollable desire. "I need inside you now." I growl pulling away and setting her down. "Clothes off. On the bed, hands and knees." A smirk plays on her lips as she quickly complies pulling her shirt over her head and her jeans down her legs. She stands in black lace, hand on her hip staring at me intently. "I said all of it. Now."

"G.T. let me clean you up first." She says breathlessly.

"No." I rip the tape off of my hands and grab a shirt off the floor wiping my face with it. Clean up will have to wait, she watches me with wide eyes. I quirk my eyebrow. Waiting.

She slowly reaches behind her back unlatching her bra, the cups fall to the ground revealing her beautiful tits. The hard points of her nipples are just waiting to be sucked and played with. She turns around and glides her panties down her legs bending at the waist giving me a great view of her ass and pussy. "You're ready for me. Come here." I command finishing the removal of my clothes.

My lips claim hers and Angel dissolves into the kiss. I abruptly pull away. "Hands and knees." She slowly climbs on the bed and sticks her delectable ass up in the air. I bend down behind her and bury my face in her pussy. Her taste invades my mouth and my dick grows painfully hard. Her sweetness coats my tongue and her ass moves from side to side and in small circles, her gasps and mews, music to my ears.

I place one finger at her entrance and tease her, only sticking a small bit in at a time. I smile when her fluid trickles out of her pussy. She pushes back trying to get my finger deeper inside of her and I pull out completely taking my tongue away too. Her head whips around staring at me with hooded eyes.

"Who's in charge, Angel?" Her head drops.

"You."

"That's right." I slap her right ass cheek with enough force to leave a small red mark, but not enough to hurt. Her body rocks back and forth. My tongue moves back to her luscious pussy, diving deep, along with my index finger moving it just enough to find that special spot inside and I rub.

She tightens around my finger and I pull back licking her pussy, but staying away from her clit. She moans and her head falls down to the pillows on the bed. I pull completely away then plunge my dick fully inside of her in one thrust, her back arches off the bed. I place my hand on the center of her back pushing her back down. "Oh God…" she moans.

"No… G.T. baby." I smirk and start moving in and out of her tight pussy, her juices covering every inch of me. I watch myself glide in and it sends electricity coursing through my veins. My spine comes to awareness and my balls draw up tight. I don't hold back. I can't. Each thrust deeper and harder than the next. Each one feels like I'm trying to climb inside Angel's body and never escape. And right now, that's exactly what I want to do.

My hand reaches around to her clit and I rub it methodically and strong. Angel tightens around me and screams my name loud enough to shake the walls. Sweat trickles down my back falling into the crack of my ass and I become relentless. Each thrust tears any self-control I had away.

"Come again." I say flicking my fingers on her clit continually.

She moans and just like that, detonates clenching around my dick. Two more rough thrusts and she milks me for everything I have. I slowly keep pumping until all the aftershocks subside.

I pull out slowly and watch my cum trickle out of Angel's body. Fuck. She collapses down to the bed with her eyes closed. I should get a wash cloth and clean her up, but the thought of my cum being inside of her clouds my judgment. I pull her into my arms and kiss her soundly. We fall into an exhausted sleep.

THREE DAYS LATER

POUNDING on the door jostles me awake. Angel's warm body is curled against mine and I don't want to fucking move. She has had a rough few days and I don't want to wake her yet. I move slowly away from her body and put my jeans on not bothering to zip them up.

Opening the door, Becs is standing there with his hands in his pockets. "Yeah."

"Gotta tell Dewey our answer. Leave in thirty." He smirks and walks away.

I shut the door and head to the bathroom. Since the party, the brothers gave Angel and I some room, which meant we haven't left the bed and I've loved every fucking minute of it. After a very tearful goodbye with Bella, Angel's smile radiates daily. I love that I'm the one that put it there.

Dewey's been blowing up my damn phone about this fucking deal. He put it on the back burner after the shit went down, but now he's back and will soon be pissed.

While the load is a shit ton of money, for what he wants, it's not worth it. The risk is too great for the profit. Ravage is all about profit, but the risks need to fall in there too and what's best for the club. This would take the entire club down and it's not something that we are willing to do.

I look at the bed and the beautiful woman lying in it. Her blonde and black hair cascades over the pillows as she lies on her back, head turned. Her arms rest under her pillow propping her up. I love how calm and peaceful she looks in my bed.

I brush her hair over and lightly kiss her forehead and she awakens. "Hey." Her voice groggy.

"Hey. Gotta go to work. Be back later." She smiles.

"K." I lean down kissing her soft lips. I pull away and she catches her teeth in her bottom lip pulling it tight. I shake my head, the little temptress.

"Bye."

"Be careful." She whispers as if she shouldn't say it.

"Always." I smile and close the door behind me. Sooner we get this shit taken care of, the sooner I can get back and bury myself in my girl.

"Well look-e-there! G.T... he lives." Dagger laughs. I follow and touch my thumb to the side of my mouth pushing my lip tight. The guys sit around a large table in the main room. Ma and Princess must be making breakfast.

"Jealousy is always great first thing in the morning." I take a seat.

"Fuck. I'd be gone too if I were buried in that shit." Rhys leans back in his chair putting his hands above his head resting back.

"Tell me about it." I grumble thinking of the naked woman in my bed waiting for me. "Can we do this shit so we can get back?"

"Already pussy whipped." Pops shakes his head and I glare at him.

"Not whipped. Just like my pussy." I pull out a smoke, roll it between my teeth and light it.

"Alright. Serious for a minute." Pops yells, we all lean up to the table and nod our heads. His voice low. "Gotta pull all resources and find Paine. This shit's not going away and when he comes back, it'll be worse. I've got a meeting with Princess's friend Deara and her crew in a couple of days. I'm also pulling my contacts and getting them on our side. This shit is done. I want it done. Now."

Ma and Princess come walking to the table and Pops stops and smiles. "Hey boys. Here ya go, eat up." Ma says putting plates of food in front of each of us. Princess leans down kissing Cruz.

"Casey still asleep?" She asks me pointedly.

"Yeah. Wore her out." I laugh shaking my head.

"I want a chat when you're done with your run." She says walking away.

"What the fuck was that shit?" I bark to Cruz.

"Don't ask me." He shovels food in his mouth. "I'm sure you did something to piss her off."

"I'm sure I did." After eating, we set off to find Dewey.

Casey

I AM in the epitome of adult hell. It has to be. It has to be a place where adults go when they've done something terribly horribly wrong to pay their penance. I don't know how the hell I got roped in to coming here. I don't know how the hell I allowed myself to. I take that back I do know how. A pair of baby blue eyes that look so full of hope and want that I couldn't say no. Now I'm paying for it.

"What the hell is this place?" I stare in wonder looking around at all the huge ass contraptions that are filled with air and bouncing all around. On one wall is a huge climbing wall with ropes hanging down from the ceiling and kids climbing up. In the far corner, games line the walls with lights flashing. Colors. Holy shit. I've never seen so many colors in one building.

"This... is Fun Time." Princess answers sighing in defeat. "I only bring Cooper here every once in a while."

"I can see why. This is insane." The noise billows out from everywhere, screams, music, whistles, horns... everything.

"He'll only play for about an hour and then he'll be tuckered out and sleep for a while." She smiles. "It's my bonus for putting up with this shit."

We walk in and my eyes scan the entire area. Kids

run in every different direction with adults in black and white referee shirts trying to get them to stop running to no avail. Some parents pay attention to their kids while others are on their laptops without a care in the world.

"Aunt Casey... You pay with me?"

Cooper looks up at me and I have no choice but to answer. "Of course." And take his small hand. We walk through the maze of kids, parents and toys and people turn and stare at us. I have no doubt it's not to see mine or Harlow's beautiful faces or Cooper's adorable one. No. It's the two brooding men standing behind us who got suckered into coming.

Tug and Buzz walk with their hands in their pockets, scoping the place with scowls on their faces. When we decided to go, G.T. and Cruz were already working and since we are not able to go anywhere without guys, Buzz and Tug got the short end of the stick. Damn do I feel bad for them. Shit. I feel bad for me. I am happy though that Tug and G.T. worked out their issues, makes life a whole lot easier.

Cooper pulls my arm. "Come on!" He yells and we take off.

After what feels like hours instead of the few minutes we are actually playing, Cooper turns his sights to Tug and Buzz pulling them into the mass of bodies.

"I like bringing you three. Less work for me." Harlow laughs eating her nachos.

"Yeah. Next time I'll know what my answer will be." I smirk. I watch all the little ones run around and have fun. It's seriously a lot to take in. A little girl with blonde pigtails runs in front of us falling to the ground. I leap up and pull her up as she starts crying. "Are you okay?" I ask. Worried that she has hurt herself.

"Mommy!" She screams as loud as she can and a large woman with blonde hair comes directly in front of me. Somehow Tug is right behind me in a moment.

The woman eyes me bends down and picks up the little girl. "You alright, baby?" She coos.

"I falleded." She cries.

"It's alright." The woman looks at me. "Thank you." And leaves. I try my damnedest to tap down the thoughts of Mia, it proves difficult, but I do it and smile at Harlow.

"You okay?" She asks grabbing my hand as I sit back down.

"Yep."

"Hey what do ya say we go out tonight and have some fun?"

"Like what?" Fun sounds good.

"We'll go over to Studio X, have a few drinks, learn a few new tricks and the guys can come hang out when they get back."

"Sounds good."

We move from one noisy place to the next, but at least this one has booze and lots of it. I throw back my shot, slam my glass on the table and watch the woman slide up and down the pole.

"She new?" She is nothing like what was here before I left. This woman is timid and shy to show her body. If that's the truth, she's got the wrong job.

"Yeah. Only been here about a week. Still getting the hang of it."

I nod and watch as the woman's hands shake as she unclasps her bra. As soon as her song is finished, she gathers her clothes faster than I ever thought possible and exits out the back. I raise my eyebrow at Princess.

"Told one of the other girls I'd give her a chance. This is it." She shrugs. "Blaze is next."

I smile. I hadn't seen her since before I left for school and it's no one's fault but my own. Just like everyone else, I didn't call. I should have. Next to Harlow and Bella, she's the closest thing I have to a friend. The thing I love about her is she's so self-contained. She's strong, independent and doesn't take shit from anyone. And she doesn't sleep with brothers. Shit, she probably goes a few towns over if she wants some just in case.

She's a very savvy business woman and seriously smart. When I left she only had a small bit of college left, I'm sure by now she's graduated. She told me once that if men wanted to pay for her school, let them. And she has. Music begins booming even louder through the speakers and out walks the famous Blaze, but in real life Taryn McKnight is only known by a few.

Her body is curved to perfection, boobs spilling out over her top. What gets me about Blaze is the confidence she radiates while she's up on the stage. It amazes me that she has that same confidence when she walks off. Drives the men wild. Every single one of them right now would give every penny they have to spend one night with her. But she never has.

Blaze's body sways to the music. Her hands move up and down her body from the tips of her toes to the top of her breasts and into her brunette hair that cascades down her back. She wraps her leg around the pole and does these twirls and slides, proving just how damn strong her legs and arms really are. She has to have the whole room panting because I'm right there with them. G.T. can't get here soon enough.

Blaze's clothes fall to the ground piece by piece. I look over to a very enthralled Tug, who is adjusting his jeans and smile. To me, those two would make an ideal couple, not that I plan on being matchmaker any time soon. Hell, I barely have my own shit together. Blaze finishes her dance and the lights on the stage go black. Cheers and whistles bring the house down and Harlow smiles.

"She's something. I want to go say hi." I yell over the noise. Harlow takes my hand and pulls me through the sea of men trying to get a piece of Blaze. Even I know that she's already locked up backstage so none of them can get to her.

Harlow nods at the bouncers and pushes through the doors. She greets the girls and heads straight to the back door that is shut. She knocks.

"Who's there?" Blaze calls.

"Your girlfriend!" I yell back and the door flies open.

"Casey!" She screeches and pulls me into a hug, the silk robe she wears clings to her sweaty skin.

"Hey girl. How the hell are ya?"

"Good, really good." She pulls away and looks me up and down. "I heard about your baby. I'm sorry."

"Thank you." We enter the room and she locks the door behind her. One would think that she is paranoid, but with all the men that want a piece of her it is for her own safety. It's something she has to do to protect herself, along with carrying a 9mm. I sit on her couch with Harlow by my side. Blaze sits in front of us in the chair; legs crossed appearing to be the perfect lady.

"I'm sorry I didn't come. Princess told me about the service, but it was for family and it didn't feel right."

It is like déjà vu hearing those words come out of her mouth. Didn't I just say them a few weeks ago? "You are family. Anything you can come to, I'd..." I stop and look at Harlow, who lifts her chin. "We'd love for you to be there. Did you finish school?" I ask.

Her face brightens. "Yes. The degree is mine."

"You're still gonna work here?"

"For a while. Money's too good to give up and the more I save now, the better. But I'll be figuring something out soon."

"I'm sure you will." It reminds me that I need to find out if I can get my job back at the shop. With everything going on, I haven't had a chance. I need to make it my top priority.

"Hey Princess." Blaze turns to her. "Some of the girls were saying that a woman's been coming here every night looking for you. Shaina. You know anyone by that name?"

"Yeah. Diamond's kid. She didn't leave on such good terms with the club, probably wants to see if she can smooth it out on my side."

"She's been pretty adamant and drinking, a lot. Cali said that he had to escort her out one night." She shrugs. "But this is all hearsay. I didn't see any of it."

"Because you're locked up." I laugh.

"Damn right. I can't be too damn careful." Blaze has had men follow her home from the club, write her letters, send her all kinds of gifts, some worth thousands of dollars. It's quite nuts. But Blaze handles it with grace and saves all the gifts as a savings account. More power to her.

Banging at the door pulls our attention away from our conversation. "Yeah."

"Cali." He grunts and Blaze opens the door. Tug stands with his arms crossed next to him.

"Princess got a visitor. Someone named Shaina. Please do something with her or I'm gonna fucking make sure she never comes back here again."

"Thanks Cali." Harlow says standing up. "Wanna come?"

I look at Blaze. "I have another set I have to get ready for. Go ahead and we can talk after." She smiles.

"Sure." I hug Blaze and follow Harlow out to the main bar. Shaina is sitting with her legs crossed staring down at the bar. She jumps when Harlow touches her arm.

"What do ya need?" Harlow asks politely.

"I need the money from my dad."

"I don't know anything about money honey. You'll either need to talk to Pops or your mom. I haven't got a clue."

"You have to get it for me. You have to."

The fear in her eyes is evident and swarming. "What's wrong? And who do you owe it to?" Harlow asks as if she inquisitions people every day.

Shaina looks away. "Come on." Harlow says pulling Shaina's arm and bringing her into her office. Shaina sits down in the seat across from Harlow, I sit in the other.

"Spill." Harlow says lacing her fingers together in front of her, her body screaming power.

"Not a big deal. Just need the money my dad put aside for me, I'll pay it and it'll be done."

"Not good enough. Who and how much?" Shaina looks to me.

"Hey. If you want her help, you gotta answer her questions." I shrug and she sags slowly breathing in and out.

"About three months ago, I got involved with this guy. He's part of a club outside of Sumner. We were dating for that time and then he disappeared. He owed the club twenty-five grand and they want their money or they'll kill me."

"What club?" Harlow asks sitting up in her chair.

"T-Darts."

My heart rate picks up and I ask the next question. "What was his name?"

"Jace." My heart plummets.

"Alright. Let me get this straight." Harlow continues as if the ground didn't just shatter underneath me. "You dated Jace, he disappeared, and he owed T-Darts money and now they are after you."

She nods.

"Who's after you specifically?"

"There have been quite a few that have come by. Guns, Montgomery, Taft and Paine."

My heart plummets. Nowhere in the time that I knew Jace did I think he knew Paine in any kind of way. The man had no tattoos on his body at all. His attitude was more of a business man than the men I grew up with. Things are not adding up.

"You've met face to face with Paine?"

"Yeah. Several times. He's threatened me in more ways than one." She shivers and rubs her arms up and down. I look at Harlow and she stares back at me conveying the same message without speaking. If Paine wanted her dead, she'd be gone, especially if they were alone. He either wants her to come to Ravage or this is a set up. I'm hoping for the first.

"I'll talk to them, but they'll want to talk to ya. Leave me your number." Shaina's eyes flash up.

"I need to stay at the club. They're going to kill me." Harlow pushes out of her chair.

"Then you shouldn't have gotten mixed up with them. I said I'll talk to them, but that's about as good as you're gonna get right now."

"What do I do?"

"Watch your back. Go." Harlow orders. Shaina reluctantly gets up from her chair and moves to the door.

"Diamond would want you to protect me." She says opening it, walking out, and shutting it behind her.

"Something's not right." I say immediately. Harlow puts her finger over her lips to shush me and I follow. She opens her door and Shaina is gone.

"She leave?" I hear her ask Tug.

"Yeah."

She closes the door and walks back over to me falling into the chair that Shaina just sat in. "No something's not right at all. It just happens to be a coincidence that she hooked up with Jace and now owes them money? She is Diamond's daughter and Paine's not stupid. And, Shaina wants nothing to do with the club, so why now?"

"You think she's a rat?"

"Could be." Harlow reaches for her phone punching in some buttons. "Hey baby. What's the plan? You still comin' here or you want us to meet you boys at the clubhouse?"

"That's fine. Hey when we get there, we gotta talk

about some stuff. Can you get all the guys?"

"Nothing's wrong. Shaina just came by and we need to talk."

"It's long and you need to ride. I'll see ya in about an hour."

She hangs up the phone. "Well, that'll get me a spanking, not that I mind." She laughs.

AFTER EXPLAINING everything to the brothers, they say they'll handle it. Which for me is good. That's one thing that I love about this club, they handle all the problems. I don't have to.

As I lay in bed with G.T. wrapped around me tight, I feel safe, protected and loved. Something I'll never get tired of.

"WAKE UP ANGEL." G.T.'s words whisper in my ear and my eyes flutter open to the most beautiful blue ones I've ever seen.

"Morning." I whisper and grin.

"We're going out riding today. Get ready." It's been so long since I've been on the back of a bike. G.T. was cleared to ride a while ago, but he didn't want me on the back yet until he got his bearings. I'm guessing he got himself together. Excitement races through me. "Damn girl. Don't break your damn neck." He jokes watching me pull out my jeans and leathers practically falling to the ground. I dash into the bathroom braiding my hair down my back and wrapping it up tight. I apply just a bit of makeup, knowing I'll more than likely sweat it off.

Walking out of the bathroom, G.T. pulls his boots up and laces them. His eyes meet mine and a sexy whistle caresses his lips. "Damn Angel. You look fucking hot." I blush, my body getting flushed. "But there are two things missing." I look down at my leathers; boots and jacket are all exactly where they should be. Nothing is missing.

"What?" I question and look over to G.T. on bended knee in front of me. I gasp my hand slapping my mouth, tears spring to my eyes and my gaze falls onto a very sparkly ring in G.T.'s hand. "Oh. My. God." I mutter, my eyes focus on his. Inside of them, love is bursting through, sucking me in like a vise.

"Angel. I love you. I've loved you for so many years and I need to make this official. I want you by my side always. I want you in my bed next to me every night. I want you to be my wife. I *need* you to be my wife. Will you marry me?" I stand there stunned. My lips try to move, but nothing comes out and I think I may have forgotten how to breathe. Years, I have loved this man and now he will really be mine. I never thought this day would come. Never thought he would want this step. Always dreamed he would, but never thought it would be a reality. And here it is, staring me in the face. G.T.'s eyes are pleading with me, but there is one thing that needs to be clear.

"It'll be only me from now on. No one else touches you, ever." I say with all the confidence I can muster, but it comes out breathy, the shock still evident. But he needs to answer this question. It's too important.

"Absolutely baby. There is no one else for me. You are it. You are the reason I breathe. You are the reason I live. I love you." He smiles and my breath leaves my body again and I suddenly feel a bit dizzy. I close my eyes pulling myself back together, as much as I can.

"Yes." I find my voice, but it's quiet and croaky. My entire body shakes and there is no way to control it.

He smiles showing me his beautiful dimples and I want to lick them. He reaches out and grabs my shaking left hand pulling it up to his lips and kissing my ring finger. He slides the gorgeous ring on to my finger and I breathe in deep, blowing it out slowly. The diamond is square and encased in the band which is either white gold or platinum, I'm not sure which. Small diamonds are embedded in the band going all the way around. It is the most beautiful thing I've ever seen.

"I picked this ring so you could still wear your gloves because I plan on having you on the back of my bike every damn chance I get. And I'm a selfish bastard and want it on your damn finger even when you're working on an engine, gloves will protect it." He smiles seductively and kisses the diamond he just placed on my finger.

"It's beautiful." I pause. "The most beautiful thing I've ever seen. Thank you." I stare into his crystal eyes; he stands and his full lips slam to mine, passion and love exploding though his kiss. His hands encase my face and I pull my hands up resting them on his. This kiss is tender and loving and special. I give him all of me down to my soul.

He pulls away, both of us breathless. "One more thing." His forehead presses to mine far too briefly as he lets go and heads to the closet opening the door wide. My eyes travel to his delectable ass, my mouth becoming dry. I lick my lips; the taste of cherries exploding on my tongue. He bends down and turns around with a large white box in his hands. My body begins to sweat. I know what is inside that box. It's amazing that the ring knocked me on my ass, but this, this just feels like too much.

He slowly pulls the top off of the box and pulls the tissue paper away. I stop breathing and stare at the beautiful work in front of me. A gorgeous black leather rag with intricate crisscross ties around the edges lay in the box. G.T. picks it up by the shoulders holding it up. The patch on the front says Angel and I blush. He turns it around and my mouth goes dry. On the back is the Ravage top rocker just like his and on the bottom it reads 'Property of G.T.'

I don't even bother trying to stop the tears or even when I break into sobs. He really is mine. "I had this made for you. It's time for you to be my wife and my ol' lady."

I nod my head unable to formulate the words and try to control my breathing. "Time to put it on Angel." I slip out of my current jacket and turn around for G.T., who slides the soft leather across my body. It smells of leather and oil and I relish in its smoothness under my fingertips.

I turn around and smile at him wiping my face dry. "What do ya think?" I say my voice regaining some of its punch.

"I think you are the most beautiful fucking thing I've ever seen in my life." He pulls me close crashing his lips to mine and I can't breathe. He sucks every bit of air out of my body and my knees grow weak. He wraps his arm around my waist holding me tight to him and I clutch onto his shoulders feeling his muscles flex under my touch. He pulls away looking into my eyes.

"When we get back, I'm fucking you all night long. I will be so damn deep in that tight body, you will always know you are mine. *My* girl. *My* ol' lady." Shivers rake my body and I smile up at him wanting that more than words could say.

"Is that a threat or a promise?" I tease, biting my lower lip and looking up at him batting my eyelashes.

"A fucking promise. Let's go before we are really fucking late and they start pounding on the damn door." I nod and check my makeup, thankful I didn't put much on. I slap some cherry lip gloss on smacking my lips together. G.T. holds his hand out and I take it happily, shutting and locking the door behind us.

We walk into the main room to cheers. The core brothers of Ravage and their ol' ladies stand around smiling knowingly. Harlow comes barreling through the crowd moving people out of her way. "Let me see." She yanks my hand eyeing the beautiful ring. "It's gorgeous." She looks up at her brother. "You did good."

"You didn't see it?" I ask because surely he ran it by his sister. Right?

"No. Jackass here wouldn't let anyone see it, so don't be surprised if you get mauled with everyone wanting to see it."

He shrugs. "I wanted you to be the first to see it, Angel." My sweet, sweet biker man.

"Come here!" Ma yells pushing Harlow out of the way. She is the only woman on this planet that could get away without a fist to the jaw. I go willingly into her open arms and embrace her whole-heartedly. "I am so damn happy right now. You make him so happy and that's all I ever wanted for him. But for you, I've always thought of you as a daughter, now we get to make it legal." I choke back the tears. I will not cry anymore. Even happy tears.

"Turn!" Harlow says loudly and I know what she wants. I slowly pull away from Ma and turn making my leather shown to the world. More whistles and hollers come from the group around me. Then they are all on both G.T. and myself, every ol' lady and brother taking their turns hugging us and kissing us on our cheeks.

Becs is one of the last ones to come up to me. He wraps his arms around me and I breathe in deep, pulling him tight to me. He leans in close to my ear. "Your dad would be so happy for you girl." I nod into his shoulder. "Your man went and talked to your dad." I pull away looking into his elated eyes.

"What?"

He smiles. "He went and talked to Bam. He's a good man, Angel." I close my eyes and let the words sink in.

"Angel." I whisper.

"Club name after all." Becs says kissing me on the cheek and falling back in with the crowd. I turn and see G.T. talking to Dagger. I know I shouldn't. But I can't help myself. I charge towards him and jump into his arms. He catches me and I latch my lips onto his, wrapping my hands through his hair and pulling him as close as I can. His hands grip my ass and pulls me tight to him.

"Alright you two." Pops calls and I pull away from G.T. His lips are swollen from mine, making me smile. "If we don't ride now, we'll never go."

Everyone nods and I set off for a ride with my family.

CHAPTER SIXTEEN
GT

"Thanks." Pops shakes hands with Lambrouni's men followed by Becs and myself. A man sits in the chair, his head slumped down, hands bound behind him and feet bound together. The black bag over his head conceals his face.

"Dagger." Pops says, lifting his chin. Dagger walks over to the man kicking him on his foot.

"Wake the fuck up." The man jumps and starts in with a bunch of gibberish that none of us understands. Pops nods to Rhys who leaves and brings back the asshole otherwise known as Jace. He stumbles in, his face battered and bruised. I'd be surprised if anyone even recognized his ass. Not that I give a shit.

His eyes flick over to the man with the bag, who is continually mumbling. "Did you miss your daddy dearest?" Dagger asks grabbing the man's head and pulling it back.

"How the fuck did you find him?" Jace's grunts between breaths.

"Skip it. Tell me how the fuck to find Paine and he walks out of here. Or don't and I fucking kill him while you watch."

"You won't fucking kill him. He didn't do shit."

I smirk to Cruz. "Fucker really doesn't understand this shit does he? We thought you were one of Paine's boys. Surely he showed you how shit works in our world."

Cruz walks up behind the man grabbing his head in one hand and a knife in the other. The knife traces along his jaw and slightly cuts his skin leaving a trail of blood. The cut is only superficial, but Jace needs to know we mean business.

Jace grunts but doesn't move. "Dad!"

The man's head jolts up. "Jace. What's going on?"

"It'll be alright, just stay still."

"What the hell have you gotten yourself into, Jace? You haven't been running around with your cousin Jared? Have you?"

All us brothers glance at each other.

"Does Jared have another name?" Pops yells.

Jace shouts. "Don't answer that." But his dad doesn't listen.

"Paine. Stupid fucker. Why my brother ever got involved in a gang I'll never know, but he brought his fucking kid into it too. That's what this is about isn't it Jace?" The man shakes his head. "I told you to stay away from him!"

"Dad shut the fuck up!" Jace yells and Rhys slams his fist into his gut.

"What do these men want, Jace?"

"Alright enough, with the fucking male bonding shit." I cut in, fed up with this circus. "Jace tell us where Paine is or I fucking kill him. I'm done with your shit."

"He's right. Either way you die today. Take your father with you if want to, but you're fucking going." Becs says crossing his arms over his chest and I nod.

"Dagger." Pops lifts his chin and he pulls the man's arm hard, probably out of the socket. He screams.

"Fuck." Jace says as Rhys holds him and I land a few punches.

"We can keep this up all fucking night." I bark shaking my fist out.

After what feels like forever, Jace gives us an address. But with his prior record, I need to make sure. I pull the gun out of my holster and hold it to the man's head. "You want to rethink that address boy? Cause if you're fucking around with me, I fucking hunt your father down and kill him, no questions asked." I click the gun and the man starts babbling again.

"I swear that's the last fucking place I saw him. If you can't find him there he has a girl and a kid that has a place out on Ebert Road, he'd be there." I remove the gun from the old man's head.

"What about the money that you owe and now Shaina? How the hell does she fit in to all of this?" Cruz asks.

"Diamond's daughter and she was easy. Wanted to hurt her daddy... blah... blah..."

I ask the questions that I need to know the answer

too. "Why Casey? What does she have to do with any of this shit?"

He smiles and he will pay for that after he talks. And surprisingly he does and he almost seems to get off on it.

"Paine knows all the little biker brats." I nod to Dagger and Rhys who pull on his arms and he screams then laughs. "You just don't get it. Paine wants you all dead. He doesn't give a shit about that land, it's about pride. You're such dumbasses."

I slam my fist in his gut. "You're not telling me why." I move over to his father and cock the gun to his head. "Tell me."

"Planned out. Moved in a week before she did. Pretty much lied about everything. She was pretty easy to convince, surprisingly." Then he started laughing harder. "Then when she lost that bastard of a baby." I'd heard enough as the fury of a father courses through my body. I pound his face over and over and over until it hangs there, blood dripping from it.

I look over at Pops, who nods at me. I point the gun at Jace, pulling the trigger with ease. He falls immediately to the ground.

The old man screams. "Now. We let you go and not a word of this to anyone, or we come and find you. Even if he's right and gave up Paine, we will kill you, make no mistake about it." Pops states and nods to Dagger, who picks the man up and takes him away.

"What do ya think?"

"Not the first. Let's go to the girl and kid." Becs moves to the door. "Get Tug and Breaker here to clean up this fucking mess." He looks down at the man covered in blood and I for once can breathe. The fucker is dead.

THE HOUSE IS MODEST, nothing elaborate, but that's how someone hiding tries to blend in to the community. Night has fallen and lights shine throughout the house, but I don't see any movement. I move around the house trying to get a better view, my brothers doing the same. The curtains are drawn, but the light penetrates through them, allowing us to see inside.

I text the brothers saying I see no one. And I get five other texts saying the same thing. I move quietly up to the door, stand to the side and test the handle which turns. The door creaks open and I hear it. A ticking. "Fucking Run, Bomb!" I yell jumping away from the door just as a huge explosion fills my ears.

My head hits the ground. I smell fire, sulfur and something else I can't place. My head feels so fucking heavy, but I fight to stay awake. I roll to my side and hear my brother's yelling. I look over and Cruz, Dagger and Becs are carrying Rhys. "Fuck." I push up on wobbly legs and head over to them.

"He was right there when it went off. He must not have heard you yell." Rhys' body is black, but there is no blood.

"Call Doc have him meet us. Now." He barks as the guys take Rhys to the cage.

"You alright, son?" I stand looking at the huge pile of burning rubble.

"Yeah. We gotta get the fuck out of here. Now."

CHAPTER SEVENTEEN
Casey

G.T.'s BEEN GONE ALL DAY ON CLUB BUSINESS AND IT'S BEEN great. Not that he's gone because I miss him, it's just when he's here I'm always preoccupied. Today, I was able to get more than my assigned homework done and work on this massive business plan that one of my professors assigned. I feel very accomplished.

I lay out on a picnic table enjoying the sun shining down. It'll be dark soon, but I need the fresh air. Brothers from the Clayton chapter of Ravage have been here all day while the guys have been gone. I feel their eyes on me constantly, but ignore them. They know I belong to G.T.

Harlow and I made them sandwiches, but mostly they did their thing and we each did ours. Harlow said that Coop needed a rest, so she decided to lie with him while I bask in the last bit of sun for the day.

It's amazing how things have changed so much in

such a short time. I really never thought that G.T. and I would be able to get to this place. There was just too much hurt there but for some reason we have. And I've never been happier.

"Hey Casey." I hear whispered through the wind. I sit up and look around. Shaina is standing on the side of the garage next to one of the entrances.

"What?" I do not know what is going on between her and club. I do know that she is a ball full of trouble that I don't want to be a part of.

"I need your help."

"With?"

She looks behind her and I can't see anything. A little girl about the age of four pokes her head around the corner her eyes scared. I jump to my feet. "Who's kid?" I say walking towards them.

"Mine." A man's voice comes from behind them and my body goes on instant alert and I let out a painstaking scream that would get anyone's attention. Jared. What the hell? Before I can say a word, his hand comes up cracking me hard across the face. My knees give out and I fall to the ground, but continue to scream knowing it's my only salvation right now. He picks me up and wraps his hand around my throat. I kick and scratch anything that I can get my hands on. Something gets stuffed in my mouth and tight arms grip my body making me immobile.

"Stop right fucking there." I hear screamed in the background. The man slams his head into mine and I see black.

MY HEAD THROBS as I move it back and forth slowly. I hear soft moans and realize they are my own. My arms are laced with pain and my shoulders are on fire. I try to open my eyes, but they feel heavy and gritty, like sand paper and everything around me is grainy and blurry. I blink repeatedly trying to clear the fog, look up and realize quickly why my arms and shoulders hurt so badly.

My hands are wrapped with a thick metal chain and I'm being held so my feet barely hit the ground. I move my arms slightly and the chains clank together loudly, but do not budge. I look down at my body, my clothes are torn but still covering me. Next to me, Shaina is in the exact same position, but her head is slumped down to her chest and there is no movement from her.

Looking around the room, it's utterly black with only a small bit of light shining in through a small window and underneath the door, giving me a sliver of hope. It's enough though to look around, but really there isn't much to see. The concrete walls are gray and bare, the only thing in the room is Shaina, the chains and me.

Shaina starts to groan and mumble incoherently. I keep quiet not trusting this woman a bit. I have no fucking clue if she's working for these assholes and I'm not taking any more fucking chances, especially with her ass.

"I'm so sorry." She groans louder now and if I weren't tied up, I'd beat the shit out of her. I try to keep my anger in check, it will do me no good right now.

"Casey? Are you okay?" She whispers.

"Why did Jared kidnap me?" I growl.

"Jared? I don't know who that is?" Her voice scrapes out and I glare at her.

"What do you mean you don't know who he is? You brought him to me Shaina!"

"I brought Paine and the T-Darts." Dread washes through me. Jared is Paine. Great. Just fucking great. Confusion along with fear creeps up, but I tamp that shit down. Now is not the time to freak out. I got out of one bad situation. I can get out of another. I just have to think.

"How many?" At least I can do something about the confusion.

"Only three that I know."

"How did you get in the club and why did you let them take me?" I ask staring over at her.

"Some newbie was by the door and I told him who I was. He let me in." Her voice got quiet. "They were going to kill me."

"So you say what the hell, instead of going to the brothers, I'll trap one of their girls." I cut at her. Who the fuck does this shit?

"I wasn't thinking."

No shit you weren't. Fuck. I'm bait that much is clear. I pull on the chains feeling a small bit of give, but not much, the links grind into my skin leaving a burn. I will not be breaking out of these any time soon. Just then the door slowly creaks open, my head turns to the sound and I blink repeatedly from the sharp light invading the space.

"Aww. You ladies are awake? Swapping childhood stories I bet. One being a biker's kid... the other a biker kid wanna be, whose father didn't want anything to do with her." My eyes widen, my body grows ridged and my mouth falls open. I stare in utter shock at the man in front of me, unable to form any words. I saw him before, but at this moment it is really sinking in. I can't believe the man that I had drinks with is the same man that had kidnapped me. How in the hell did Jace know this man?

"Casey. It's a pleasure to meet you... again." He smiles and walks around my body, his fingertips reaching out to graze my hip. It takes every bit of willpower not to flinch from his repulsiveness. My heart beats so fast it threatens to burst out of my chest. "I've been looking forward to this moment for a while now. See, when we hung out at the bar I could see in your eyes that you wanted me. And that's a good thing 'cause now you are mine. Mine to do whatever I want with. You will never see any of the Ravage assholes again and you definitely will never see that pissant G.T. again."

I listen to his words, but do not let it show on the outside that they are cutting me deep. How in the hell did I not see this? My mind begins running at the speed of light trying to piece this twisted ass puzzle together.

"O' by the way. I'm Paine or Jared, but only my mother calls me that." He runs his grimy hands over my leather rag and caresses the softness. He pulls out a knife, my body tensing, which I fight to stop, but fail unsuccessfully.

My mind is racing. Paine is Jared. This means that Jace and Paine know each other and this whole damn thing was a set up from the beginning. Was it? How do they know each other?

"Ahh... I see those little wheels turning, but you'll get

answers in time. Maybe. First things first. This shit has to go." I bite my lip hard tasting blood and try to contain the words as he slices the leather off of my body and throws it like trash into the corner of the room. My mind is unable to process what is going on. He runs the knife between my breasts and I continue to stare straight ahead. Something inside of me is saying that I need to channel Harlow.

I'm nothing like her, but over the years watching her in action. I have learned a thing or two.

"Maybe I should cut this shirt off too, so I can see those tits. I love me a good set of tits." I ignore him and his hand whips out hard lashing me across the face. I hold the whimper in, but my breathing is now labored. The pain is agonizing, but I will not shed a tear. I will not give him that satisfaction.

"You will react when I touch you. If you don't, I'll beat you until you fucking do!" He yells punching me in the stomach knocking the air out of me in a whoosh. This time the groan and gasp that comes out of me is unstoppable.

"We're gonna teach you to be a good little girl like Shaina here." His boots click on the concrete floor as he moves away from my body and through my peripheral vision I see him standing next to Shaina. "See, she knows how to fuck and will be doing it a lot. See here in the T-Darts, I don't believe in monogamy and neither do my boys. We all fuck you. And Casey, we will fuck you." His hands snake up Shaina's arm and her body begins to shake.

The thought of Paine or his men touching me makes my stomach roll and bit of vomit comes to my mouth. I swallow trying to get the bile back down. I'll kill myself before I let this man hurt me.

"I kept telling those assholes over there that I'd make them pay if they didn't give me my fucking land, but for some reason they're didn't believe me. So, I'll make them give it to me. Then I'll keep you because I fucking can." He growls loud. The door opens, my eyes shoot up to it and a cold chill falls down my spine. Two men enter the room, both large and imposing. Both with cold dead eyes that say to me, they could care less what they do to either Shaina or myself. "Great. Time to start sharing." He slaps me on the ass hard and moves away.

GT

I HOP out of the cage to three brothers from Clayton running up to me quick, a frightened expression on their faces. "Some guy fucking took her!"

"What the fuck are you talking about?" These assholes are trembling, either from adrenaline or fear and if I think what they are going to tell me is true, it had better be fear.

"Some guys about two minutes ago took Casey, you probably fucking passed them. Black van, tinted windows. We shot and ran up on them, but they fucking took off before we could get to them."

"Why the fuck are you not on your bikes?" I growl grabbing two of their necks. These fuckers are lucky I need to find my girl or I'd fucking snap both of them.

"We were and then you pulled up." One of the men says in a hurry.

"Did she have her rag on?"

"Yeah."

"Get on your fucking bikes and find her! I'm coming!" I turn to Buzz. "The chip in her rag. Track it. Text me where she is." He nods running into the club house.

I look at Pops. "Go get your girl, I'll stay with Rhys. Cruz, Dagger, Becs, Go!" He yells and we are off. To where I don't have a fucking clue. Right now I'm following two numb nuts who supposedly know what fucking direction my girl went. Even though they are brothers, they are from another chapter and they don't know how shit works around here. After I get my girl, I'll fucking show them.

This time riding does not calm or soothe me. Every twist of the throttle sends a slice of fear through me. Every tick of the clock is a second that I can't fucking protect her. I only have one guess who has her and that's Paine. And if I'm fucking right... It scares the fucking shit out of me. I've heard of the way he treats his women, and it makes my fucking stomach roll. He is keen on inflicting pain and having very unwilling participants in the bedroom. Even having his brothers join in repeatedly without the woman's consent. Once he scarred a woman's body so bad, she ended up taking her own life because she didn't want to live with the reminders of what had happened to her. I can't let that happen to my Angel.

I keep my phone cradled in my crotch looking down

repeatedly waiting for the coordinates and hoping that the little device fucking works. I hadn't had a chance to check the little chip out yet and Angel doesn't fucking know it's in there.

Buzz came to me when I told the guys I was giving her my rag and said something about this little techy chip shit that could track my girl if I ever needed it. He said it could get sewed into the leather and she'd never have to know it was there. I went along with it, not thinking I'd ever fucking need it. Now I hope like hell the damn thing works. It's the only fucking way right now; I'm going to find my girl.

My crotch lights up and I'm sure vibrates, but I can't tell from the vibrations of the bike. Lucky I kept looking down at the fucking thing. The address listed is in the total opposite direction that we are heading. I make a quick turn and pull away from the guys in front, who slow, turn and follow along.

We make it quickly to the address killing the engines and moving quietly up to the big brick building. It's two stories with lots of fucking lights on, bikes and cages lining the outside of it. Windows have light shining through them, but I'm unable to see any shadows inside.

I pull out my guns, screw the silencer on, and check the clips, putting one away in my holder. Each step I take is one step closer to my girl. I move in slowly, careful not to make noise or step on anything that may bring attention to me. My brothers stay right by my side. I breathe in and out to slow my ever beating heart. I've done this shit hundreds of times, but knowing my girl is the one I'm looking for puts this on a whole different level of fucked up.

Becs and Dagger motion with their hands that they are going around back with one of the Clayton brothers. That leaves Cruz, myself and two of the Clayton brothers to take the front. I turn the handle of the door opening it and move quickly away from it waiting for shots. When they don't happen, I step in and see two men, I raise my gun, pull the trigger with precision and shoot one and Cruz the other. They tumble instantly to the ground unmoving.

We move through the building looking around every turn, the musty smell invading my nostrils. Our backs are either pressed to each other or against the wall at all times. I take a step and a creaking sound, almost like a moan, echoes through the room. Shit. I look around quickly not seeing anyone. Turning the corner, two men stand with their back to us with no idea that we are about to end them. Shots easily to their hearts have them crashing to the ground in heaps.

Moving down the hallway, I turn into the first door. Immediately I see three men who pull their weapons cursing at us rapidly. Cruz and I shoot back quickly, dodging their bullets and they fall dead to the ground. Sweat begins to run in my eye and I swipe it quickly with my hand. Fuck. I hate nerves.

We move quietly down to the next door, when a gun is placed at my temple from the opposite side. "Don't move." The asshole growls and I slowly breathe in and out.

Cruz doesn't give him a chance. He steps around the corner putting a bullet right between the man's eyes and taking out the guy standing behind him. Everything is eerily quiet and there is still no sign of my girl. I breathe in and out, nodding at Cruz.

We creep slowly down a long hallway our backs to the wall. Our boots tap lightly on the linoleum, but it can't be helped.

We look in each of the rooms that we pass by, lucky that the doors are open but not seeing anything. We move to the last door and my heart picks up. My gut is telling me that Angel is behind this door. I lift my boot and kick the door in, pushing myself through, my brother right on my tail.

My breath catches, two women one being my girl, hanging by chains from the fucking ceiling, clothes stripped away from both their bodies, feet barely touching the floor. Looking at Angel's face, I see no signs of tears, but her eyes are dead. Void. Almost as if she has drifted to somewhere inside of herself, her safe place.

"Well. Look who showed up to the party." Paine moves quickly behind my girl clenching his gun that is now pointed directly at her head. "I'm guessing you got through my men or else you wouldn't be here right now." He shakes his head ruefully. "It's astounding that you even found us."

"You fucker. You're dead." I growl pointing my gun his direction. Angel's eyes stare at me and spark at hearing my voice. Her head rises lightly.

I hear moaning from the side and without moving my eyes away from my girl, I know it's Shaina. "Oh my God." Shaina voice gasps the chains clanging from her struggles. "Get me out of here!" She yells but is ignored. I'm too busy looking at Angel, whose arms are a strange color of white from the loss of blood to them.

"You're not getting out of here Paine, may as well give it up." My voice comes out strong and authoritative, even if inside the level of hate and fear are wrapping around me like a snake squeezing every bit of life out of me.

"You think I'm gonna roll over and play dead?" He laughs sadistically. "Fuck no. If I'm going out, I'm taking this one with me. You'll know what it's like to feel pain the rest of your miserable life."

I'm unable to get a clear shot because the worthless piece of shit is guarding his body with Angel's. Paine pulls Casey's hair back tight, her head snaps backwards. He holds the gun up to her temple with a slight reach and her eyes latch on mine. Inside of them I see a spark of determination. I know something is coming. I clutch my gun ready for it.

Out of nowhere, Casey's leg swings back kicking Paine hard in the nuts and he stumbles back with a grunt holding himself, falling away from the girls. I aim and shots go off from Cruz, myself and Paine all at once. When Paine hits the ground with a thud, I rush to my girl and grab her around the waist, pulling her up to get the pressure off her arms. "You okay." She nods carefully, but no words escape her lips. I rip my shirt over my head and cover her body with it holding it in place. Cruz rushes over to Paine checking his pulse. "Dead?" I ask quickly.

"Yep. Fucking dead." That is for Diamond and my girl. Fucker.

"Call everyone. We need cutters to get them down now. Get over here and hold them up so their arms can get blood back to them." Cruz dials the phone giving instructions. Becs and Dagger come rushing in, guns raised.

"Fuck. We missed the damn party." Dagger lowers his gun placing it at his back.

"Dagger, hold Shaina up to get the blood back in her arms." He does so and Angel starts shaking in my arms. I hold her tighter.

"It's alright Angel. I'm taking you home." I repeat soothing words to her over and over again. Her eyes slowly shut and her head falls to my chest. I want her fucking arms cut down now.

"He... Jace..." Her words stumble and are incoherent, but I know exactly what information she just became privy to. Dammit. The fear in her eyes and the sound of her voice guts me like nothing I've ever felt before. I would do anything to take that pain on myself and wipe it from my girl. I want that fucker alive again just so I can fucking kill him all over again.

"I know. It's okay. It's all over." She slowly nods, but the fear is still prevalent in her eyes damn near ripping my heart out. "Everything clear on your end?" I ask Becs.

"Yeah. Took out four men."

"We took out seven." Cruz says coming back putting his phone in his rag pocket. "On their way, be here in ten."

IT'S BEEN four days since she was taken and I haven't let her out of my fucking sight. And she hasn't let me either. Angel's been up and down with what happened to her. She doesn't want to talk about it, but at night, she has this tormented scream that rattles my core. I've pressed for answers, but she closes up. She swears that she wasn't raped, but other than that, I can't get shit out of her. Even Princess has tried, but still nothing. All I know is that I love her and I'll do whatever she needs. I know the connection between Jace and Paine has really messed with her head. I just hope not too much.

The discussion on how I found her went much better than anticipated. I thought I'd get shit for it, but she didn't even bitch about the chip inside of her cut. She even told me she was grateful for it. It just made me hold her tighter. I don't know what the hell I ever did to deserve her, but I'm glad I did.

Princess, on the other hand, when she found out, went on a fucking rampage. She felt around her rag trying to find the chip, but that's her. I'll let Cruz handle that shit. My hands are full enough.

With Paine and most of his crew gone, we can now breathe a bit. First it was Rabbit and then Paine after us for all they were worth. I need a fucking break. I'm ready to ride with my girl behind me and relax for a change.

Shaina is one big hot mess that Princess has been dealing with. I can see why Diamond kept her out of the life. She can't handle it, at all. Even though neither Shaina or Angel are talking, my gut is telling me that Shaina was hurt much worse than Angel. If that's so, then she has every right to feel that shit.

Today, I'm getting my girl away from this clubhouse and we will ride to wherever the wind takes us. We are both in need of a fucking break. She says she has school work to do today, which she always says, but never does. But it needs to fucking wait. I need her wrapped around my body and the road in front of us. She needs it too.

"I really don't want to go." She says pulling on her leathers and pouting.

"You're going."

"But... Never mind." She finishes lacing her boots and pulls her old leather jacket on. I know she doesn't want to wear it and I can't blame her and I know what she wants. "Ready." Her voice is glum and down. I smile reaching into the closet.

I pull out her rag and hold it up with my hands. "You're missing something." Her eyes flash to her rag and tears form in her eyes.

She stands and walks over. Her arm reaches out to the leather and she rubs it in between her fingers. She pulls it to the side and notices all the new lacing I had done throughout it. "You fixed it?" She whispers softly.

"Of course I did." Everywhere that bastard cut, I had lacing woven through the leather connecting it until it was all one piece again.

"I love you." She says looking into my eyes.

"Love you too, Angel."

CHAPTER EIGHTEEN
Casey

In the last two days, G.T. has been my rock. After our day long ride, I felt a bit more relaxed. But as soon as we got back to the clubhouse, I felt it happening again. The twitchy, jumpy anxiety that creeps into my body that I can't shake. I know Paine and Jace are dead. G.T. wasn't supposed to tell me because it is club business. But after talking to Pops he got the green light to tell me about Jace, they both agreed that I should know.

Thank God for that. I don't think I could go on every day without knowing that those men wouldn't be passing me on the street one day, ready to capture me, hurt me or kill me. Even though I saw Paine drop from the shot, I can still feel him and every time I do, I need a shower to scrub off his hands.

But, even with them gone, I can't help but jump at the noises, the bangs on the doors and even when my damn phone rings. It's not only what happened to me. All that Paine really did to me was touch my body on the outside and terrorize me with words about killing G.T. I hear those words replay in my dreams and wake up in cold sweats. Nothing can happen to G.T. ever. And I will prob-ably never get over the Paine-Jace connection. But that's not what really gets me.

It's what I witnessed him doing with Shaina that I can't ever seem to shake. It's replaying in my head when I'm awake, when I'm asleep, and every moment of the day. Her screams, sobs and pleas roll over and over in my head. I couldn't help her. I couldn't do a damn thing to save her. I just had to listen and watch when Paine ordered me too or he'd shoot both of us on the spot. I had to buy time and hope we were found alive.

I want to talk to Shaina, but G.T. doesn't think it will be good for me. I can't blame him. I know I've been just going through the motions of life. I tell him I have to do my school work, but I don't care about it. All I really want is to lie in bed and have G.T. hold me. And I also know I won't get away with it for much longer.

Princess for one is about at her wit's end with me and that's one end no one wants to be at. It's only a matter of time before she blows and takes me for a ride. G.T. doesn't know what to do with me; hell I don't know what to do with me. But he's been so understanding and loving that it kills me when I break in front of him. The look in his eyes, he's lost and I can't find him right now. I need to find me.

I jump when there's a knock on the door, but blow out a deep breath. "Who is it?" I ask cautiously.

"It's me, Casey. Or is it Angel now?" The corner of my

mouth turns up slightly at the sound of Doc calling me Angel. I slowly unlock the door and turn the handle. "Hey. You wanted to see me?"

"Yeah. Come on in." I move away from the door and shut it when he enters. My heart pounds inside my chest so rapidly I fear it may burst. My hands sweat and I wipe them down my jeans. Doc turns and holds out his hands.

"What can I do for you?" I stare at the man not knowing where to start. I've never asked someone for help like this and I find it difficult to put the words together. I'm not sure what I need, but I hope that Doc does. He eyes me and quirks his eyebrow. "Angel, I know you've had a rough road. Is that what this is about?"

I nod my head and look at the floor. I breathe in and out trying to slow my heart down. My words come out in a rush. "I-don't-know-what-to-do-Doc-I-can't-sleep-for-shit-I-thought-I-was-totally-over-Mia-but-with-every-thing-that-happened-with-Jace-and-Paine-she-keeps-creeping-in-my-thoughts-I-worry-about-Shaina-and-I-can't-take-it-anymore." I stop, but don't look up at Doc, don't want to see whatever look he's got, pity, condemnation... Who knows?

"Angel." His voice is calm, but I still avoid him. "Casey." His voice is more firm and authoritative this time and my eyes cast up. He smiles. "Sweetheart. This is normal. You've had a hell of a rough go. The first step to getting better is to ask for help. The fact that you picked up your phone and called me, tells me that you want to get better. Your mind is in a place that it needs to find peace."

I don't bother stopping the tears as they fall when he speaks. "Now, we need to get you in with a therapist." I looked at him in shock. There is no way I'm telling a stranger my stuff. I can't even tell G.T. everything, let alone some person I've never met. "I can see that you don't like the idea, but do you want to get better?"

I do. I really do. I don't want to live like I have the last few days or even worse sink down to where I was when I lost Mia. The doctors at the hospital said I should talk to someone and I wish I would have taken their advice, but at the time, I was in denial. "Yes."

"Then we get you the help you need. Do you feel more comfortable talking to a woman or a man?" I pondered his question for only a moment.

"Woman."

"Alright a colleague of mine would be perfect, Dr. Anderson, and I think you two will get along well. I'm gonna give her a call and set up an appointment for you. Alright?"

I nod. "Thanks Doc."

"Anytime." He walks in front of me and stands close. "Look at me, Casey." My eyes slowly cast up a smirk playing on his mouth. "You did good. I'm proud of you." He reaches around, wrapping his arms around my body. I reciprocate and for a moment just relax into his arms.

The door swings open, I jump, gasp and pull quickly out of Docs embrace.

"What the fuck is going on here?" G.T. roars and our eyes meet.

"Stop. It's not what you're thinking."

"Really, Angel. What am I thinking right now?" He glares at Doc. "Get out!" He yells and then turns to me. Doc doesn't move.

I walk to G.T. and place my hand on his chest. "Calm

down. I need Doc to help me." I breathe deep. "With everything going on, I can't figure out how to do this. I asked him to help me."

"You called him and you couldn't tell me?"

"I'm sorry. I should have. But G.T. it was really hard picking up the phone and calling him in the first place, so can we please not fight about this?" He sighs and wraps his arms around me, pulling me into his body. He kisses the top of my head and I melt into him.

Doc clears his throat. "I'll be in contact soon with your information." I try to pull out of G.T.'s grasp, but he's not having it.

"Thank you." My words muffled by G.T.'s shirt. He nods and walks towards the door.

"Sorry, man. Don't like you having your hands on my girl." G.T. says, pressing his chin to the top of my head.

"Take care of her, G.T." He says, closing the door behind him.

"Talk to me." His voice is firm, but very much laced with concern.

So many thoughts wrestle in my head, but I just speak from the heart. It's time it comes out. "I feel like I did when I lost Mia. Lost. Broken. I go through the motions of the day, but it's not like it should be. I need to figure this out before it gets worse. And it will get worse. I've been there. I can't go back there. And I need to talk to Shaina."

"Are you sure you're ready for that?"

"Yes." No, not really, but it's a step.

"You gonna tell me what happened?" He asks pulling me to the bed as I curl up in his lap. I don't want to tell him what I saw, but I need to. Need to tell someone. I pull his shirt and get as close to him as I can.

"He..." my voice choked out. "...touched me." His body tenses. "Not what you're thinking. He ran his hands over my body and said things that echo in my head. Mainly the threats about killing you and letting me watch." I breathe G.T.'s scent in deep, feeling a small bit of comfort. "But... It's not me that I can't stop thinking about. It's Shaina." His hand rubs up and down my back soothing me. "He took from her what she was not willing to give. Her screams echo in my dreams. When I close my eyes, I hear her pleas for him to stop and for someone to help her. For *me* to help her. And I didn't. I couldn't. I was so damn helpless." Tears fall and I wipe my nose with the back of my hand. "I need to tell her that I'm sorry. I need her to understand that I would have helped her no matter what, if I could have. I need her..." Sobs break through and I cling to his shirt. G.T. absently starts rocking me like I'm a child, the motion is a welcome distraction.

"I just need to talk to her, please." I plead with him.

"Alright Angel. I'll set it all up. She's staying here right now. Pops wanted all of us to stay close after what happened."

"I know." I want to tell him to take me away from here. Not that I don't like the clubhouse, it's just too many noises all the time and I don't think it's helping me.

"We are packing up and moving into our house tomorrow. Tonight will be our last night here, hopefully for a long time."

My head pops up and I bat the tears away. "Really? We get to leave?" I say, surprised.

He smiles. "Yeah. I finally get to take you home, babe.

Away from all of this, where it can be just you and me. I'm not doing any runs for the next two weeks, so it's just you and me for the most part."

I squeeze him tight. "Thank you." It does not pass me that I never got my fight about moving in with him, but I'll let it go. He is after all going to be my husband.

"Anything for you and I'll do whatever you need to make you feel better."

We hold each other for the longest time. When he releases me briefly, he grabs his phone and dials. I hear the one-sided conversation to Princess setting up a meeting with Shaina tonight. I can't help the nerves that kick in. I don't want her to hate me because right now I hate myself enough for the both of us.

When my phone buzzes, I jump but answer it when I see Doc's name. He set up an appointment with Dr. Anderson for me in the morning and G.T. says he'll take me. Things have to be looking up. Right?

SHAINA'S FACE is faded black and blue with partially healed cuts covering her cheeks and forehead. Her eyes widen as I enter the room and I still myself, waiting for the screams that will come out of her mouth, aimed at me. G.T. is at my back as I walk in the room. I didn't want him to come in, but he insisted. He didn't want me to go to the basement alone. He promised me that he would not be far away.

Shaina gets up from the chair and walks towards me. My eyes widen and panic sets in getting ready for the blow. When Shaina's arms wrap around my body, she squeezes and we both unleash the tears that need to fall. We stay locked in an embrace for a long time, both needing to feel the pain of Paine. And both understanding what it was like in that room. No one else will ever know the terror we felt and still feel, but Shaina got the worst of it.

When she pulls away from me and looks into my eyes, words fall from my lips. "I'm so sorry, Shaina. So very sorry."

"Shh... It is not your fault Casey." She grabs my hand and moves us to the table and chairs. We sit. G.T. stays far enough away to give us privacy, but close enough in case something happens. "You didn't do this. That asshole did."

"But I couldn't stop him."

"No, you couldn't. I couldn't either. I'm not gonna lie and say I'm okay, cause I'm seriously not. But I do know that it's not your fault. At all. You cannot think any of this is."

"I feel so damn guilty."

"Why? Because you're not Diamond's daughter? That's why he wanted me Casey. You heard him. He wanted to make Diamond pay from the grave. Instead of that, he made me pay. There was no changing his mind. Nothing. What happened to me is a result of who my father was."

"You can't blame your dad." I whisper.

"I don't know how I feel right now about that. I'm not sure how I feel about a lot of things. But one thing is for sure, I do not blame you in any way. You are probably the only reason he didn't kill us immediately. I know we were buying time, but it doesn't make it any easier."

"I'm going to talk to someone. I think you should too." I say wanting to suggest it but not step over bounds.

"Princess said the same thing. I'm not sure what to do right now. I'll figure it out though. You do not worry about me. The only thing I ask of you is that you keep in touch with me. I need to know that you are okay."

I am stunned by her words. If anything, I thought she'd want to hightail it away from the club and never look back. Not want to keep in contact with me and certainly not to make sure that I am okay. If anything it should be me voicing my worry for her. "Of course. But you have to do the same."

"Absolutely. I'm going to go to my mom's cabin for a while. It's quiet up there and I need time to figure this out."

"You sure being alone is a good thing?"

"For me. Yes."

I nod my head trying to understand, but I'm not her and I don't make choices for others.

"Keep in touch. Okay?"

"Okay." I rise from the chair and hug her tight. A small bit of weight lifts off of my shoulders but worry still encases me. I hope the doctor will be able to help.

"How'd it go, Angel?" G.T. asks as we walk out of Dr. Anderson's office. He wanted to come inside with me, but I needed to do it on my own. To be honest, I'm glad I did.

Dr. Anderson is a slender woman with dark brown hair that is cut in a pixie cut. She has the glasses that scream doctor. But what I really like about her is when I walked in, she oozed comfort. There is something about her that makes me feel like I can talk to her and open up.

I surely didn't think that would happen, but with her it did. And boy did I open up to her.

"It went well." I smile. "She's easy to talk to and I like her."

"I'm glad you're seeing a woman." Like I didn't already know this. Not only did I choose a woman for myself, I did it for him as well. I'm not stupid. "You want to talk about it?"

"I feel good G.T. I'm ready to move." I say excited for the first time since it happened.

"Me too. Let's get you home." He smiles putting his hand on the small of my back and pressing me into my car.

For the first time in a while, warmth creeps through my body. Home. Something I haven't felt in a long time. Now, I'll have a home with G.T. Now if I can just shake all the rest.

"THAT'S THE LAST OF IT." G.T. says dropping the box to the ground with a thud.

"Thank you." I say looking around at the space that G.T. wants to make ours. The term bachelor pad doesn't seem right, but it's the only thing that comes to mind. When we walked in, the house was so damn musty that it suffocated me until G.T. opened some windows and got the funk out.

Food boxes, beer bottles and clothes were strewn throughout the place and I did a quick clean just to move around. Furniture wise, there isn't much, couch, chair and huge TV. I'll need to pull some things out of storage soon.

The bedroom is the same, barren, with a bed and dresser. The first thing I did is grab the sheets and bedding and strip them off. G.T. laughed as I went straight out to the trash and chucked them into the can. I do not want to know who or what has been on those sheets and it will be the first order of business to get a new bed. If this is our new life, I'm not doing it on a bed that God knows what happened in.

"Angel, let's go get a bed and some other shit you want. I want you to make this your place. But none of that pink shit." He smirks and I damn well know that if I find a damn pink pillow, he'd suck it up and have it, at least for a while.

"Please. I want a place to sleep tonight." I joke and he laughs.

AFTER SHOPPING AND DINNER, we lug everything back into the house and I mean lug about ten bags of new, clean things. The bed is being delivered in one hour and I'm tired. Really really tired. Sleep hasn't been good for me these past few nights.

I yawn and lay on the couch, a feeling of calm washes

over me. The sounds here are soft and I find myself relaxing. I fall into a deep sleep.

My eyes flutter open as G.T. picks me up and carries me in his strong arms down the hallway. I look in the bedroom we just walked into. The bed showed up while I was sleeping and G.T. made it with the new sheets we bought. "You set it up?" I whisper surprised.

"Anything for you, Angel. Sleep." He lays me down softly pulling the blankets up over my body. The bed dips down and G.T. climbs in behind me wrapping his arms around me. I snuggle into his warmth, feel the soft sheets and close my eyes for the most peaceful rest I've had in a long time.

I watch my Angel sleep, her breathing slow and deep. I'd do anything to take away her pain. I'd gladly put it on my shoulders and carry it for her. But unfortunately I can't, and it makes me feel so damn helpless.

It kills me that she couldn't talk to me about what happened to her. Like I'd ever think less of her if he actually did touch her. But who knows what the hell goes on in a woman's head. I'm just glad that this doctor is someone she feels that she can talk to. I shouldn't be hurt that it's not me, but fuck I can't help that shit. All I do know for sure is I'm glad she picked a woman to talk to. It was hard enough waiting for her to get through her session. If I'd had to wait while she was in with another man behind closed doors, I would have lost my shit.

I keep in the back of my head all the time to be careful with her. I will not push her. I will show her every damn day that I want her and will always find her beautiful no matter how she feels about what happened.

The memories of that day are etched into my brain and I'd do anything to bleach them out. There are nights that I wake up with a jolt, visions of her hanging by her arms, but I mask that shit quickly, not wanting to scare my girl. She's been doing so damn good. She's so fucking strong and I love her more and more each day.

When she wanted to see Shaina, I wanted to flat out refuse. There was no fucking way I wanted her to relive that shit and seeing Shaina would definitely do that. It was selfish, I fully admit. But I had the best intentions at heart. I just want to shield her and protect her as much as I can. Several times I've thought of locking her in a room and never letting her leave. But I know she'd never let that fly. I chuckle to myself at the thought.

It'd actually be nice to see that fire. She's been so mellow. Strong, but subdued.

All I know is that I love her and I will do anything and everything I can to help her get through this.

CHAPTER NINETEEN
Casey

ONE MONTH LATER

"G.T.! STOP IT!" I LAUGH AND TRY TO PUT THE POTATO salad in a big bowl to serve, slopping it all over the place. "They're all due here any minute." I screech as his hand wraps around my waist and travels up my shirt gripping my breast. I drop the spoon not wanting to make a bigger mess.

"They can wait." He growls in my neck. After talking with Dr. Anderson several times a week, I feel much better. More like my old self. She is helping me work through my grief for Mia, even though I'll never get over her loss. I'm also beginning to release what happened with Jace and Paine. It's amazing what a month can do. After leaving the clubhouse, sleep got so much better. It comes easily, not that I still don't have the occasional nightmare, but they are becoming few and far between.

I went back to work at the garage and I think that helped me a lot. Being under the hood of a car always soothes me. I've managed to keep up with my classes and actually do pretty well with this online thing. G.T. set up the spare room as an office with a desk for me to study. G.T.'s house feels like *our* home.

When I initiated sex for the first time after the incident, G.T. pounced and he has not let up a moment since. I thought I would have more of an issue with sex, but talking to the doctor has helped. One day, I just decided I wanted it and it helps me feel closer to G.T. which is something I desperately crave.

"Quick." I answer turning in his arms and connect our lips.

"YOU'RE HERE!" I grab on to Blaze pulling her into the house. I didn't think she would come, even though I invite her to everything. But she's here and I'm grateful. The brothers and their ol' ladies have been here for two hours and the booze and food is flowing. I have come to realize that I love throwing parties.

"I'm here." She says wrapping her arms around me. I do the same, squeezing her soft body.

"Come in and eat." I pull her into the kitchen and everyone's eyes in the room land on her. She is very beautiful and the men and women alike can appreciate her beauty. She squares her shoulders and gives small smiles and waves hi with confidence. Even though she has seen the brothers at the club, she doesn't interact with them often.

"I'm not really hungry and I can't stay too long."

"Bull. You stay, eat and have some fun. You need to stop hiding out all the time." She gives a small smirk but doesn't respond.

"Beer Pong!" Bubbles, Becs ol' lady, yells out. I roll my eyes slightly.

"What are you eighteen?" Harlow chastises. "Oh shit... What the hell." She throws her arms up and stumbles over to the cabinet pulling out a stack of red and yellow Solo cups. She fills twelve of them partially full. "You got a ping pong ball woman?"

"Hell if I know!" I say going to find G.T., who is now sitting outside on the deck with his brothers, Cruz, Becs, Dagger, Rhys and Zed, who all smirk when I walk out. G.T. full out smiles, his eyes locking with mine. "Hey babe. You got a ping pong ball."

"Oh shit. Really Angel?" I shrug.

"Bubbles wanted to play, Harlow went along with it and now I'm out finding a ball."

"I've got balls for ya." Dagger says to the side and G.T. growls.

"You wanna keep those fucking balls?" He asks Dagger, who busts out laughing. "Come on babe. I'll get it."

We are on our second round of beer pong and shit, Harlow must have practiced. She keeps hitting them all and focusing her fury on me. I've had several shots of beer, but still holding strong.

I look across the room seeing Blaze and Tug in what looks to be a serious conversation. Blaze's hands are moving all around in front of her and Tug's arms are crossed over his chest, in the I-am-man-you-listen, stance. G.T. does it a lot, so I'm very familiar with it.

I try to read their mouths, but to no avail. I'm sure it has nothing to do with the amount of alcohol that I've consumed. I want to know, but it really is none of my business.

My eyes flash to the hottest man that I know, *my man*. His eyes catch mine and I can see them dancing. I wink and he smiles, God I love those damn dimples. I feel the strings trying to connect us and pull me to him, but I also know that if I go, he'll probably end up carrying me through the house to the bedroom. Not that I mind. I just need to take care of all of our guests.

Life sure has a lot of twists and turns in it. Some you expect and others may devastate. I'm not entirely sure how G.T. and I got to this place, but I wouldn't want to be anywhere else.

GT

"THANK FUCKING GOD THEY ARE GONE." I slam the door behind Rhys and Dagger, they seem to always be the last ones to leave the party. Which is normally fine, but tonight I have an Angel to be inside.

I turn and march straight towards Angel her eyes

grow wide and her breath catches. I haven't been able to keep my damn hands off of her for more than a few minutes since she let me back in. I fucking love being buried inside of her. She's my drug, my addiction.

I grab her around her waist pulling her to my body and she gasps, her hands flying up to my chest to hold on. I slam my lips to hers, tasting her cherry lip gloss and eat every bit of it off of her lips. She has made me love cherries. She kisses me back and holds steady, her hands thread through my hair and give it a small tug. I growl.

I cup her ass pulling her up and she takes the invitation, wrapping her legs around my body. I carry her straight to the couch falling down on top of her. My hands travel down her body to the hem of her shirt pulling it up quickly and off of her. Our lips take a small reprieve but continue after the obstruction is gone.

I unhook her black lacy bra, tossing it to the floor and knead her tits as she moans in my mouth. I tweak her nipples and roll them with my finger and thumb causing her back to arch off the couch.

Pulling away, I look down at my beautiful girl. She has her smile back. It seemed to have taken a small vacation there for a while, but whatever Dr. Anderson is doing, is working. She is opening back up and showing me the Angel that I love.

I undo her pants and pull them along with her underwear off in one swoop. She moves up to unlatch mine. "No. Stay." I stand and remove my clothes quickly lying back on top of her.

"I'm gonna fuck you now, babe." She nods unable to form words from her lips.

"Yes, please." She whimpers and moans.

I waste no time and slam home, inside of her, stretching that tight pussy as she screams. Her short nails dig into my flesh and I fucking love it. I crave it. I want her to mark me. I want to make her mine.

After our screaming releases, we barely make it to the bed and drift off into a happy, peaceful sleep.

Continue Reading for the Epilogue...

EPILOGUE
Casey

TWO WEEKS LATER

Bliss. Who'd have thought? I sure didn't. But it's amazing how life changes. My arms hold G.T. snug as the roar of his Harley's engine rumbles between my spread legs. My pussy vibrates as I push it closer into G.T.'s tight ass. The wind whips through my hair as my lid and shades block the bugs from crashing into my eyes. I learned as a child to keep my mouth closed, only to open it when needed. Damn if that brisk wind didn't give ya a sore throat.

But this is what I love. I love being on the back of my man's bike feeling the world drift by. Nothing is a blur. Everything is in full vivid color and I eat every second of it up. G.T. surprised me this morning saying he wanted to take me for a ride and I quickly obliged. There is no better place on earth, than where I am at this moment.

My mind drifts to the past few weeks and the rollercoaster that I've been on. There have been so many downs, but also ups to try to balance it out. One thing is for certain. I love this man. I love him down to the depths of my soul.

I hold him tighter; his hand leaves the handlebars and squeezes my hand telling me he's feeling it too. I let everything go, and enjoy the ride.

LATER THAT NIGHT

THE BLARING noise coming from my phone wakes me from a peaceful sleep. The room is cloaked in darkness with only a small bit of moonlight coming in through a break in the curtain. Letting out a groan, I roll over and peer through squinted eyes to try to read the red digital clock that is burning my pupils. 3:37 AM. What the fuck? This had to be bad. My body falls back to the bed, but is on instant alert, unease and adrenaline begin to pump through me causing my heart to hammer in my chest.

Stretching out my arm to reach for my phone, I try to find it quickly before I wake the beautiful woman draped around me. Grabbing the denim jeans I had dropped on the ground the night before, I dig into the front pocket. I clasp my hand around the plastic device, tug it out and bring it to my face to read the caller. Pops. Shit, this really can't be good.

"What?" I grumble into the phone and pray it is nothing. Hopeful mom has the flu or Low is having a meltdown about something. Ravage has been through the wringer lately and we are due some down time. Past due.

"Get the fuck here! Cops just left. They fucking raided the clubhouse and destroyed everything!" Pops yells in the other end of the phone.

I move out of bed careful as I can, not to jostle Angel. I shove my legs in each pant leg; the harsh denim material wakes me up even more as Pops words roll around my head. A million questions and finally I focus on one.

"They find anything?" I ask, knowing we have our skeletons we need to keep hidden at Ravage.

"I don't fucking know. They didn't arrest anyone, but that doesn't mean shit."

Pops is pissed. This is just a never ending cycle lately. We handle one situation just to have another blow up in our faces.

"On my way." I hang up the phone and jam it back into my pocket. Turning to look at Angel, her eyes are shut, eyelashes fanning across her delicate cheeks. She looks so calm and angelic. I hate waking her, but she needs to know I'm leaving. Leaning down I kiss the top of her head and call out her name softly. With a grumble, she wakes and pouts her cherry lips.

"Baby, I've gotta run to the club. I'll be back in a bit."

Her eyes flutter open "Okay babe. Love you."

Kissing me, she drifts back to sleep.

I snatch a cotton shirt off a hanger in the closet, slipping it on and stepping out of the dark room into the hallway and shove my feet into my boots. I walk out of our home preparing myself for whatever is going on now.

Jumping on my bike, I rev up the motor, the vibration doing nothing to calm my nerves and thoughts. I just need to get there, get the facts, and help the brother's make a plan. Pulling back the throttle, I gun it to the clubhouse, the roar of the engine echoing on the deserted streets.

Can't a man just get a moment of peace?

GET the next book Consume Me NOW!

ABOUT RYAN

Ryan Michele is the *Wall Street Journal* and *USA Today* **Bestselling author** of over 40 romantic suspense novels. She found her passion bringing fictional characters to life, being in an imaginative world where anything is possible. Her knack for the **unexpected twists and turns** will have you on the edge of your seat with each page. She is best known for **her alpha, bad boy bikers and strong, independent heroines who refuse to back down.** When she's not writing, you can find her on her swing, watching the water ripple in the pond and daydreaming about her next book.

Join my Reader Group: https://www.facebook.com/groups/RyansSultrySinners/
Sign Up for my https://www.subscribepage.com/918BackmatterSignUps

facebook.com/AuthorRyanMichele

twitter.com/Ryan_Michele

instagram.com/author_ryan_michele

BB bookbub.com/authors/ryan-michele

ACKNOWLEDGEMENTS

Thank you to every single one of you reading this book right now. I appreciate the time you took to sit down and go on Casey and G.T.'s journey with me. Casey had to deal with some serious emotions throughout the book, but I am so damn proud of her outcome. And G.T., I swoon over that man.

Thank you to everyone who took a chance on *Ravage Me*. I know some had an issue with Princess being way aggressive, but she is who she is. When I sat down to write her, she could be nothing less than badass.

Bloggers, Thank you for your posts, shares, likes and great conversations. I appreciate all the time and effort you put into promoting me and my books. If there is anything you need, please email me at ryanmicheleauthor@gmail.com .

Betas—My lovely wonderful, fantabulous betas! Lori, Sarah, Becky, Megan, Becky 2, Heidi, Dawn, Chas and Jade. I adore each of you and thank you from the bottom of my heart! Thank you for putting up with my craziness and my questions! Thank you for helping me make *Seduce Me* shine!

Lori—You are a wonderful person. I'm honored to be able to call you my friend.

Jade—Thank you for the AWESOME teaser pictures! You are the BEST!

Ena—Big Hugs! Thank you!

Ravage MC Hotties group on Facebook—THANK

YOU! A special thank you to Mari and Juliana for starting the group! I appreciate your faith in me. Colette, thank you for the hot ass pictures you post daily! So much inspiration. I love them!!! To everyone in the group, I am so grateful for each of you. Thank you for sharing and liking my posts and just overall interacting with me on there. I love hearing from all of you!

Clare—THANK YOU!

JJ—I know it was long, but thank you Ms. Comma Queen.

My family- I love you. Thank you for all your support!

I have made some really good friends with several amazing authors. Words cannot describe how indebted I am to you. Thank you for answering my thousands of questions and bullshitting with me. I am honored to be part of a community that shows such love for one another. THANK YOU BABES!!!

Editor: Laura Hampton
Cover Artist: Cassy Roop, Pink Ink Designs

Thank you for reading!

Ryan
Michele